PITTY party

An Enemies-To-Lovers Romance by

TIFFANY ANDREA

Paperback ISBN: 978-1-990724-39-8
eBook ISBN: 978-1-990724-38-1

Cover Design by: Burden of Proofreading Publishing featuring graphics by Msanca and A7880S via DepositPhotos.

Interior Graphics by Design & Beyond via Canva

www.boppublishing.com

*For Dr. Anwar and the staff at **Boyne Veterinary Clinic**. Thank you for caring for our sweet fur baby like he was your own. You went above and beyond to not only care for him, but to ease my mind through the process. A simple thank you feels insufficient, so I hope a book dedication somehow shows the depth of our gratitude.*

I know your job can be challenging at times, so please never forget the difference you make in the lives of your patients and their owners. Your dedication to caring for each animal you see makes this world a better place.

P.S. Steel says thank you for making him a happy boy again.

TABLE OF CONTENTS

As with all of my books, they are free from explicit sexual content and violence, but they often dive into more serious topics. This book, while it is light-hearted and sweet, which I always strive for, does have mention of a few darker subjects. If there is potential for anything like that to bother you, please read the warnings below. If not, happy reading, and I hope you enjoy Frankie and Oscar's story.

A large part of this story deals with the trauma surrounding having a stalker, as well as some mild (not descriptive) scenes of violence. The content is still PG-13, but if this may bother you, please reconsider reading this book.

1

FRANKIE

Call of the Wild

"**U**m, somebody? I could use a little help here."

I rush out of the exam room at the sound of Rhonda's plea, expecting to find a dog fight or an escaped python in the vet clinic's lobby. To my surprise—and relief—she's attempting to wrangle three little grey puppies wobbling around behind the reception desk.

Dr. Ellis comes to a stop beside me to take in the scene.

"The woman who just left found a box outside with puppies and a note." Rhonda hands the small piece of paper to Dr. Ellis, who skims it and passes it to me.

Dear Dr. Ellis,

I brought my dog in to see you last year and you treated her without judging her breed or reminding me about Ontario's pit bull ban. Your kindness meant a lot to me, and I knew you truly cared about animals, not discriminatory laws. That's the reason I know her babies will be safe with you. I'm sorry to dump them on you, but I can't afford to keep them anymore. Please make sure they find good homes.

Sincerely,

Desperate pit bull mom

The woman's observation doesn't surprise me at all. Most vets I've been around love animals, but Dr. Anton Ellis goes above and beyond. His care and concern for all living things is obvious in every interaction.

One of the three little babies, who can't be more than seven weeks old, staggers up to me and paws at my leg. I can't resist bending down to pick him up. He's so wrinkly because his skin has grown faster than the rest of him, so he looks like he's wearing a fur suit that's two sizes too big. He's the cutest thing I've ever seen.

"This is the last thing we need today." Dr. Ellis lifts the remaining wandering pup, now that Rhonda has captured the other. "They are cute, though."

I look down at the sweet guy in my arms, revelling in his puppy breath and tiny pink nose. "They are. A blue pit has always been my dream dog." I scratch under his little chin and he nuzzles into my shirt. There's something so instinctual about protecting an abandoned puppy. Maternal, even.

"Well, here's your chance to have one. The letter did say to find them good homes," Dr. Ellis points out.

I gape at him, trying to come up with a reason to say no. Aside from the province's breed-specific legislation, I'm not sure I'm in the best place to bring home a dog. I don't have any family or friends in the city. My schedule is crazy. My next semester starts in a few days, so between classes and volunteering here, I'm not home a lot. But when I am, I'm alone... and that reality still terrifies me.

Maybe having a dog for security is a smart option. That would give me some peace of mind, knowing I have that extra alarm system. It has nothing to do with him licking my chin or wagging his little tail. No, it's practical. Totally mature and responsible. A rational decision if I've ever seen one.

"If you don't take him, he'll end up in a rescue. We can't keep them here, so I have to find somewhere that can re-home them."

"Wow. Laying on the guilt trip a little thick, huh?" I giggle when the puppy tickles my neck with his short whiskers.

"Come on, Frankie. Look how much he loves you. And when you're working here, you can bring him with you until he's old enough to stay at home," Rhonda adds.

Rhonda, her husband, and Dr. Ellis are all equal partners in the animal hospital, so it's not like I have to run her plan past the big boss. Plus, with my discounted rent and scholarships, I can probably swing the extra expense thanks to a lot of overtime through high school. The companionship and added security are invaluable.

"Okay. Who can say no to this little face?"

Rhonda smiles wide and pulls her shoulders up near her ears. "There's nothing like an impulsive puppy adoption to make you feel alive!"

I chuckle at her excitement. And at her valid point, because I haven't felt this excited about anything for a long time. "What about the other two?"

"Don't worry about these guys. I'll take them until I can sort something out with a rescue." Dr. Ellis spins toward the back of the building and nods for me to follow him. "Let's grab you a few supplies to get the little guy settled."

We spend thirty minutes packaging up some food samples and giving my new roommate a quick physical to check for any obvious health issues. Good news is, he seems perfectly fine. Whoever abandoned them took good care of them. That's a slight comfort.

When we're finished, I scoop up my fur baby and cuddle him into my chest, then hook the bag of goodies onto my arm. "Okay, I'll be back in on Wednesday. Wish us luck."

With a quick exchange of goodbyes, I exit the animal hospital to my car. With my pup in the back seat, we drive to the nearest pet store, where I stock up on the other supplies the little guy will need. The more I browse the aisles, the more excited I get to have a creature of my own to pamper. It's so different from helping to heal injured animals, then sending them home for someone else to love.

For the first time in months—probably years—I move through an entire store without constantly scanning my surroundings. It's unnerving once I notice, but just as things have been since I first moved to Toronto four months ago, the coast is clear. So instead of dwelling on how my new puppy is a potential distraction, I revel in how he tickles my skin and seems to love me already, even before I've fed him.

Who says the way to a man's heart is through his stomach?

After we check out and I spend a sizable chunk of money, we drive to my home on Boston Avenue. My stomach drops when I round the corner.

A moving truck.

It's been so nice that the house attached to mine has been unoccupied since I moved in. Now, not only will I have to share a wall with other people, but their stupid moving truck is blocking my parking spot. We only have permitted street parking, so I have no choice but to park down the block instead of my usual space mere feet from my front door.

They haven't even lived here for one day, and I'm already annoyed.

I walk back to my house, carrying my new roommate, trying to allow his presence to ease the irritation I'm feeling. But as I get closer, I notice something that even puppy cuddles can't fix. My new neighbours are students. Not just students, but they look like either freshman or sophomores. Boys. Meaning this is probably their first time living off-campus. Likely the first time having their own house without parental or university supervision.

I can only hope they are mature, dedicated students who take their education seriously.

As I climb the stairs to my front porch, that hope is dashed.

"This house is sick, man. We're going to have some epic ragers," one brunette guy says.

Two other guys high-five each other. The level of frat-boy vibes they give off is strong enough to aggravate me from thirty feet away.

The lone blond guy, who looks like a buzz-kill in track pants, steps out of the back of the moving truck with his arms full of boxes. His face looks to be frozen in a perpetual scowl. A gorgeous scowl, but still a sour expression if I've ever seen one.

That's all I stick around to see before I walk in my front door and lock it behind me. With the puppy still in my arms, I perform my routine inspection of the main floor and upstairs.

Once I've checked every closet and under each bed, I breathe a sigh of relief. I return to the living room, and my nameless pup starts whimpering.

"Are you hungry? Come on. Let's see what goodies Dr. Ellis sent for you, hmm?"

I walk toward the kitchen, but he doesn't follow me. Instead, he wobbles over to the front door, still whining. It never occurred to me he'd be potty trained already. It also never occurred to me that dog ownership would mean unlocking and opening my door more often or going out after dark.

Maybe this wasn't such a good idea.

But looking at his adorable face, I can't possibly regret my decision.

"Come on. You can explore the backyard." I scoop him up and take him to the back door, unlocking it and stepping outside.

The entire yard is only about three by five metres, and half of it is paved with patio stones. The other half is grass and a foot-wide strip of gardens lining all three sides of the solid privacy fence, featuring large, leafy hostas. It's not a dream yard, but it provides enough grass to suit a dog's needs, as long as I walk him.

He rushes to the edge of the grass to do his business. I'm honestly shocked he didn't pee on my floor.

"Hi, new neighbour," a voice calls from the opposite side of the fence.

I stand silently for a moment, trying to peek through the very narrow cracks in the fence, but I can't see anyone. I keep listening, hoping he's talking to someone on the other side of his yard.

"Well, I'm Blake. Nice to meet you, too."

I stay frozen, waiting for the other person in this conversation to reply.

"Hellooo? Please, don't make this awkward."

The top two inches of a brunette's head pops above the eight-foot high fence. And that makes me realize he *is* trying to strike up a conversation with me.

"Oh, sorry. I thought you were talking to someone else." Though, I'm really just sorry I didn't run inside as soon as the dog emptied his tiny bladder. "I... uh... I'm Frankie."

"Frankie? Interesting. Is that short for something?"

Again, I blanch, asking myself how honest I should be with this perfect stranger. I quickly decide it's not worth the risk, so I reply, "Yep, it is. Nice to meet you, Blake, but I've gotta get back inside. I've got a hungry guy waiting for dinner."

I turn to walk up the three stairs, but before I even lift my foot for the first stair, Blake replies.

"Don't be a stranger, Frankie."

But that's exactly what I intend to be.

2

OSCAR

Time of Our Lives

"The neighbour chick sounds hot," Blake says, dropping onto the sofa I was just trying to move. "We should invite her to our party. She says she has a guy, but you know that doesn't mean anything."

I roll my eyes, more than a little annoyed by my friend. "You wanna help with this, or should I just move it with you on top?" I ask, gesturing at the sofa.

"You know what we need? Music." Without acknowledging my question, he pops up and rushes out of the room.

I thought my brain was chaos, but Blake's is a whole other level. It's hard to keep up with him. We may have that commonality in an ADHD diagnosis and using martial arts to help with mental discipline, but that's where our similarities end. He's social, outgoing, and never quiet. I'm reserved, discerning, and prefer to spend hours with my guitar than other people. Yet, somehow, our friendship works.

Even if I'm left to move furniture on my own while he flakes off to hook up his playlist to the built-in Bluetooth speakers. Speakers that are now pumping out techno music. Not my first choice for a moving soundtrack, but that's just another difference between us.

"This is going to be epic," Austin says as he drops a box of textbooks on the living room floor in front of the built-in bookshelves.

"Are you to blame for this?" I ask, pointing up at the thumping speakers.

Given that he's the resident tech expert, I'd be willing to bet Blake didn't figure out how to connect his phone that fast. Technology is not his strong suit.

"Lighten up, Ozzie. Maybe we'll find you a girl to help you loosen up a little."

I scoff at that for a couple of reasons. One, I *hate* that nickname. Two, the last thing I need is a girl to loosen up. Unlike my three roommates, I don't have the same unrelenting drive to pursue a new girl each week. My unrelenting drive is reserved for the muay thai gym, *proper* music, and finishing my degree so I never have to take another test.

I continue moving the second-hand sofa we inherited into a better position. "Let's get moved in before you start playing matchmaker, eh?"

"It wouldn't kill you to—"

"Party's set for next Friday!" Blake whoops as he re-enters the living room with Keith right behind.

At least *he's* sweating like he's actually been working.

Austin turns and high-fives them both, then attempts to do the same to me. I leave him hanging.

"Buzz kill alert," he chides. "Somebody get this guy a drink."

Again, I roll my eyes and seriously reconsider my living arrangements for my sophomore year. "I'm not drinking. If you're planning to have people here in a week, you can at least, you know... help?"

Keith throws his arm around my shoulders, confirming he was, in fact, working—and sweating. "We'll get it done, Ozzie. Classes don't start for four days. Relax."

Relaxing is one thing I don't do. Ever. My brain doesn't allow it. I'm either asleep or on the move, at all times. I don't bother trying to explain that to him. He has a normal brain that experiences silence. It's hard to relate to someone who doesn't quite get what it's like living with thoughts that never shut off.

"This is our first time with real freedom. No parents, no RAs, no dorm rules. Just chill. This year will be epic." Keith removes his arm, then drops onto the sofa beside Blake. "Let's just enjoy the moment."

"I'd enjoy it a lot more if we got all of our stuff from the truck and returned it, so we're not blocking the whole street." And I'd be happy if I never hear the word "epic" again for the rest of my life.

Without waiting to see if any of them get the hint, I return outside to gather the rest of our things. As I walk up the ramp into the back of the truck, I glance over at the neighbour's house. Every single window is blocked by blinds or curtains, so I don't have the slightest hint at what's happening inside or who lives there. I saw the blonde wearing scrubs walk in earlier. She had her arms full of stuffed bags and looked to be cradling something, but I only caught a glimpse.

Blake may have based his assumption on her voice, but from what I saw, he's not wrong. She is objectively hot, even in something as unflattering as scrubs. She didn't look any older than me, though, so I wonder what line of work she's in.

I chalk off the curiosity to my overactive brain and get back to work.

Keep busy. Stay focused. Don't let my mind wander. And definitely don't waste time thinking about the neighbour.

The start of a new school year once you get to university age is anti-climactic. Three hours of classes and a quarter of my summer savings spent on textbooks. At least I was able to sell a few back from last year, but since I only worked two months over the summer, I don't have a lot of spending money to play with. Especially when I'm paying $1000 a month for rent.

That's why my coaching job at the gym is so important. I didn't spend thousands of dollars of my grandparents' money to go to Thailand and get my muay thai clinic certifications just for kicks. No pun intended.

I was lucky enough that Tyrus was looking for a muay thai coach at his kickboxing gym, so as soon as I mentioned I got my certifications, he hired me on the spot. Getting hired is only a minor detail compared to arranging my schedule around my classes to make me worth employing. Most of my classes are mid-day, so I can coach in the mornings and evenings, depending on demand.

Not only is today my first day of classes, it's my first day at my new job too. And I'm already running late.

I bound down the steps of our front porch with my gym bag slung over my shoulder, excited for the new challenge coaching will present. Anything challenging keeps my brain engaged, making it easier to focus on the task. It's when things get easy that they become an issue. That's part of the appeal of muay thai. No belts to give you a sense of accomplishment. There is always something to perfect and always something else to learn.

"Brad?" a woman's screaming stops me in my tracks before I reach the sidewalk.

Not only her screaming, but the grey dog running toward me makes me pause as well.

"Brad?" she shouts again.

I look up to see the blonde run out from between her house and her other neighbour's. She looks beside herself with worry. The small dog jumps up at my leg, but I shake it off, noting its name tag dangling from its collar. Looking at the shape of his face, I recognize it for what it is.

"Brad?" she calls one last time, still partially shielded by her porch.

"You named your dog Brad?" I ask, trying to keep the tiny terrorist from wiping more dirt on my track pants.

She peeks her head around the corner of her porch, scanning both directions until her eyes land on me. "Y-yes…"

"He's right here. Attacking my legs."

"What?" She steps forward, turning her focus to her dog. Then she jogs over and picks him up, clutching him to her chest. "Thank you."

"Your dog is a menace."

Suddenly, every ounce of worry and nervousness she demonstrated a second ago disappears. Her eyebrows, which are several shades darker than her brassy blonde hair, narrow together. "He is not. He's twelve pounds."

"A twelve-pound menace. You know about BSL, right? Pit bulls are illegal to own in Ontario."

Her eyebrows inch closer together, creating deep lines between them. Her dark eyes glower at me with a surprising intensity. "He's not a menace. You're part of the reason breed-specific legislation exists."

"Because I'm logical and don't get suckered by puppy-dog eyes?"

"No. Because you're judgmental and feed on stereotypes instead of seeing things at face value!"

"If you want to live with a vicious dog, that's your business, but don't expect me to call the coroner when it's eating your rotting corpse."

She scrunches her face and pauses, as if she's picturing that graphic scene. "Oh, don't worry. I won't be asking you for any favours, *neighbour*."

I step inches closer, but that causes her to step back a couple of feet. Her dramatic reaction doesn't deter me from what I want to say, though.

"Keep him in your yard or I'll report you to the city. You're lucky I wasn't some kid that he ripped the face off of."

"Are you serious?" she shouts, but immediately shrinks back. "He's *twelve pounds*. He slipped out through a hole in the fence that I didn't know was there. Get over yourself."

"Get over myself? You're the one with the illegal dog that you can't keep control of." I scoff, finally remembering why I'm outside to begin with. "Some of us are law-abiding citizens and have jobs to keep, so if you don't mind…"

I don't give her the chance to shout anything else at me before I'm walking down the road toward the gym. Now I really need a chance to work out some of my frustration.

Oh No He Didn't

The nerve of this guy. How *dare* he lump Brad in with other dogs who have been trained to be vicious. He was curious, not malicious. Since he's so small, he snuck through a hole behind a plant in the yard, and I didn't notice he had gotten out until thirty seconds after the plant stopped rustling. My heart stopped when I feared for a moment he was lost. What kind of irresponsible dog owner loses their dog after four days?

I was already sick and tired of these party animals next door after spending the weekend listening to their stupid music pounding through the walls and incessant hollering. Like they can't just text each other from different floors of the house like normal people. I was willing to let it go, but now that this guy has threatened my dog, he'll learn that I won't just roll over.

Actually, I probably will. If I upset him, he'll be more inclined to report Brad. And I really don't want to move again. Nor do I want to draw attention to myself.

This sucks.

Life was peaceful here. Until this entitled motley crew of frat boys came on the scene.

"This is why I prefer animals, Brad. People are the worst." I lie back on the couch and let Brad curl up on my chest. I take deep breaths, watching as he rises and falls along with each inhale and exhale. He's the embodiment of love and peacefulness; he's nothing like the stupid neighbour made him out to be.

But I won't put my dog at risk to prove a point.

"Guess I better go block off the fence, huh? We don't want to upset the blond grump again."

Though, instead of getting up to repair the hole, I stay and enjoy Brad's snuggles for a few more moments. I have to admit, after my first day of classes, it was nice to come home to something other than silence. Even if he's proven he isn't fully house-trained, mopping up a tiny pee puddle is a small price to pay.

A few minutes turns into an hour, and I've accomplished nothing. But I've also felt a calmness I haven't experienced for years, despite the angry neighbour confrontation. And that feeling is one I'll protect at all costs.

"How have your first few days of classes gone?" Dr. Ellis asks, stroking Brad's head.

I lean back in the office chair, enjoying being off my feet for a moment. "Fine. My vertebrate anatomy class seems really fascinating. Well, they all do, to be honest. I have another one on genetics that I'm excited about."

"Sounds like a full course load. Are you sure your volunteer time here won't get in the way?"

"No!" I practically shout. "Sorry. No, it won't. My time here is important to me. I'll stay as long as you'll have me."

"Third-year demands are a lot more than the first two. You've never had to balance a class schedule with your time here, so if it gets to be too much, just let me know. You do good work and we're happy to have you, but I don't want you burning out." He gives me a gentle smile. "Oh, but an update on Brad's siblings. They were both transported to a rescue in New Brunswick, so they'll be able to place them in homes there. You know how hard it is for bully breeds here."

I sit upright, smiling back. "That's good news. Speaking of, Brad got out through a hole in the fence yesterday and ran up to my new neighbour." Just the memory of the encounter makes my blood boil. "I won't even get into how over-dramatic he was, but he told me if Brad gets out again, he'll report him to the city."

Dr. Ellis sighs. "That's definitely a risk of owning him. You'll have to be really careful, Frankie, because no matter how gentle or sweet he is, some people will see him as a monster." He stands straight, lifting Brad from the desk and cradling him in one arm. "Tell you what. Let's go microchip him just in case, but promise me you'll be careful."

"I will. That would be good peace of mind, though." It might not stop him from getting out again, but at least knowing he's registered to me will ease my mind a little because he won't just get tossed in a shelter with no one to advocate for him.

Watching Dr. Ellis work, noting his care and concern for every little thing, is such a great learning experience. He's in his early 30s, I'd assume, but he's been working as a vet for six years already. Not only is he passionate about animals, but he runs a program for vets to address mental health issues that are abundant in the field.

He's been a wonderful mentor, and some days I wonder if everything that happened over the last few years led me here for a reason. As if all the stress and fear and turmoil was pushing me to find Dr. Ellis... and now Brad.

"Why Brad? I meant to ask earlier?" he asks after injecting the microchip between my dog's shoulder blades.

"It's stupid. But... the day I got him, I was in the backyard and one of my new neighbours—not the cranky one—started talking over the fence. It got me thinking that I didn't want them knowing I live alone, so I needed to come up with a human name for the dog. Later that night, we were watching *Happy Feet Two* and when Will the Krill came on, I just… He's voiced by Brad Pitt. Get it? Brad Pit… bull?" I flash a toothy grin, just to really drive home my lameness.

Instead of teasing, he just laughs. "That's a good one. I like it. And now you can say Brad's at home waiting for you. Smart."

"Exactly." For some reason, his understanding makes me feel less self-conscious about it.

Since he's best friends with my landlord, who also happens to be dating my aunt, he's familiar with my situation, and I don't feel like I need to hide things here. That's part of the reason why my volunteer time is so refreshing. Not only do I get to work with animals, but I don't have to pretend to be someone or something that I'm not.

I get to be the anxious, paranoid mess that I am, without fear of judgment.

"Mrs. Harman is here, Dr. Ellis," Rhonda says, peeking her head through the door.

"Oh, thanks Rhonda." He feeds Brad a treat, reinforcing his good-boy behaviour. "Do you want to put this guy in the back? Then you can help me with Rusty."

"Sure. And thank you for this," I say, picking up Brad, acknowledging the microchip.

Two minutes later, I've secured Brad in the surgical recovery area and returned to the exam room. A heavily pregnant Mrs. Harman is beside herself because her beloved Siberian husky ate half a package of her birth control pills… which she clearly isn't in need of at the moment.

Dr. Ellis does an initial assessment, asks Mrs. Harman questions, and does his best to comfort her. After he's administered a hydrogen peroxide solution to force Rusty to vomit, I'm tasked with holding the bucket in hopes we'll find undigested pills. It's glamorous work.

Once Rusty has purged his stomach and relaxes on the table, we begin a routine blood draw. I cuddle the vocal husky who is not enjoying the poking and prodding.

"Okay. Let him relax." Dr. Ellis hands me a cotton ball, then picks up the vials of blood to take for analysis.

He exits the room, leaving me to comfort the upset dog and his distraught owner.

"Dr. Ellis is wonderful. Your dog is in great hands." I give Mrs. Harman a reassuring smile, but she can do little more than sniffle and nod.

This is one of the hardest parts of this job. Watching people so worried over their beloved pets and not being able to ask the animals what exactly is wrong. Not to discount the challenges of being a human doctor, but it is a bit of a head start when someone can explain what hurts.

The hardest part of being a vet, though, is when there's nothing more we can do. I don't suspect that's the case with Rusty here, but his owner obviously loves him. Now that I have Brad, even after a few days, I understand on a new level.

Rusty trails a slobbery slurp up the side of my face that tells me he's quite content now that nothing is stabbing him. I tug my shirt upward to wipe my face right as Dr. Ellis returns. He explains timeframes for test results and encourages Mrs. Harman to take Rusty home, reassuring her he'll call with results as soon as he receives them.

She insists that she'll drive right back if she needs to and again says that she'll do whatever it takes to make sure her dog is okay.

Her intense determination to care for her dog makes one thing clear: no grumpy neighbour is going to come between me and Brad.

4

Celebrate

First week of sophomore year is in the books. Also, my first week at my new job, which was far more enjoyable than sitting in classes, trying to concentrate on what the professor was saying. I may be passionate about the subject, but that doesn't mean listening to someone drone on about the principles of macroeconomics is exciting.

Tonight, though, we're hosting our first party at our new house. Rather, my roommates are hosting, and I'll be suffering through it. It's not that I don't like partying; I just don't like it nearly as much as the rest of them. Never mind. I hate parties. It's often forced small talk, worrying people can't hold their liquor, and dragging my drunk friends home at the end of the night. Now, the only difference is I don't have to drag them home, but we'll be left with the mess tomorrow morning, and I'm supposed to coach a private client at 7am.

"Ozzie!" Austin cheers as he approaches. "Are you ready for this?"

"So ready," I deadpan. "It's gonna be so lit… or whatever."

"I'm sensing sarcasm, but you're right. So many hot chicks have tagged me in their getting ready posts…" He grasps my arm, but considering his only workout comes from typing and clicking a mouse, I barely notice.

"Liquor delivery," Keith yells from the front hall.

He and Blake enter the kitchen seconds later, each carrying a box of liquor bottles.

"Do you think twenty-four bottles will be enough?" Blake asks.

"Twenty-four? How many people did you invite? A hundred?" I can already feel the tension building in my head.

"Yeah, that's about right. I announced it in my screen-writing class, and Keith put up flyers."

"Oh my G—"

"Relax, Ozzie. It's all part of the experience," Blake interrupts.

"You realize we paid a five-thousand-dollar security deposit, right? That if we break stuff, we don't get that back?"

Maybe it doesn't bother Blake because he's here on his rich dad's dime—likely to ease some of his own guilt for cheating on Blake's mom and imploding their family—but I have to pay my own way. My parents' stipulation was that they'd save enough to pay for my first year, then I was on my own. They kept up their end of the bargain, which I'm grateful for, but now I don't have my father's corporate credit card to charge a thousand dollars' worth of liquor on just for fun.

"I've got you covered. If we break stuff, your security deposit is on Dear Ol' Dad. My treat." Blake winks at me, then unscrews the top of a bottle of vodka and pops open an energy drink.

Great.

The Bluetooth speakers start pumping out a harmonica tune that takes me a second to recognize as a Pitbull song. That makes me think of the neighbour and her dog. I was probably a little hard on her the other day, but I hope she keeps control of that beast before it hurts someone.

"Ozzie!" Austin interrupts my random train of thought. "What are you drinking?"

"Water. I have to work early. No way am I going in hungover and dehydrated." I swipe a bottle of water from the counter and exit the kitchen to escape to my room while I still can. Suddenly, I don't feel like partying at all. Twenty people would have been manageable. A hundred people are too many.

The guys all mutter a few things behind me, but Pitbull drowns most of it out.

I settle in my room with the door closed, resigning myself to staying in here for the night.

Within a matter of minutes, the volume is cranked up, people start arriving in taxis and funnelling through our front door. I watch the people walking up our front path from my window that overlooks the street. Like a loser, sitting in my room in the dark.

About two hours later, I'm lying on my bed, humming the chords to a song I want to learn, and my bedroom door inches open.

"Occupied!" I say, trying to drown out the music that is much louder now with the open door.

Since I'm still here in the dark, the offenders don't seem to realize they're not alone until they're leaning on the bed beside me a second later. Though, even then, they're so busy sucking each other's faces, they still don't notice.

"Um, hi. Do you mind?" I interrupt. It would have been nice if they heard me five seconds earlier, but I get a kick out of their utter panic.

The girl scrambles to her feet, and from the light in the hallway, I can see her straightening her short dress.

The guy is quick to follow, standing and fixing his pants. "Sorry, man. I didn't know anyone had dibs on this room."

I stand so I can make sure they leave without any issue. "Well, if by dibs, you mean I pay rent for it, then yeah. Dibs. In fact, my friends all have dibs on the other rooms too, so maybe you can take your girlfriend back to the place you have dibs on, hmm?"

"She's not my—"

"Not the point. Take your… whoever she is and go."

He doesn't argue with me any more than that. He turns and leads the girl out by the arm. Just to make sure they don't try to duck into my friends' rooms—even if they fully deserve whatever would happen to their beds—I follow the couple down the stairs.

The party is in full swing, which I didn't need to confirm visually, since I could hear the commotion upstairs. There has to be at least seventy people on the main floor.

"Ozzie, my man," drunk Blake shouts from three feet away, but I still barely hear him. "Come down for a drink finally? You're missing all the fun."

I'm trying here; I really am. It's not my intention to be the resident party pooper, but this is not my idea of fun. Still, I'm not about to stop my friends from doing what makes them happy. So I reply, "Yeah, just going to the kitchen." I pat him on the shoulder, which almost knocks him over, but a willing brunette holds him upright.

Just so I'm not an outright liar, I go to the kitchen and grab another bottle of water. Then I walk out the front door for some fresh air. The entire house smells like alcohol and sweat. I spend a third of my waking hours in a martial arts gym. I thought I'd gone nose-blind to the smell of body odour, but apparently not.

The stale city air outside makes me miss home. Not only that, but I look up and can't see a single star. My siblings and I always watched the stars with our grandparents, so they've always been a reminder of home. The light pollution here makes it impossible to see a single one.

A noise draws my attention to the neighbour's, where I see someone and the illegal dog exiting the front door. The person is wearing baggy track pants and a black hoodie with the hood pulled up, so I can't tell who it is… until she turns around and I see long blonde hair framing her face. Her pale skin glows under her porch lights, making her look like she hasn't seen the sun in months.

She pauses on her porch after locking at least three locks and scans to her right, then back until her eyes land on me. She does not look happy to see me. The way she stomps down the steps confirms that thought. "Did you know that playing music loud enough to disturb your neighbours past 11pm is against the local bylaws?" she states as she nears my spot on the sidewalk.

"Nope. I didn't. I've only lived here for a week."

"Well, that's funny. You knew the bylaws about my dog. Isn't that convenient?"

"Actually, BSL is a province-wide legislation, not a bylaw. Anyone who has ever watched the news would know about it." I step closer to her, testing my theory from the other day.

She steps back, as I expected, but her dog rushes forward, making me jump back.

"Woah, you need to control him."

Instead of clawing at my pants like last time, he stops in front of me and flops on his back, exposing his belly.

"Yeah, he's a real menace, isn't he? Ahh… watch out. It's the scary, child-face-eating dog. Everybody run." She rolls her eyes, which I barely catch because I'm trying to keep an eye on her creature.

"That puppy is sooo cuuute," a random girl squeals behind me. She comes running from nowhere and practically dives to the ground to pet the dog.

I'd tell her to be careful, but I have no idea who she is and really don't care if the dog chooses her face to eat.

My neighbour isn't watching the girl in the glitter dress gush over her dog. She's staring at me. "Turn your music down or I'll call the city," she says, looking far less confident than she sounds.

"You want the music turned down?"

She glances down at this girl who doesn't appear to be in a hurry to go wherever she was headed, then back at me. "Yes."

"Come on, then. I'll take you to the guys in charge."

"Wai—" She scans the area again, even going so far as to check behind her. "Why can't you do it?"

I really focus on her face to say my next words. "It's not my party."

What does he mean it's not his party? It's *his* house, isn't it? Maybe I misunderstood, and he's a friend who helped the other guys move and visits often. But that can't be it, because I've seen him come and go early in the morning. Nobody visits at 6:30am.

Why would he live in a house where they're having a party and not actually party? Maybe his grumpiness extends to his roommates too, and he wasn't invited.

"Can't you go ask them to turn the music down? Why do I have to?" I ask.

"You're the one who has a problem with it. Not me."

I hate that he makes a perfectly valid point. "Fine."

Normally, I wouldn't be going into a stranger's house under any circumstances. Especially not with a bunch of drunken college students. But I'm not about to back down from the unspoken challenge this blond guy has issued. Like he wants to see if I'm brave enough to do it.

I pick up Brad, who has been well loved by the girl finally getting up from the ground. She didn't acknowledge me or the neighbour guy, so aside from pouting over Brad leaving, I don't think she's bothered by us walking away.

Into this house.

Together.

The music inside is ten times louder than outside, prompting me to tuck Brad in the neck of my baggy sweater and cover his ears. What's the appeal? Don't people like to talk? You can't even hear yourself think over the thumping bass.

My grumpy neighbour places a hand on my arm, startling me. He immediately pulls his hands back, holding them up in front of him in surrender. Instead, he leans forward to shout in my ear. "This way." He hooks his thumb toward the kitchen.

This house is similar to the one I'm staying in, so it feels somewhat familiar and less like I'm venturing into uncharted waters. We step into the kitchen, where the music is a slightly lower volume, and find all three guys I recognize from their moving day.

The most muscular one of the trio, who is the only one who seems to have noticed us, shouts, "Ozzie! Where's your drink?"

Ozzie? Interesting. I glance over at "Ozzie" to find him scowling. It's kind of reassuring that it's not just me who brings out this side of him.

Instead of answering, he tosses his empty water bottle into the recycling bag hung over a cabinet door. "This is our neighbour… uh…" He looks at me.

"Frankie," I answer.

"Frankie," he repeats, looking at me with the same measure of curiosity. "Right. This is our neighbour Frankie, and she has a request for you." He takes another bottle of water from the counter, twisting off the top, but before he lifts it to drink, he tips it toward me in offer.

That surprises me. Enough so, I pause for a second, looking into his green eyes before shaking my head.

"What kind of question?" the same guy answers. He's tall— probably around six feet—with bronze skin and a closely cropped fade. He has a dazzling smile, which might be more appealing if it wasn't paired with bloodshot eyes.

"Oh, where are my manners?" Ozzie interrupts. "Frankie, this is Keith. That's Blake"—he points at the brunette with his back turned to us—"and the curly-haired guy over there is Austin. I'm Oscar." He turns back to face Keith and adds, "Not Ozzie."

Keith smirks at his friend before settling his eyes back on me. "What can I do for you?"

For some reason, the crowd of people, the music, the guys staring at me, and the puppy wriggling in my sweater all become overwhelming. My breaths become more shallow and rapid. I can't find the right words, or any at all, for that matter. "I... uh... Could..."

Breathe.

"She asked if you can turn the music down. Something about a bylaw infraction," Oscar finishes with his eyes locked on me.

I focus on him and the comfort of having Brad against my chest until my breathing slows enough to respond. "Right. It's late... and loud. Would you mind?"

Keith smiles, waving Austin over to join our conversation. "This is Frankie. She says the music is too loud."

"Oh, my bad. Sorry about that, Frankie." He reaches down and pats his pockets, not finding what he was looking for. "Wait, Frankie? Backyard Frankie? You talked to Blake."

"Who said my name?" Blake asks, stumbling over to his friends and draping an arm around each of them.

"Me. This is Frankie," Austin adds, elbowing Blake in the ribs.

I'm so confused right now, because Blake and I exchanged about four sentences. It hardly seems worth mentioning.

"Frankie! Woah. I was right."

I don't know what that means, and I'm not sure I want to. As I scan the four pairs of eyes looking at me, I get the impression it means something to them.

"Blake, give me your phone," Austin orders.

"I dunno where it is."

Austin rolls his eyes and reaches behind his friend, pulling the phone from his back pocket. With a few taps of the screen, the music's volume decreases to a reasonable level.

"Thank you," I reply. "I'll leave you guys to your… party."

"What? No, don't go. Stay. Hang out a little," Keith suggests.

"This… isn't really my scene. And I have my dog." I tug the neck of my sweater down enough to reveal my little grey fur ball.

He wriggles and squirms until I pull him out; he's thrilled by all the people around, judging by his wagging tail.

"Ozzie, is this the vicious pit bull you were talking about?" Austin asks, brushing his curly hair out of his face. "I can see why you were so worked up. He's terrifying."

I bite the inside of my cheeks to stop myself from laughing. Austin's upturned lips almost make Oscar's scowl funnier.

"He's not now, but he will be someday."

"No, he *could* be someday. So could a German or Belgian shepherd."

For some reason, that comment seems to make Oscar pause, and I can only hope he understands that Brad isn't a threat.

"Anyway, thank you for the music," I add, "and the invite, but I'm going to head out."

"Just stay for a bit. We want to get to know our new neighbour," Keith offers again.

Another girl in a tight dress and sky-high heels walks up to me and starts gushing over Brad. Her appearance makes me feel even more self-conscious of my own. Sweats aren't exactly house party attire. Granted, I've only been to one house party ever, so I'm no expert.

The glamorous girl asks if she can hold Brad, but I don't think it was really a question, because she tugs him from my arms without waiting for an answer. She walks into the living room and immediately, I hear several other girls squealing, saying how Brad is so cute. Now, thanks to the low music, I can hear most of what they're saying.

"So this is what it feels like to not be the most desirable guy in the room, huh? I've never had this problem before," Keith says.

I chuckle this time, and it feels good. Surprisingly, I'm feeling at ease around this random group of guys who you'd never guess were friends by looking at them. It's weird. Nice even.

After Blake, Austin, and Keith refill their drinks, Austin leads me into the living room and clears a space for me to sit. He's shockingly hospitable, but I don't get the impression he's flirting with me. I mean, all the other girls here are gorgeous, and here I am in a black hoodie, covered in dog hair, two steps removed from climbing into bed. That makes me appreciate his kindness even more, because he's not acting with ulterior motives.

Oscar trails behind and settles on the armrest of the opposite sofa, next to a pair of girls who are lost in their conversation until he sits down. I watch as one girl's eyes light up when she sees him, but despite her not-so-subtle nod to her friend, he doesn't seem to notice. He's watching me.

Somehow, even in his casual track pants and T-shirt, he looks put together. Like he's in his element and not wearing something he picked up off his floor to walk his dog. He's not as bulky as Keith, but he's muscular. Lean. Fit. Hot. His hair is styled in what I can only describe as a modern pompadour; closely shaved on the sides, but he has some length on the top that he keeps brushed back. It's soft, with no signs of any product. Almost like he's so insufferable and cranky, not even his hair dares to cross him, so it just stays put.

"Tell me about yourself, Frankie," Austin interrupts, dropping onto the floor in front of me.

I might think that was weird if there weren't a half-dozen other people on the floor playing with my rambunctious dog.

But now that the attention is back on me, the discomfort creeps back in. I don't like sharing details about myself. The safest bet, so I don't seem rude, is to share surface-level information. "I'm studying animal physiology, hoping to become a DVM."

"I might just be too drunk, but what's a DVM? Department of…?"

"Doctor of Veterinary Medicine. A vet. I want to be a vet," I ramble. I gather some fabric from inside my sweater pocket, clutching it with both hands.

After that detail is glanced over, the conversation eases into random tangents about the latest celebrity news or viral TikTok videos. Everything that is so far out of my element, I sit as a silent observer. So does Oscar. He doesn't laugh, offer any insight into the conversation, or even change his facial expression. He just sits, fidgeting non-stop, ignoring the girls who so desperately try to get his attention.

His friends surprised me tonight. They all seem nice, outgoing, and maybe a bit immature. He, on the other hand, comes across as brash, cranky, and opinionated. None of which are redeeming qualities.

Brad eventually shows signs that he's tired from all the attention, so I take that as my cue to leave. I grab his leash that has been dragging behind him all this time and say good night to the crowd of people—most of whom I have no idea what their names are.

In a surprise move, Oscar is the one who gets up to walk me out. He doesn't say anything, but he opens the door and trails behind us as Brad and I descend the steps, then down the short path to the sidewalk.

"Um… Are you walking me home? I think I can find it."

He halts his steps. "Just want to make sure your dog doesn't attack anyone on the way."

After the last ninety minutes, I'd assume he was joking, but he sounds dead serious. "Ugh. Go back to your cave or wherever you crawled out of. And keep the music down," I call over my shoulder as I walk up my steps.

He doesn't reply. He just stands there and waits while I unlock my deadbolts and pull Brad inside.

5

OSCAR

Don't Stop the Party

Can someone please explain to me why I just walked this girl home? Or why I'm now standing on the sidewalk, watching as each light in her house systematically gets turned on and off, like she's inspecting every room.

She has piqued my curiosity. That's the answer.

When Austin asked her to tell him about herself, I assumed her first words would be about the boyfriend Blake mentioned last week. She didn't say a word about him. And she looked as out of place amongst the crowd of people as I felt.

For me, conversations are exhausting. Surface level ones, anyway. The amount of mental energy it takes to focus my mind on one voice is more than I can spare most days, so I drift in and out of discussions. That perceived disinterest makes people think I'm rude or anti-social. Really, my brain is just going in a hundred different directions, and because that's such a mental tax, it does make me anti-social, but I'm not trying to be.

I'd rather be alone with the endless trains of thought running through my head than be around people who don't understand. The guys understand. Especially Blake, since he deals with the same thing, but he thrives on having people around. I do not.

So that also begs the question why, instead of retreating back to my room and standing guard over my bed, I stayed in the living room, suffering through what was no more than vapid gossip. None of the other girls made me curious. Not even a little.

What is it about this girl that irritates and intrigues me?

That's a question for another day. It's nearly 1am and I have to be at the gym in six hours.

I climb the stairs back into our house, only to be greeted by Keith's raised eyebrow as I tug off my shoes.

"You invited a girl. I'm proud of you, mate."

"I did not invite a girl. She was having a fit over the music, so I told her to come ask herself. I'm going to bed." I sidestep him to reach the staircase, turning back to add, "Keep the music down, eh? Some of us have work in the morning."

Keith flashes his enviable pearly whites and winks. He might have been right about being the most desirable guy in the room, but I'd never tell him that. His ego is already big enough. "Good night, Ozzie."

I turn to head up the stairs, grumbling, "Don't call me Ozzie."

Thankfully, my bed is empty and undisturbed when I reach my bedroom. I collapse on top of the blanket, pull on my noise-cancelling headphones, and try to silence my brain.

Normally, when I know I'm going to the gym, I hop out of bed and get ready. I'm no stranger to short stretches of sleep, so my reluctance to get up is not because I'm tired. Today, I'm lying in bed, unwilling to move, and I don't have a reason why. I just feel stuck.

My window of opportunity to get to the gym on time is shrinking, and I still can't find the motivation to get up. Until I hear a noise outside.

I sit up and pull my curtain back to discover Frankie in her front yard, picking up pieces of garbage. Garbage I'm assuming came from our houseguests last night.

I hop out of bed, change into some clean sweats, and brush my teeth as fast as humanly possible. Then I grab my gym bag and rush out the door.

Why? I don't have an answer any more than I did when I walked her home.

"You're up early," I state as I approach her.

She startles and turns her head just long enough to make eye contact, then returns to her task. "I came out to walk Brad, and a literal tonne of garbage is in my front yard. So, thanks for that," she snaps.

Even though I'm running late, I would have offered to help because I felt bad. But after that greeting, I'll pass. "You know what literal means, right?"

She ignores my question, instead continuing on her rant. "And the more frustrating part is the amount of trash that got thrown over my fence! Like *my* backyard was *your* personal dumpster."

Yeah, if she hadn't come inside and witnessed my version of partying last night, I might be more forgiving, but she did, and she's still choosing to make this personal. To blame me for things I had nothing to do with.

"Thanks for being neighbourly," I reply with an equal amount of irritation.

She scoffs as I turn to walk down the street. I've got a job to do, and it's not helping an ungrateful neighbour.

My client didn't even show up this morning, which has me worried about getting the numbers up so I can keep my job. I send out a mass text to everyone I know—family and friends—encouraging anyone nearby to come check it out. The only person who replies is my cousin Caleb.

When I was home through the summer, he was staying with my grandparents after returning from France. I convinced him to work out with me after he said he needed something to keep him active as he approaches thirty. I thought he was hopeless for the first few weeks, but he's getting better. Having him for one-on-one training will be good now that he's moved down to the city too.

After I shower, I talk to Tyrus for a bit. He tells me about the plans for my programme, and a little more about what he wants me to focus on. This is the only place I *can* focus, so whatever he wants me to do, I'll find a way. I tell him as much before heading home.

The guys are all still sleeping when I return around noon. The house is trashed. There are both partially full and empty plastic cups, bottles, and cans on every surface of our main floor. I was in such a rush this morning, I didn't realize how bad it was. Bad enough, I can't ignore it.

I open the cupboard and pull out a trash bag and a blue recycling bag, then get to work. Half of the job is carrying the drinks to the sink and dumping them. There goes half of Blake's dad's liquor purchase down the drain. Something tells me neither of them care.

It takes me an hour to rid the house of the garbage, which I take outside to throw in the bins. Looking at Frankie's front yard, I wonder how bad the back is. Before I comprehend my own movements, I'm walking up her steps and knocking on her door.

No answer. She was wearing scrubs this morning, so she might be working. But now my mind is stuck on this task, and I won't be able to accomplish anything else until it's done.

I walk around the side of her house, but like our yard, there's no gate to enter the back. The only way to access it is from inside. Or...

Next thing I know, I've got two trash bags stuffed in my pockets, and I'm hopping the eight-foot fence into her yard from ours. She wasn't kidding. There's the same amount of cups here as there were in our living room. Some idiots have no respect for other people's property or the environment.

My big brother, Ethan, is a ranger at a provincial park. He's spent over a decade learning about conservation efforts and encouraging people to be in touch with nature. He instilled the same values in me, which is why I worked with him while I was home this summer. The frustration I felt over disrespectful campers and backpackers is on the same level now.

I move quickly to clean everything up, tossing one bag over the fence, then another. Before I hop back over myself, I take a minute to look behind the plants bordering the yard to find the hole Brad supposedly slipped through. She could have been making that up to excuse her carelessness. Lo-and-behold, behind some big leafy plant, right at the opening between the houses, there's a spot dug under the fence.

It's been days since Brad escaped. Why hasn't she dealt with this yet?

Whatever her reason—she's lazy or she just doesn't care— I won't stand by and let that dog escape again. I shift dirt and mulch from other places in the garden, careful not to disturb the other plants. Once I fill it from this side, I climb back over into my yard, pick up the trash bags, and walk into the house.

Unlike earlier, now all three of my roommates are awake. Staring at me. Studying me, by the looks of it.

"What?"

"Where did you come from?" Blake asks, resting his forehead on his palm, hunched over the counter.

"The yard. Someone had to clean this stuff up." I hold up the bag of trash, hoping it's clear how displeased I am.

"Yeah, but I just looked outside two minutes ago and you weren't there. I know I'm not still drunk."

"Could be," I retort, grabbing the bags and walking to the front door without answering.

Now the next problem is that because of bi-weekly trash pickup and our whack of moving boxes, our recycling bin is full. So, on my way to fill the other side of the fence hole, I drop the second bag in Frankie's bin.

Satisfied I've done my good deed for the day, I return inside my house, again facing a firing squad of questioning looks.

"You cleaned up her garbage?" Keith asks.

"No, I cleaned up *your* guests' garbage from *her* yard."

"Ladies and gentleman, here we have a real-life superhero. Under the cover of darkness—"

"Shut up, man. I just don't want her complaining to bylaw about us."

"Mm-hmm," he hums at my back as I retreat upstairs.

I pick up my guitar as soon as I enter my room and start strumming the chords I was trying to figure out last night. I can read music, but mostly I play by ear. Trial and error. There's something about the challenge that keeps me engaged.

But in the middle of the chorus I'm just getting a handle on, Austin shouts up the stairs, "Ozzie! You have a visitor."

'm so furious, I'm shaking. Or maybe it's not fury. It's fear. That overwhelming, all-consuming feeling of vulnerability and exposure. The space that's meant to be mine has been infiltrated by a meddling neighbour.

Austin answered the door and quickly ratted out the culprit. Note to self: Don't share anything with Austin you want to be kept secret, because he cracks at the first sign of pressure.

Though, for some reason, I'm not surprised it was Oscar. He's the one I yelled at this morning... which was probably unnecessary, but I *was* furious then.

He bounds halfway down the stairs, which lead down to the front door, but stops halfway when his eyes meet mine. Then he slows his pace to saunter down the remaining ones.

"I'll let you two discuss whatever" —Austin waves his finger between us—"you need to... discuss." Then he disappears toward the back of the house.

"You went in my yard?" I seethe the second Oscar reaches the main floor.

"You're welcome." His facial expression doesn't falter.

"That's trespassing. You had no right to invade my—" I stop myself short to take a breath. "It wasn't your place to break into my backyard."

He raises his eyebrows, but the rest of his face remains neutral. "First, I didn't break anything. Second, I tried knocking on your door, but no one answered. So I did what I had to do. Problem solved." He shrugs one shoulder, and his casual dismissal of this issue replaces every bit of fear with anger.

"No, problem not solved, Oscar. Now we have an entirely new problem. Loud music and trash might be a bylaw issue, but trespassing is a criminal one."

For the first time, his expression indicates genuine surprise. Paired with his raised eyebrows, his mouth now gapes open. "You want to call me a criminal for cleaning up garbage and fixing the hole in your fence? Seriously?"

Now, I'm sure my face matches his. "Fixed the fence?"

"It didn't look like you were going to do it, and I didn't want that dog to get out to torment someone else, so I filled the hole. If you want to call me a criminal for that, go ahead. In fact, my boss's brother is a cop. Want me to call him? He can slap some cuffs on me to make you feel better?"

I'm not really sure what to say now. As much as I'm upset about him coming into my space, I don't get the impression he had bad intentions. The opposite, really. And I should be grateful for that, but I will not thank him for nearly scaring the life out of me.

When I came home, I anticipated spending the next few hours cleaning the yard, but it was spotless. Not a single cup or wrapper to be found. Instead of that filling me with relief, my only thought was how someone I didn't invite had gotten into my yard. A fully fenced yard with eight-foot solid fencing. Experience has taught me not to discount any point of entry, but knowing someone had gotten in terrified me.

So he's not a criminal, but it's not okay, either.

"Don't come into my yard again. Ever." I put a lot of effort into glowering at him so he understands how serious I am.

"Message received. Is there anything else you'd like to accuse me of, or are we done here?"

I scoff at him, and with that, he closes the door.

He really fixed the fence. After I confronted Oscar four days ago, I came into the backyard to see if he really did what he said. It wasn't a big job; I just hadn't gotten around to it because I figured I'd keep Brad on a leash to err on the side of caution. But now he's able to enjoy the secure backyard and I don't have to worry.

That doesn't mean I'm going to thank Oscar for doing it, though.

"Get the ball," I encourage my little dog, who is filling out nicely, though still a far cry from a menacing pit bull.

"Frankie, how's it going?" Blake calls over the fence.

I can see a bit of movement between the fence boards, but the gaps are so small, I can't tell what he's doing. "Hi, Blake."

"She remembered my name. Score."

I smirk, hearing the excitement in his voice. "It's one syllable. Not exactly testing my brain capacity."

"Let me read into it." He pauses for a second, then sighs. It sounds like he took a sip of something refreshing. "So, what brings you out here on this fine September evening?"

"Brad. I'm just letting him run around a bit."

"Ah, the neighbourhood menace, Brad. I don't know if anyone told you yet, but that's a weird dog name."

I take a second to appreciate how easy talking to Blake is. My instincts may not be stellar, but he doesn't scare me. In fact, it's actually nice to have someone to talk to. "Yep. My boss told me. I didn't think it was weird at the time."

"Nah, it's weird. It's like naming a dog John or Steve."

"I'm sure there are dogs named Blake."

"Oh, she cuts deep." He makes a comical gurgling sound. "Right to the heart. Savage."

"I don't know if anyone has told you, but you can be pretty dramatic."

"Yep," he repeats. "My roommates tell me every day." He screeches a chair across the patio stones, and it appears he drags it next to the fence. "I'm majoring in screenwriting. You know, for movies and TV? I hate acting, but love the drama. Looove iiit!" he sings.

I giggle at his theatrics. "That makes sense. I think you'll make a great screenwriter."

"Meh. Thanks. You know what name a lot of dogs probably have?"

Okay, I guess we're going back to this now. "What's that?"

"Oscar. That sounds like a good dog name. *Here, little Ozzie.* See? It's a winner."

The mention of his name makes my stomach flip, and I'm not sure if it's from lingering upset over his trespassing or something else. Still, I want to learn more about him without having to interact with him because I'm curious about what makes a person so infuriating.

"Is he always cranky?" I ask, reaching down to pick up Brad, who is pawing at my leg.

"Oscar? Nah. He's a good dude. Maybe he's really serious sometimes, but he'll also make you laugh harder than anyone. He just struggles with change, so he's been a bit off since we moved in. Solid friend, though. He's the kind of person who will push you beyond what you think you can do."

All of those things surprise me. Oscar making anyone laugh, being a good friend, or struggling with change. Not the vibe I got at all.

"He felt pretty bad about the other day... but don't tell him I told you that."

That is also surprising. I doubt he'll ever speak to me again, so keeping that to myself won't be a problem. Just to clarify which of our encounters Blake is referring to, I ask, "Felt bad about what?"

"When he hopped your fence. He was just trying to make things right, you know? I… uh… Sorry about the mess, by the way. We'll keep things more low-key from now on."

That makes me feel worse for getting so angry with him, but in my defence, he didn't help his case at all. And I'm still not okay with him hopping the fence to do it.

"Your secret is safe with me." Now I know at least fifty percent of my neighbours can't be trusted with a secret.

"Tell me something else about Frankie. You're studying animal something and you have a vicious dog with a weird name. What else is there to know?"

I haven't opened up to a virtual stranger for so long, I forgot how. Last time Blake ambushed me with conversation through the fence, I was alarmed and just wanted to run away. But now that I've put a face to the voice, and he's been forthcoming with me, doing the same doesn't feel so scary.

"Nothing too exciting. I go to school and I volunteer at a vet clinic. I'm in my third year, but this is my first semester in Toronto."

"Oh? Why's that?"

That's one thing I don't want to be forthcoming about. Dirty laundry I don't want aired.

"I had a scholarship offered here, so I decided to take it. Plus, I had a good volunteer opportunity with a vet who is doing great work for vets' mental health programs, so I'm learning a lot more than just caring for animals."

"Vet mental health? But… doesn't like… being around fluffy things all day cure everything?"

I stroke my own dog's ears, allowing him to do that for me at the moment. "It's a hard job. For every few pets you send home with their owners, there's one who never gets to go back. Especially in an animal hospital, where a lot of cases are more serious or more urgent. So for people who love animals as much as most vets do, it's really taxing."

"Gotcha. Makes sense." He pauses for a moment, and it sounds like he pushes the chair back. All of a sudden he grunts, then says, "How did he jump over this thing?"

When I look up, I see two hands clutching the top of the fence.

"I was going to pop my head over to say hi, but I'm not Oscar. He's some kind of superhuman. Don't tell him that, either. It will add fuel to his *muay thai is superior to jiu-jitsu* argument."

"Muay—"

"Come on. We're supposed to meet Oscar at the gym after his class," Keith calls through the back door of their house.

"Lovely chatting with you, Frankie. Pretend you can see my bow and you're flabbergasted by my gentlemanliness."

"Oh, yeah. Thanks for the chat." I want to laugh at his antics, but now I just feel like I started conversing with him and he's disappearing right as things got interesting.

"Later," Blake shouts as I see their back door close behind him, leaving me with a slew of unanswered questions.

If Blake claims Oscar is a good guy, just serious, what is it about me that makes him so miserable? And more importantly, why do I care?

Guilty By Association

"Did you know that statistically, vets have high suicide rates?" Blake asks, parking himself on my bed.

I spin in my desk chair to face him. "And this is important because?"

"Frankie is studying to be a vet."

My shoulders tense. "Are you saying you think she's suicidal?" I'm not an idiot. I heard him telling Keith at the gym last night that he was talking to Frankie again. Sure, I was curious, but I'm not going to waste time analyzing why. And I certainly won't ask Blake what they talked about.

"No, I'm just saying it wouldn't kill you to be a little nicer to her. She's cool."

"Uh-huh. 'Cool' is exactly how I'd describe her." I add air quotes and an eye-roll to emphasize my sarcasm.

"She asked about you," he adds, challenging me with one raised eyebrow.

I won't give in. "Good for her. Do you have anything important to tell me?"

"We're having another party next Saturday, but it won't be as crazy. Turns out Dear Ol' Dad actually does check his credit card statements, and he wasn't thrilled about the $1168 liquor store charge. Go figure." He shrugs, but in typical Blake fashion, turns it into a joke. "I think five hundred bucks is more reasonable for next time."

"Right. I'm sure Fletcher will appreciate your restraint."

He stands and rubs his hands down his thighs. "He'll be proud I've learned my lesson. Like any good father would." With that, he exits my room, but I don't feel any peace in his absence.

Every time he mentions his dad, it makes me feel bad for him. Not only did his father cheat on his mom, but he turned it around to blame his actions on Blake because he was "too much of a handful." A phrase a lot of neurodivergent kids hear far too often. If only people realized how much of a *handful* having an uncooperative brain can be. Add that on top of constantly being told something out of your control is "too much" and it can take its toll.

Being reminded of his terrible parents makes me appreciate mine.

This conversation also leaves me wondering, what did Frankie ask about me? And why does that matter?

The past ten days have been a blur. Between the demands of my classes, assignments, work, and training, I've been going non-stop. That's how I operate best, but it also leaves me feeling like there aren't enough hours in a day. So tonight, I promised my friends I won't be a recluse, and I'd actually come to their party.

But the second I walk downstairs to find twenty people in our living room, it takes every bit of self-control not to turn around and go right back upstairs. There's a collection of girls hovering around the sofas that are crowded with guys around my age. I only recognize Austin's distinguishable curls and the girl who was more interested in the dog than anything else last time she was here.

I wonder if Frankie will come up with something new to complain about and show up again tonight.

The weird thing is, I'm kind of annoyed the music is so quiet, making that unlikely. We haven't spoken a word for two weeks. Blake has talked to her a few times, but he never admitted what she asked him about me. I'm too stubborn to ask. So instead of trying to make amends and be neighbourly, I've avoided her.

If she wants to call me a criminal for trying to help, then what do I care?

As I enter the kitchen, another group of girls, who all look identical, surround my other two roommates. Not only do they all look similar, they talk, walk, and act the same. You can't tell one from the other. In my experience, all the girls who end up at these random parties that aren't hosted by the campus jocks are ones trying to climb their way up the social hierarchy. Ones trying to *earn* an invite to parties hosted by campus jocks or resident rich kids.

"Ozzie, my man. What are you drinking?" Keith walks around the kitchen island toward the fridge, pulling it open. "I grabbed these just for you." He hands me a light beer with a satisfied smile on his face.

"You're an idiot." I laugh, swiping the can from his hand. "But just because I don't have to work tomorrow, I'll drink it."

"Thatta boy. You know I wouldn't be caught dead drinking it. It was bad enough buying it. I had to wear a face mask."

I don't tell him that I would have preferred he not buy it, deciding instead to pop the top and take a swig just to see the smile of satisfaction on his face. We might have different priorities, but Keith is still a good friend, so I appreciate him trying to include me. Even if my experience with alcohol has only ever exacerbated my ADHD symptoms and is not a feeling I enjoy. I won't drink to get drunk, but I'll have a beer and hang out with my friends.

I chat with Blake and the girl standing beside him for ten minutes until her obsessive recounting of campus gossip bores me near death. On my list of things I'm interested in, who is sleeping with whom this week is as close to the bottom as discussing my sister's period.

After I chug my beer, I decide to escape into the backyard, which is thankfully empty. Since the party population is so much lower this time, I guess no one else felt the need to escape.

"Blake?" a familiar voice calls through the fence.

"No. Oscar."

"Oh." She says a lot more than the one simple syllable with her tone.

"Sorry to disappoint."

"I didn't say I was disappointed," she snaps.

"Right. Maybe you didn't say those words, but you made it pretty clear."

"You think you're some expert on me now? Like you know me and can tell what I'm thinking without me saying it?"

Silence. Well, not really, because sounds of the city hum in the air; everything from honking and car sounds to a shouted argument somewhere down the street. Despite not being able to see her, the lack of conversation hangs over me like a rain cloud. I'm not sure how to respond to that, so I revert to my default Frankie setting: irritated.

"If you want to talk to Blake so badly, why don't you just come to the front door and crash the party again instead of lurking in the backyard like a creeper?" I finally ask, and every ounce of confusing, petty jealousy seeps into each word.

"I'm not a creeper," she shouts automatically. Like that word in particular triggered some angry, defensive side of her.

"Says the creeper calling over the fence."

Metal scrapes concrete, making me squint from the sound.

"I don't know why you've had a problem with me since day one, but I suggest you get over it. Get over *yourself*," she seethes.

I can't see her, but I can picture the steam coming from her nostrils, all while her angry dog snarls beside her. It still doesn't intimidate me in the slightest. It's not the first time she's told me to get over myself.

"Front door is open if you want to talk to Blake."

With those parting words, I clear two steps at a time and duck in the back door, sliding it closed behind me. But the second I return inside to the humid air and the constant buzz of conversation, I realize that arguing with Frankie is the most interesting thing I've done all night. Even when we can't get along, I'd still prefer talking to her than any of the other girls in here.

This isn't my scene. The guys knew that from last year, because I didn't go to parties unless I went to make sure they all found their way home. I get overwhelmed by the music and conversations and smells and sights. It makes me want to crawl out of my skin to make it all stop.

As I get to the bottom of the stairs to disappear to my room, I hear a knock at the front door.

I refuse to accept that the flutter of excitement I feel has anything to do with it possibly being Frankie. But when I open the door, there's no denying that's the cause.

She stands on the other side, dressed in an Eagles T-shirt and black sweatpants.

Interesting.

"Blake's in the kitchen," I say instead of a proper greeting. We're beyond exchanging pleasantries.

"I didn't come to talk to Blake."

She doesn't elaborate, so I prompt, "Okay?"

"I came to talk to you." She narrows her eyes at me, but if she thinks she's intimidating, she's way off the mark.

To say I'm surprised by those words is a fair assessment. I trail my eyes down her left arm, noticing her fist clenched around a dog leash. My eyes follow the leash to find Brad sitting on our front porch, unmoving, aside from his wagging tail.

"Frankie!" Blake's voice shouts from behind me. "You made it. And Brad's here. Everybody, Brad's here!"

Even with Blake saying his name, the dog doesn't move. Once the brunette who gushed over him last time hears his name, she comes running to the door and ushers Frankie inside.

Frankie says something that sounds like Italian to Brad, who dutifully follows behind. She flashes me a pleading look, like she wants me to intervene.

What am I supposed to do? And why, after the interactions we've had so far, would she expect that?

Oh, no. My bad. That's anger. I can see it clearly now that she's standing still, glaring at me.

I'd be more inclined to step in on her behalf than I am to stick around and be the recipient of her death glare, but I don't want to do either. So, while everyone is distracted by Brad's arrival, I turn away and head upstairs. Back to my sanctuary where I can get lost in my own music and forget about Frankie.

Rain Over Me

Apparently, I wasn't clear when I told Oscar I was here to talk to him. Not long after I walked through the door, he disappeared upstairs and hasn't returned. I sat here and waited for ninety minutes before accepting that he's not coming back down.

Since days after they moved in, he's had an issue with me, and I'm sure it's more than my "menace dog" or his struggle with change. It feels personal and I want to know why.

The last time someone took exception to my presence… well, it resulted in me transferring schools, moving to a new city, and starting over. The circumstances might be different, but that doesn't mean I want to leave the situation unchecked.

It appears we're not resolving things tonight, even though I'm still angry. I'm mad Oscar called me a creeper. Mad he's decided to hate me for no reason. And now I'm especially mad because there's nothing I can do about it. It's not like I can march upstairs to confront him.

Can I? No. That *would* make me a creeper.

I tap Blake on the shoulder, interrupting his conversation with a girl he introduced earlier as Jessie-Lee. "Sorry, guys. I'm just uh… Yeah, I'm going to head out. Gotta get Brad home."

"Are you sure?" Blake asks, turning away from his new lady friend.

"Yeah." I consider telling him that I came to talk to Oscar, but I don't want him making it an issue or going up to get his cranky roommate, who clearly doesn't want to talk to me. "Enjoy your night," I say to everyone within hearing distance, including Keith and Austin. Then I walk out the door into the cooling early autumn air.

My Sunday morning volunteer shift at the animal hospital always seems to be the craziest. Most vet offices are closed on Sundays, so we end up with an influx of people bringing in their pets for one reason or another, desperate for help. It's hard when not all of them can be saved.

Today we had a few different pets, from a hedgehog to a macaw, so it was a great learning experience, but we also had to say goodbye to one family's beloved cat. By the time I walk out the door into the rain, shielding Brad in my coat, my heart is heavy. My little pup has only been in my life for a few weeks, but from day one, I loved him enough that if I lost him, I'd be devastated. That was made abundantly clear when he got through the fence and Oscar threatened his safety.

Just thinking about Oscar's infuriating behaviour makes me tense as I walk to my car. But that's not what causes the surge of panic to rush through me before I reach my driver's side door. The problem is, I don't know what does. Brad reacts, scrambling to poke his head out of my coat.

I freeze, pulling the hood of my jacket back enough to scan my surroundings—something I've been a little too lax with lately. There are so many vehicles around, but the falling rain makes it impossible to see inside any of them.

Should I go back inside? Risk running to my car? Am I just being paranoid?

I take a deep inhale after scanning the area one last time and dash for my car. I press the unlock button when I'm only a few feet away and hit the lock button as soon as I open the door, so it seals us inside when I close it. From the safety of my car, I again search for anything out of place.

Nothing.

I'm just being paranoid.

That thought doesn't calm me down, though. My heart hammers against my ribcage as I sit and wait for something to appear that justifies my reaction. My thumb hovers over the call button with 911 already typed in.

Still nothing.

No one suspiciously lingering in the bus stop. No shadows moving inside any of the neighbouring cars. Not a single reason to explain the hairs standing on the back of my neck. I don't know if Brad's reaction is to an external threat or if he's picking up on my fear.

After a few more minutes, I convince myself the events of the day just have me on edge. Brad helps ease my fears by making a nest out of a hoodie on my back seat. With no reason to hang around any longer, I pull out of my parking spot and exit onto the street, desperately wanting to be inside the safety of my own four walls.

As I drive, I keep a close eye on my rear-view mirror, watching for anything suspicious. I don't want to accept that my instincts are that far off. Instead of taking the direct route home, which takes less than five minutes, I continue south so I can make a wide circle, only making right-hand turns. After my third right-hand turn, I realize a black sedan has made each turn a few car lengths back. When I turn back onto Dundas Avenue and the car follows again, I continue eastbound, headed to the nearest police station.

Before I reach the next block, the car turns right onto another side street, out of view. My shoulders are tense and my palms sweaty from the sixty-second ordeal. I attempt a few steady breaths to slow my racing heart, deciding to continue to the police station anyway.

I pull into a street parking spot in front of the station, continuing to watch my side mirror to be sure the person following me doesn't reappear.

Several police officers run in and out of the precinct, rushing inside or to their cars. Their presence, despite not being aware I'm even here, is comforting. After five minutes, the mysterious car hasn't reappeared, so with less fear choking me, I make a second attempt to get home.

On top of the physical effects, my mind is racing, so my thoughts are not focused on the road, where they should be. That's exactly why a figure suddenly appears in front of my car at the crosswalk turning onto my street.

Or should I say *our street*?

I slam on the brakes, causing the tires to screech along the pavement.

"Hey! Watch where—" Oscar's words stop when he makes eye contact after my windshield wipers clear the window.

I don't even know what to say. I feel like the world's biggest idiot and actually feel sick that my distracted driving could have just ended in tragedy. Sure, I may not like the guy, but I don't want to run him over with my car.

What choice do I have but to issue a heartfelt apology?

I roll down my window, wincing as some of the cool rain splashes my face. "I'm so sorry. Do you want a ride home at least? To… make up for almost killing you?" I laugh in an attempt to ease the awkwardness.

It doesn't.

Oscar raises an eyebrow and steps over to the window. He leans over, placing his hand on top of my car. "Sweetheart, if that's how you drive, I'd rather take my chances on foot." Then he stands straight, glances in both directions—which is unnecessary on a one-way street, but he did almost get mowed down—and dashes off in the rain.

After a few seconds, I shake off the surprise from his response and roll my window back up. I have no choice but to drive forward, passing Oscar jogging along the sidewalk. A fresh surge of embarrassment courses through me as he turns his head to watch me roll by. Like he needed another reason to hate me.

And what was with the derogatory *sweetheart*? Like he's patronizing me for having an error in judgement. Or for almost flattening him.

Whatever. What's done is done. All I need right now is to get inside and hide out until I have to go to my classes tomorrow. I can use that time to get my head right so I don't nearly kill anyone on my way to campus.

I pull into my usual parking spot in front of the end-unit row house I call home, hop out, and lock my car. Oscar is only a few dozen metres away now, jogging down the sidewalk to my left. He runs along easily, despite his soaking wet grey track pants and gym bag slung over his shoulder. As much as I want to yell at him for disappearing last night without giving me a chance to talk to him, I don't really have a leg to stand on after being the cause of his near-death experience. Now is not the time to try to claim the moral high ground.

The reality of the entire situation has me rushing inside before he gets any closer. Besides, I'm far too embarrassed to admit why I was distracted in the first place. I highly doubt Oscar is the type to garner a modicum of sympathy anyway. And the last thing I want is his pity.

10

OSCAR

Get It Started

Can't say I've ever been hit by a car before, but today, I came close. It was partly my fault for not paying attention because I was lost in my head. Oddly enough, I was thinking about what Frankie might have said if I stuck around last night. Maybe her taking me out would have been poetic justice, but in this case, I don't think the punishment would fit the crime.

"Who peed in your protein shake?" Blake asks as I stomp into the foyer. "You mad at the rain?"

I roll my eyes, not really in the mood for conversation. "Nah, I'm mad that our house got trashed again and because I almost got run over."

"Run over? By what?"

"A car," I deadpan. "Frankie's car."

"Was Frankie driving it?"

I have serious concerns about this guy sometimes. "Yes, she was driving. Probably distracted by that dog in the backseat."

"What's your problem with Brad?"

"He's illegal."

Blake returns my eye-roll, then takes a sip of his incredibly pale coffee. "I know you're a stickler for the rules, man, but he's not hurting anyone. Take it easy on her."

"Take it easy on her? She just tried to run me over. With. Her. Car."

Instead of standing around, arguing with my friend over a topic we'll never agree on, I tell him I need to shower and change. He leaves it at that, but there's a good chance he'll bring it up again later.

For now, I'll get dried off and spend the rest of the day struggling through course work. It's hard enough when my brain isn't inundated with a thousand different thoughts, but right now, it'll be near impossible.

Thursdays are my busiest day this semester, but the payoff is that my roommates all have evening classes. At least I get the house to myself after hours of coaching and classes. That thought propels me out the door, knowing I'll be able to come home to some much needed peace and quiet.

That promise of some peace is crushed when I exit the house to find my angry neighbour in her front yard.

"Do you have to put your garbage bins there? Every time it gets windy, I end up with trash blown all over my yard."

I stare at Frankie, who is currently picking up plastic cups littered across her grass. She's in regular clothes, and I'd have to be blind not to notice how different she looks in leggings and a fitted jacket than scrubs or sweats. Especially when she bends over to grab a cup from under a plant lining her pathway.

When she stands back up, I clear my throat to answer, "Where do you suggest we put them?"

"On the *other* side of your house. Is it really so hard?" She still refuses to make eye contact with me, and I don't know if she's just that angry or she wants to avoid talking about her attempted vehicular manslaughter.

Based on our previous encounters, it could have been first-degree murder. Wouldn't surprise me one bit if it was premeditated.

"Right. Let me show you something." I wave for her to follow me the few feet to the other side of our house. To the exact spot where the neighbouring row house attaches. "Should I just ask them if I can keep the bins in their living room or...?"

She scoffs, spinning on her heel to walk back over to her yard. "You could at least make sure they stay closed so your trash isn't blowing all over my yard."

Yeah, we could, but I bet if Blake had been the one to walk out the door just now, she wouldn't have come at him with her fangs out like a rabid pit bull. She seems to reserve this reaction for me.

"Talk to Blake about it. He'll be happy to help," I reply with a little more bite to my voice than I intended.

But really, why is it always me she accuses? It's not my fault we had a wicked wind storm overnight. I'm not the Big Bad Wolf she seems to think I am, huffing and puffing to make her life miserable.

She's been to both of our parties. I've had nothing to do with either of them, yet she still blames me for everything. Even after I tried to help, she still had a problem. I'm starting to think we rented a house next to the most frustrating woman on the planet.

Instead of hanging around for her to find something new to complain about, I continue down the path without offering to help again. I reach the sidewalk and add, "Keep your eyes on the road this time so you don't kill anyone, eh?"

Her glare transforms into a more softened expression as her cheeks flush. If I have to hold her dangerous driving over her head to keep her from ripping mine off every time I walk out the door, so be it. I'm sick of her assuming the worst of me while my roommates, who are actually the ones to blame, get off scot-free.

They can be the ones to deal with her from now on.

My mom called to check in when I was on my way home, which helped ease my mind. Some people would call me a momma's boy—Blake does—but she's always been supportive of me and taught me to embrace the things that make me different, rather than silence them. Without her and my dad advocating for me, I probably wouldn't have made it through high school. I love my parents, and I'm not embarrassed to admit that.

So when she asked about our accommodations, I didn't hesitate to tell her about our frustrating neighbour. My mom is the type of person to launch an entire revolution when she feels something is unjust—which is often something as trivial as the price of her morning coffee—so I had to talk her down from driving here to tell Frankie off. I have no doubt my mom would have put an end to the conflict once and for all. For some reason, I find that disappointing.

Just because Frankie's pit bull attacked me, doesn't mean I need to send mine after her.

Now, having vented my frustrations to my mom, I can spend the rest of the evening in peace. At least, that was my plan before Austin walks up the stairs from the basement, wrapped in a blanket, with his hair tied in a poofy bun atop his head.

"What are you doing here?" I ask, a little snarkier than I should have.

He sucks in a loud sniffle. "Sick. Dying. Send help."

"Have you been here all day?"

"Uh-huh." He starts hacking his head off, covering his mouth with his blanket.

"Do you have any meds? Need me to grab something?" Yeah, I want him to feel better, but I also want to stay as far away from him as possible. I can't afford to get sick, so I'll run to the store to create some distance if I have to.

"I need drugs, Ozzie. Hard drugs. Decongestants. Nasal spray. Throat lozenges. Bourbon. The smelly stuff you can rub on my chest. All of it."

So much for a quiet night alone to get some work done.

"Go back to bed. I'll run out and grab you something." I walk toward the front door to create more distance, then yell back, "But I'm not rubbing anything on your chest."

"You're a champ, man. I'll take whatever I can get. Hard drugs, okay? The good stuff," he confirms as he rounds the corner to go back downstairs.

"Got it."

I slip on my shoes, then open the door, only to find that it's pouring out. I also find my neighbour pulling her car up along the curb. At least I was still on the front steps, so she couldn't run me over.

She steps out with a hoodie pulled up and makes her way across the sidewalk toward her pathway, but she freezes before reaching the cobblestone.

If looks could kill... I'd be safe and sound, because that doesn't look like the angry glare I was expecting. Her soft dark eyes and light pink cheeks look almost angelic, but I'm not foolish enough to fall for it.

"Do you have some weird addiction to walking in the rain?" she asks, her voice barely loud enough to hear over the water pelting my surroundings.

"No," I reply, approaching the end of our pathway. Honestly, I'm not thrilled about going out in the rain because I could still end up sick, which I was trying to avoid. I was lucky enough to escape a head cold from coming home the other night. "Austin is sick. He wants hard drugs."

Her eyes widen as rain saturates her hood. "You're going to get him drugs?"

"Hard drugs." I nod. "Decongestant. Nasal spray. Throat lozenges." I don't mention the chest rub, because I'm still trying to rid that vision from my head.

"Oh." She lifts a hand to her chest. "Do you want a ride?" she asks, her cheeks deepening in colour.

"Would I be any safer inside the car than out?"

"Forget it. But don't blame me when you can't find any of the 'hard drugs' you're looking for at this pathetic drug store." She rolls her eyes and hooks her thumb to point toward the exact place I was headed.

She steps forward to walk past, but I stop her with words that surprise us both.

"Actually… would you mind?" Once the sentence spills out, I refuse to acknowledge that my decision has anything to do with her and everything to do with not wanting to miss time at work because I'm sick.

"Fine. Get in." She presses the unlock button on her key so the lights flash.

I glance back at the house, double checking that Austin isn't watching out the small basement window. He'd no doubt relay this encounter to Blake, who would find a way to irritate me over it. The coast is clear, so I jog around the passenger side and hop in. The seat is so close to the dashboard, I nearly get stuck with my knees in my chest.

"Sorry. You can move it back." Frankie shrugs, sliding the key in the ignition. As soon as the engine turns over, the small screen lights up, indicating the car is connected to her phone's playlist.

I honestly expected her to be the type to listen to talk radio or complete silence, so I'm surprised to hear a Spanish Pitbull song pump through the speakers. I glance at her, but I don't ask.

It's just one more annoying thing that she and Blake have in common. One more difference between us.

One more reason I stay silent from the second we pull away from the curb until we return fifteen minutes later.

11

FRANKIE

Go Girl

"**H**owdie, neighbour," a familiar voice calls over the fence.

"Hi, Blake," I return, leaning back in my patio chair.

"What brings you to your backyard oasis this fine afternoon?"

I chuckle because he's so eccentric and ridiculous, it's hard not to love him. Unlike his roommate. "Just out here with Brad. Finished up some work I had to get done for a lab tomorrow. You?"

"Oh, how I wish I could get some work done. I'm stuck, Frankie. And I think it might be my cause of death. Not disappointing Dear Ol' Dad like I thought."

There's a lot to unpack in that one statement. I'm not sure if it's just his dramatic personality or his relationship with his dad is really that bad, but I'm not ready to dive into deeply personal issues. Certainly not with any amount of reciprocity. So I stick to what I know best. "What are you stuck on? Maybe I can help."

He hops up, trying to peek over the fence again, but aside from a couple glimpses of his hair, he's unsuccessful. Finally, he replies, "If you can get me out of this funk, I'd marry you and adopt a hundred children from third-world countries."

This guy is so weird.

"Not necessary. I have no intentions of getting married or having kids, so you're off the hook. No promises I can help, anyway."

Instead of gifting me with some other unpredictable response, he replies with something even more surprising. "Can I come over?"

"Um... like, over the fence?"

"I was thinking more like through the front door, but if this is my only option, I can get Oscar to give me a boost."

Few people have come into my house before, and they either own the house or are my immediate family. Call me paranoid—because I am—but that's a big step. So I surprise myself when I agree.

Two minutes later, Blake is standing at my front door, holding a wilted hydrangea he must have cut from the plant in front of their porch. "For the lady," he says, holding out the flower and bending in a dramatic bow.

I'm learning quickly that everything Blake does is over the top. "Thank you... I guess." Even if the gesture has me questioning my decision.

"Since marriage and babies are off the table, I thought I'd at least bring you flowers. Or... flower." He claps his hands once and steps inside my front door, taking in the room. "Wow, I like what you've done with the place. Which is precisely nothing."

I close the door behind him and turn around to look at my barren house. It's intentionally plain and minimalistic because I knew if I had to up and move again, it would make a hard thing easier. I'm not going to delve into those details, though. "Yeah, less to clean. Brad's in the yard. Come on." I encourage him to follow me outside, because that feels like less of an invasion of my space. "Do you want something to drink?"

"Woah, Frankie. This is starting to feel a bit like a date, but I'm a long-term kind of guy. If you're not putting a ring on it, don't get my hopes up."

My steps halt beside my fridge. Is this guy for real? "Oh-kay," I draw out. I continue forward to open the back door and find my eager little dog waiting.

He immediately runs over to Blake but doesn't jump up at his legs. This is progress.

Blake greets Brad, bending down to scratch behind his ears. After a minute, we settle at the patio table, and I call Brad up to sit on my lap, knowing he won't be able to fit much longer. Blake leans back in a sideways chair, resting one arm on the table and stretching his long legs out in front of himself.

"Okay, what are you stuck on?" I ask again.

He explains that the majority of his screenwriting class this year hinges upon him completing a full movie script, but it has to address real-life issues in a fictional way and have an unpredictable or unresolved ending. On top of that, he has to have a pitch and outline submitted next week, so he's really feeling the crunch. His ideas have all fizzled in the opening scenes, so he's back at Square One with nothing to show for the hours of work he's put in so far.

It's all way over my head. "Wow. Suddenly my genetics class seems like a cakewalk. At least with most science courses, the answer is concrete. Either right or wrong. I'm not sure I'm cut out for creative stuff."

Blake deflates and sinks into his chair. "Yeah, that's what my roommates all said. I'm so screwed."

I'm tempted to inspire him with my own experiences, but the thought of sharing that with him and giving the situation an unresolved ending in a fictional world will only make me more anxious about the limbo I'm living in. And based on Blake's eccentricity, if he went with an unpredictable ending, that would probably terrify me even more.

Instead, we sit and chat for thirty minutes. He tells me Austin is on the mend and they've essentially quarantined him in the basement until he's fully recovered. He doesn't mention anything else about Oscar or our silent trip to the drugstore, so I assume Oscar never told him. Otherwise, Blake would have brought it up—I'm confident about that.

I grill him on where he normally finds his inspiration, which genre he wants to focus on, and his favourite films of all time. Turns out, I haven't seen any of his favourite movies, and concepts for unpredictable thrillers that deal with real-life issues are not easy to come by.

By the time he goes home, he seems more defeated than he was when he walked in, so I feel terrible that I couldn't help. But whether he realizes it, he helped me take a step I didn't know I needed to, so I'm determined to return the favour.

Professor Childs opens the class by sharing a plagiarized assignment submitted by a student in one of his classes, including their photo and name. He informs us that if we don't want to be the butt of the joke for his next group of students, we better play by his rules. I don't know about everyone else, but it has me sitting straight and my eyes wide open. Not because I have any intention of plagiarizing anything, but because the possibility of being put on blast like that is terrifying.

Today's lesson, in part, focuses on animals' instinctual need to protect their young and the difference between creatures that abandon their young, like sea turtles, versus animals that protect their babies with an intense ferocity. He finishes the class with a story about poachers being killed by a pride of lions, and not a single part of me feels bad about it. I've always preferred animals to people, and while I wouldn't wish death on anyone… karma.

I head to my three-hour lab, prepared to absorb everything in my class, but my mind is stuck on Blake's assignment instead of my own.

My lab partner, Lynne, pulls my attention back to our task again.

"Sorry," I apologize for the fourth time. I'm used to my mind being preoccupied by other things, but this is completely unnecessary. My focus should be on RNA extraction, not on writing an epic thriller.

Still, when the student radio station playing at a low volume on the lab speakers starts discussing the latest world news, I'm further pulled from my task. Between my class discussions and the most recent tragedy unfolding, I have a spark of creative genius that I've never had before. My brain has never thrived in creative spaces, and unless I was given clear direction for an art project, I floundered, unable to come up with something new. This excitement I feel over creating an idea that could help Blake has me rushing through my lab tasks to get back home.

Two hours later, I'm pulling my car up along the curb to park in front of my house. I don't see any action at the neighbours', so I go straight inside to let Brad out and unwind for a bit. My little dog is thrilled that I'm home and even more excited to be let outside. He roams around the garden as I listen for any sign of people next door.

Okay… maybe Oscar was right. I am being a bit of a creeper.

Yet, as soon as I hear Keith shout something from inside the house, I can't stop myself from calling Brad inside, then walking next door.

"Is Blake here?" Frankie asks when I open the front door. Seems she's either forgiven me for the trash in her front yard or she's choosing not to mention it. Funny how when I asked Blake about it, he said she never mentioned a word to him.

"He's upstairs."

"Oh." She fails to say anything more and instead stands in front of me silently.

Awkward silence is better than arguing, but I don't have the patience for this, either. "Blake?" I shout up the stairs. Then I turn back to Frankie to add, "Why don't you just get his number, so when you have an issue, you can text him?"

"I don't have an iss—"

"Yeah?" Blake asks, jogging down the stairs. He spots Frankie and clearly doesn't need to ask me anything else. "Frankie! My FBFF. Where's Brad?"

Why is everyone so obsessed with this dog?

"He's at home. I just got back from my classes, but I was thinking about what we discussed yesterday, and I have an idea." Whatever that idea is, she seems excited about it.

I should give the two of them some privacy and go back to my room, but I'm curious. Why is it that she jumps down my throat whenever I walk out the door, but she's coming here with excitement in her eyes to share something with Blake? What's this grand idea?

"Come in," Blake offers, pointing to the living room.

Frankie looks at me as if she's asking for permission before stepping in and slipping off her shoes.

"Do you want a drink or something?" Blake asks, following her over to the sofa. "No strings attached."

"Oh, no thanks."

I feel awkward trailing them into the living room like I'm the one who's on a leash, so I continue past, taking up a spot in the dining room where I can still hear. Nothing pathetic about it. Plain old curiosity.

"So, I was thinking about your screenplay idea, and today, while I was in my biology class, I had an epiphany."

"I'm listening," Blake answers.

Little does he know, I am too.

"This is just a suggestion, so you won't hurt my feelings if you hate it," she starts. "Picture this. Set in Washington D.C., surrounding corruption in congress and ties to weapons manufacturers."

"Already a good start. D.C. might be a bit predictable, but woo me with your grand idea, Frankie. Let me have it."

"A vigilante sniper is targeting members of congress, shooting them at random. They start off months apart. Ballistics don't match, but the MO is the same, right? This has protection details scrambling because they aren't sure what to make of it. But as months go by, the attacks get closer together. Never shooting to kill, but injuring."

Now I'm too intrigued to hide around the corner, so I step into the living room and park myself on the arm of the couch Blake is on. Frankie eyes me cautiously, but I nod for her to continue, hoping it says 'don't mind me.'

"This keeps happening until they become a weekly thing, and everyone is on edge because the shooter is good."

"I like. I like. Keep going." Blake nods and rubs his hands together like an evil genius.

"Anyway, finally, the shooter breaks their silence, sending a letter to the national news, stating that they are making the members of congress live in fear the same way children in schools are, trying to force them to make some changes."

"Ohhh… savage. Very Unabomber-esque. And applicable. Definitely a real-life issue."

"Right?" She smiles wide, leaning forward to continue. "So after each shooting from then on, the vigilante sends a new letter, stating that they'll never be caught and they'll keep going until something is done to protect children."

I've never seen Frankie so passionate about anything more than hating me. Watching her face light up is like seeing a whole new side of her. Not one who starts yelling, then shrinks back like she regrets her words. She's intense and excited. And gorgeous.

Blake is invested too. He's been stressed over this screenwriting class and struggling with it for weeks. None of us have been any help. To be fair, I've watched a handful of movies in my life, so I'm not the right person to ask.

"What happens next? Do they catch the guy?"

"See, you've made the same assumption everyone else has. That the vigilante is a man, set on making a change. But in reality, it's a group of women from all over the country working together to make their point."

"Ohhh!" Blake cheers again, adding a fist pump this time. "Female power. I love it. So what happens next?" he asks, like he's waiting for the end of the greatest movie he's ever seen.

"They don't get caught. Congress re-evaluates their stance, and the 'shooter' sends a final letter stating that they're all mothers who have each lost a child to a school shooting, going as far back as twenty years. They express how they never healed from the situation because it keeps happening, and each child lost since has been like losing their own all over again."

Even I find myself nodding my head as I listen and watch Frankie's animated delivery of this off-the-cuff story. Movies don't often appeal to me, but I'd watch this one.

"This would make a great movie." Blake pushes himself to stand and bounds over to Frankie, looking like he's about to kiss her.

My stomach tightens, forcing me to look away. I knew they were friends, but...

"Put 'er there. You're a champ, Frankie. I'm going to get started on this and see what I can come up with. If I get stuck, I'm comin' over."

I look up in time to see him giving her a fist bump instead of a kiss. I ignore the flood of what feels like relief.

He rushes toward the stairs, stopping at the bottom and peeking his head around the corner. "If you ever change your mind about marriage and kids, you know where to find me." Without waiting for a reply, he disappears.

Frankie's cheeks flush pink as she looks at me. "Expect the unexpected with him, huh?"

I want to ask what that means, but asking implies interest I shouldn't have in Frankie's decisions about marriage and kids. I don't even have an interest in my own decisions on either subject. So I just stand and stare, not answering.

"I guess I'll go."

"Yeah."

She has no reason to stay. I have work to get back to and shouldn't want her to stay. But even as I pull the door open, encouraging her to leave, I'm irritated by the conflicting feelings I have over seeing her walk out the door.

Clearly, Frankie and Blake have something going on and, despite his womanizing ways, he seems interested in her. So no matter how much she might intrigue me, that's all she'll ever be. An area of interest. It's clear we can't even be friends. And I certainly don't want to try to build a friendship with the girl who has captured Blake's interest too.

It's a strange realization, watching her walk away.

I'm jealous.

FRANKIE

I Wonder

"Did you get the stool sample, Frankie?" Dr. Ellis asks. I tug off my gloves and toss them in the garbage. "Yes. You don't pay me enough to scrape liquid feces into a container, though." I walk over to the sink to scrub my hands and arms all the way up to my elbow.

"How much is enough? I thought you did this out of love for animals." He laughs, grabbing the container from the sample collection tray. "I hope my sincere thank you will suffice," he adds as he walks through the door into the lab.

I wouldn't say a love for animals is enough to make these tasks enjoyable, but that's what keeps me coming back. That's what propels me into the next exam room, where I find a gorgeous Himalayan cat alongside its gorgeous human.

"Hi, little one," I greet the cat, not having the nerve to address the guy with her. "Let me get you set up for the doctor."

The cat is wearing a crystal emblazoned harness with a matching leash and looks perfectly healthy.

Curiosity gets the better of me, so I ask, "What brings you guys in?"

"My mom insists her eyes are more watery than normal. So here I am, on a Wednesday morning, bringing her spoiled cat for a checkup." He chuckles, not looking the least bit bothered by the situation. He runs a hand through the length of his light brown crew cut, leaving it mussed.

"Oh. I'm sure it's nothing serious. Dr. Chen will be in shortly to look at her." I continue with my tasks, making sure all the equipment Dr. Chen will need is available. The entire time, I feel eyes on me, which gets more awkward by the second. "What's her name?" I ask, trying to break the silence.

"Lovely. Mine's Whit. And yours is...?" He looks at me expectantly with his smiling grey eyes.

I don't get the impression he's *trying* to flirt with me. I think he just has a charming personality without putting in any effort. So I answer, knowing I'm wearing a nametag; my name is not a well-guarded secret. "Frankie. Why Lovely?"

"Her full name is Mademoiselle Lovelyworth, but no one calls her that. My mom can be a little extra."

I look down at the cat's file and notice the extensive list of visits she's been in for—all of which have been non-issues. "Sometimes peace of mind is worth a quick visit."

"You know, I once broke my pinky finger after my sister shut my hand in the car door, and my mom told me to 'walk it off'? But the cat has a hangnail, and we have to rush her to the vet. I didn't see a doctor until my hand swelled up like Mickey Mouse." He smirks, turning up one side of his face with a ridiculously handsome dimple.

Dr. Chen walks into the room before I can try to rationalize his mother's neglect, but I'm not even sure what to say about that. We work quickly to examine the fluffy cat, not finding anything wrong, as expected. With a clean bill of health, Mademoiselle Lovelyworth gets the all-clear to go home. Dr. Chen exits the room, leaving me with Whit and Lovely.

"Hey, Frankie?" Whit asks after picking up the cat.

"Yeah?" I spray some disinfectant on the exam table, too anxious to make eye contact. I may be bordering on misanthrope, but I know what his tone is getting at.

"Can I take you out sometime? Somewhere that has nothing to do with my mother's cat's goopy eyes?"

I pause in the middle of wiping the stainless steel. "Eye goop is the least of our worries here. But uh…" My words trail off so I can try to find the right way to answer.

Objectively, he's the best-looking man I've ever seen in my life. GQ would sell a lot of copies with him on the cover. Based on our brief interaction, he's funny, charming, and kind. Clearly, he's a devoted son, despite his mother's shortcomings. Really, he seems like a catch.

Yet, going out with him doesn't appeal to me at all. There's no spark. No interest in getting to know him better. I'm not intrigued, wanting to peel back the layers of who he is.

"Sorry, Whit. I'm flattered, really, but I don't have time to date right now. My life is… complicated."

His smile never falters. "She's stunning, hardworking, and mysterious. My loss." He turns toward the door, looking back over his shoulder to add, "I'm sure I'll be back in a few weeks because Mademoiselle Lovelyworth's meow is a quarter-octave higher than normal. Maybe things will be less complicated then." With that, he chuckles and walks out of the room, letting the door swing closed behind him.

Brad and I get home just before 4pm, so I decide to take him out to the backyard to play before I make myself dinner and get some studying done. I have an essay to write about ethical considerations of genetic experimentation, which I haven't started on yet.

The neighbours' door opens and closes, and I hear someone walk down the steps. Since I made the assumption about who the person was before, I wait for whoever it is to speak first.

Neither Keith nor Austin have come outside when I've been out here, so chances are, it's Blake or Oscar.

Brad brings me his ball, but refuses to let go, so I tell him, "*Calare*." Thankfully, he drops it.

"Frankie! My guardian angel. My saving grace. The ace up my sleeve. The feather in my—"

"Hi, Blake." I laugh, wondering how many more idioms he'd have come up with if I didn't stop him. "How's your screenplay coming along?"

"If I can get Spielberg on board, it should be in line for an Oscar in a couple years. Keep your schedule clear, Frankie, because you're going to be my date on the red carpet."

"Can't say I enjoy being in big crowds or on camera, but if you make it to the Oscars, I'll be there." I feel confident making that promise, because, no offence to Blake, but I don't think my story idea is really Oscar material.

"*All* the Oscars will be jealous. I'm holding you to that promise."

I'm not sure what he means by that, but I don't ask. "Right," I drawl.

"What's new with you, anyway? We haven't had a backyard chat for a while. Gosh, you bring a girl a flower and get ghosted. That's cold."

I finally toss the ball for Brad again after he's waited so patiently. It's somewhat depressing that I never have anything "new" happening in my life, and it revolves entirely around classes and the animal hospital. I don't even have a hobby to talk about. I blurt out the only semi-interesting thing to happen to me for weeks—maybe months. "A guy asked me on a date today."

"Ooh, do tell. When's the big night? Is he hot? What's he like? Tell. Me. Everything." His excitement over that confession is a little surprising. Not that I ever got the impression he was interested in me, despite his eccentric jokes, but I didn't think he'd care much.

"No, I'm not going. I turned him down."

"Listen, Frankie, I get that it's hard to compete with me and my excellent taste in floral arrangements, but you gotta give the man a chance. Unless he's like... eighty. Or if that's your thing, I don't—"

"It's not." Seriously, I don't even know what to do with this guy sometimes. Yet, he's still the closest thing I have to a friend. I'm starting to think he's not the best person to go to for advice, though. "He just... I don't know. It didn't feel right."

"No attraction? Again, it's hard to compete with me, but not everyone can have a winning personality, a chiselled jaw, and six-pack abs. We're a rare breed."

"You're a rare breed, all right." I contemplate how else to explain my lack of interest in Whit, because I'm not sure I have a reason for it. Just instinct.

Before I can attempt to explain, we're interrupted by his back door opening.

Oscar says something to Blake about it being time to go. I can't make out the rest of it, but he doesn't sound too happy. Unsurprising.

"If you'll excuse me, Frankie. It's time I go beat Oscar to a pulp. If you never hear from me again, I was unsuccessful. It's been a pleasure."

Much like everything else that comes out of Blake's mouth, those few sentences leave me confused. Yet, the most confusing part is the concern that takes hold of my gut, clenching like a vise over the thought of Blake beating Oscar to a pulp.

Every so often, Blake and I have a friendly competition to determine which is the superior form of martial arts between jiu-jitsu and muay thai. Since he has Wednesday afternoons free and I have a gap between school and work, we agreed to have another round today. We've done this eight times since we met, and aside from once, when he lucked out with a figure-four leg lock, I've beaten him every time. Despite the blow to my pride, at least I know how to do a figure-four leg lock now.

Today, there's more than martial arts pride on the line. Blake is a great guy. Maybe misunderstood, and basically chaos covered in skin, but he's a good person. I'm happy to call him my friend. One thing he's not, though, is boyfriend material. And I'd be lying if I said seeing Frankie smile at him and light up when he's around doesn't irritate me—for no good reason. Add that to overhearing him tell her he's got a winning personality and six-pack abs, and this unjustified jealousy I'm feeling has reached a boiling point.

As we square off, each in our appropriate gear, a crowd starts to gather around us. Probably because we look like we have no idea what we're doing. Where muay thai focuses on striking and attacking, jiu-jitsu is geared toward defence, grappling, and submissions. It's common to combine the two in mixed martial arts, but we're both trained in single disciplines. These battles are for nothing more than bragging rights.

Like mine, Blake's parents got him into martial arts as an energy outlet for their "out of control" kid who couldn't focus. Also like me, he doesn't do it to be a good fighter. He does it for the discipline. As a way to achieve complete and utter physical exhaustion in hopes of finally shutting his brain off.

I wish I could shut my brain off now. "What's the deal with you and Frankie?" I ask, taking an easy swipe at him to see how reactive he is today.

He dodges out of the way, stepping back and to his left. "She's cool."

That doesn't answer my question, so I send an easy knee strike, which he blocks. "You like her?"

He smirks, again stepping to his left until we've completed a full circle. "What if I do?"

Honestly, I thought his lack of an attention span would have him moving on within a week. He has liked a lot of girls in the last year, but never for more than two days. That question sends my thoughts in a hundred different directions, which all lead back to wondering why it bothers me. He can't know that, though; I'd never hear the end of it.

"Just curious," I add, delivering another front kick his way with no heat behind it.

"Nice try. You haven't given any girl the time of day since Sonia."

I grumble at him for mentioning her. He knows that's one name I don't want to hear.

To express my annoyance, I try a slapping foot jab and make contact with his thigh. "She has nothing to do with it."

"What does Frankie have to do with anything?" Blake asks, diving forward to grab my left leg.

My reflexes would normally have helped me avoid it, but I'm too distracted to deal with the mess in my head and anticipate Blake's movements. Plus, I don't have a good answer to his question.

"Why do you care?" he shouts, straining to pull me down to the ground.

"I don't know," I yell back, doing my best to stay standing. Ground fighting isn't my forte, even when it's in good fun, so I don't want to end up on the mat with him. "You're gonna hurt her." I finally slide out of his grip and step back to reevaluate my options.

When Blake returns to standing in front of me, he's the one who looks hurt. Not physically, which is easier to ignore. I would have preferred to have landed a backfist strike to his nose than hurt him the way I just did.

"Sorry, man. I shouldn't have—"

He lunges forward, catching me in the gut with his shoulder, knocking me down. "You and Fletcher hang out to talk about what a piece of trash I am, huh?"

I don't even attempt to fight back, because it's me who's the piece of trash. I let him pull me into a side triangle choke, then I tap out.

We both collapse back into the mat, not the slightest bit winded. That was our tamest battle to date. Even the small audience around has lost interest and walked away already.

"You're the better man," I declare.

"That was weak, Ozzie. Doesn't count. You could have gotten out if you tried."

Yeah, I probably could have, but I didn't deserve to. He should have knocked my teeth out for coming at him like that. "Nah, you got me. Fair and square." I push myself to my feet, then reach down to give Blake my hand.

He takes it, which is a good sign he doesn't hate my guts. "It's not even like that with Frankie. She just needed a friend. I don't have a thing for every female I talk to."

"Then why'd you act like you were?"

"I didn't. I asked 'what if I do?'" He levels me with his cocky smirk, and it's nothing to do with him beating me just now. "You've never cared about me hurting any other girl... except your sister."

"Leave Hollis out of this," I snap.

He laughs, stepping through the ropes to climb out of the ring. I watch him leave and assess how accurate that statement is. I wouldn't let him anywhere near my sister, but I don't have a good explanation for being just as protective over a woman who has done nothing but anger me since we met.

That's a lie.

She's angered me, but she's also intrigued me. In a room full of girls who go along with everything, giggle, and cater to every whim, Frankie pushes buttons. She presses back and stands her ground. She's challenging and, as much as I've tried not to, I like that about her.

On top of that, when she's surrounded by other girls, each wearing an outfit that puts more on display than the next, Frankie shows up in sweats, with no makeup on, wearing her hair in a ponytail, and she's still the most beautiful girl in the room. Yet that's not the most interesting thing about her.

I jog after Blake, catching up to him as he walks into the change room. "You really don't like her?"

Blake pulls his gym bag from his locker and tugs out his mouth guard case. "You and I both know, even if I did, I'd screw it up in a few days. Besides, she told me about some other guy who asked her on a date today. Trust me, one hundred percent platonic."

I tug off my hand wraps just in time for my fist to clench, digging my nails into my palm. Now my jealousy that was directed toward my best friend is aimed at some unknown person. I shouldn't be surprised someone else asked Frankie out, but that doesn't mean I'm happy about it. Just one more reason why I need to get over whatever this lingering interest in her is.

Blake tugs off his rashguard and tosses it on top of his bag. "Listen, if you like her, don't worry that I'm going to stand in your way. We both know you could take me out if you had to."

"I don't. That's not—"

"I may not be a Rhodes Scholar, but despite what Fletcher thinks, I'm not an idiot. If you like her, you'd be the idiot not to do something about it. And I've never seen you as a coward."

Again, I deny the obvious because I don't want to hear his input. "Not happening, man. I'm not interested in her. I just don't want things to be weird with our neighbour."

"Right. Because you haven't made it weird at all." He grabs his shower bag and walks toward the back of the change room, whistling the tune of his favourite party song. Though, in this case, I think the intro to 'I Know You Want Me' is just meant to prove his point.

I shove down the frustration I've created for myself and head to the showers. The last thing I need is another distraction.

Hey You Girl

Blake has been acting weird for the past few days. I don't know why, but every time we've had an over-the-fence chat, he's joked about making the Oscars jealous and how he can't wait to prove *him* wrong. I'm assuming the "him" he's referring to is his dad, but with this guy, you can never be totally sure. He's really determined he's going to the Oscars, though.

Beyond that, Oscar has been avoiding me even more than normal. I've gotten enough side-eye glances from him over the past week, I'm convinced his eyes are just stuck like that. He hasn't uttered a single word, so I've done my part to steer clear of him too.

The weird thing is, I kind of miss our charged dynamic. He may have frustrated me, confused me, and downright angered me, but he's the first person I've found the courage to push back against for years. He's the first person to challenge me and make me want to be something other than a people-pleasing wallflower. But it doesn't seem he's interested in helping with my confidence re-building.

The confusing status of our neighbourly relationship is the sole reason why I agreed to show up at their party tonight. Blake asked, and he's so convincing, it's hard to say no. He even encouraged me to bring Brad, because apparently he's a real selling point when trying to persuade "hot girls" to show up. I'm not sure how I feel about my dog being a wingman, but he gives me a good excuse to leave if I need to.

As I walk up the stairs and hear the faint dance music pumping through the door, I already want to go back home.

The door swings open before I can bail.

"Brad's here!" a familiar brunette squeals, bending down to pet my dog without acknowledging me.

I'm not upset about that, though. His presence helps to make me more invisible.

We step inside, where the girl grabs the leash and leads Brad into the living room. He goes without looking back, making me question his loyalty.

"Frankie!" Austin cheers, walking into the small foyer. He looks characteristically happy.

"Austin. Nice to see you've recovered."

He stops in front of me and leans against the wall. "Thanks. I was pretty sure I had the plague. Things looked pretty grim for a while there."

Now I've learned two things Blake and Austin have in common: neither of them can keep a secret, and they're both overly dramatic.

"Well, I'm glad you pulled through." I glance behind him and see Brad flopped on his back, soaking up some belly rubs again. The other guy I search for, however, is nowhere to be seen. "Oscar in hiding again?" I ask, adding a short laugh to play off my question as a disinterested observation and nothing more.

"He went to Hollis' place." Austin shrugs before taking a sip of his beer. "He's anti-hot girls and good times this year." Without further explanation, he turns and waves me inside. "Come on. I'll get you a drink."

I look down at my fingers, picking at my nails, asking myself a carousel of questions with no answers. Most notably, who's Hollis? "Oh. Sure," I finally choke out, following Austin with a pit of disappointment in my stomach.

A totally unjustified pit of disappointment.

I should be happy the curmudgeon isn't here. The fact that I'm not leads to a lot more unanswered questions.

"Frankie!" Blake says in the same enthusiastic tone Austin used minutes ago. He's standing in the kitchen, in the exact spot he was in the first time I came in here. His level of drunkenness and the girls crowded around him is also the same. "Where's Brad?" he asks, as he always does.

"In the living room with his biggest fan. Probably making Keith feel inadequate again." I try to laugh off the stupid joke, but being here tonight just doesn't feel right. And I don't think it's because I'm not a people person.

"Don't worry. Nobody makes Keith feel inadequate. What are you drinking?"

Normally, I drink wine, paired with the right meal. The odd time, on special occasions, I'll have some Campari before dinner, but drinking just for the sake of drinking has never been my thing. Until tonight. "I don't know. What do you suggest?"

One girl clinging to Blake squeals and claps her hand. "Let me make you a cocktail."

Blake smiles at her, which she returns, but she doesn't look to me for any confirmation. She gets to work sliding bottles across the counter and pouring liquor into a glass. I watch in horror as she adds tequila, rum, vodka, gin, and a few other ingredients.

"This is my favourite. It's called an 'AMF', but I won't tell you what that stands for. I'm Molly, by the way."

I take the drink she's set in front of me, hesitant to try it, so I delay by introducing myself. "Frankie. Nice to meet you. Uh… thanks."

Molly claps again and waits expectantly for me to take a sip of this mystery drink. Blake and Austin are both staring at me with the same eager expression.

I lift the drink and smell it before bringing it to my lips, but the alcohol scent is so strong, it tickles my throat. A small cough forces its way out, making me even more reluctant. Yet, peer pressure wins out, so I finally test Molly's concoction. It doesn't taste as potent as it smells, but it's still strong. With all the eyes I can feel focused on me, I keep my eyes on the drink as I continue to take small sips until it's three-quarters empty. Now, everyone else seems to have gotten bored watching me, so they're back to the conversations they were having before I entered.

And even amongst a crowd of people, I still feel lonely.

It's that realization that forces me to peek my head into the living room to find Brad. He's busy soaking up the attention from his adoring fans.

Molly redirects my attention, offering me another drink. Blake has made his way across the kitchen, leaving me and Molly alone, so I agree. Not like I have to drive home.

I watch as she pours the same mix of liquor into my plastic cup and passes it to me. She's smiling from ear to ear as she repeats the process for herself.

"How are my two favourite girls?" Blake asks, throwing his arm around Molly when he returns with a new beer.

They really do make a good-looking couple. It's weird, because I don't have the smallest spark of jealousy over Blake—who has been nothing but kind to me—showing attention to Molly, but the thought of Oscar missing out on tonight to be with another girl has left me feeling empty.

Enough so, I chug half of my drink, then reply, "Not feeling the buzz yet."

"Molly can take care of that." He tilts his head down to whisper something in her ear, which has her cheeks blazing pink and a shy smile appearing on her face for the first time.

"Sure," she says to me. "To both," she adds, looking at Blake.

His face splits with a devilish grin as he glances down at her.

"Frankie, tell me about yourself. How come I've never seen you around campus?" Molly asks, leaning into Blake's side.

I take a minute to explain to Molly that this is my first year here, but glance over details about where I'm from or the real reason why I transferred. She asks about my program, but she's in the screenwriting program with Blake, so my major isn't in her wheelhouse. In her words, "The only science I study is science fiction."

"She might be a science nerd, but she came in clutch for my screenplay this year." He smiles at me, but instead of being grateful for the praise, it makes me more uncomfortable to be the focus of attention amongst the other people who have joined our conversation.

I down the rest of my second drink and slide my cup back to Molly. I reply while she works her magic. "Don't thank me yet. Your professor could hate the idea."

"No, I presented an outline to Kiki, and she said, and I quote, 'It has wonderful potential if you can keep the storyline focused.' That's my specialty; focus." He winks at me and adds, "So one day, the Oscars will appreciate Frankie... I don't know your last name."

Instead of answering, I divert my attention back to my fresh drink and glance back into the living room again.

The next ninety minutes pass much the same way. Awkward breaks in conversation when I'm left feeling alone inside a house with thirty other people in it, another couple of drinks, and me wishing I could be as relaxed and carefree as Brad.

I finally vacate the kitchen and go sit on the couch near Keith. It's not until I sit that I realize how much my head is spinning. It's also a surprise how heavy my eyes are... and I'm too relaxed to fight.

OSCAR

Everybody Get Up

My phone rings, displaying Blake's name.

"Are you going to get that?" Hollis asks around a mouthful of popcorn.

It's not like I'm watching the insufferable romantic comedy she's forcing me to sit through. Blake's call isn't interrupting, but I'm afraid of what he'll say if I answer. With a party happening, who knows what could have gone wrong. I have a feeling whatever he says means I'm not getting my deposit back.

"Yeah?" I answer.

"Ozzie," Blake slurs. "Are you coming home?"

I pause, thinking about the implications of my answer. Is he asking because someone wants to use my room? I got a lock for the door, so I wasn't worried about that, but you can't discount a determined drunk's abilities. Or the more likely explanation, he's hoping I'll come to fix something. Finally, I just ask. "Why?"

"Frankie's drunk."

I push myself to stand, drawing Hollis' attention. "Is she okay?"

Blake laughs a long, obnoxious, drunken laugh. "I knew you had a thing for her." He hiccups and mutters something to someone next to him. "She's asleep and I can't find her keys. We were going to put her in your room."

I know Blake has good intentions, but I'm not okay with her being unconscious in my bedroom. Or anywhere other than behind her locked door, to be honest. "I'll be home in thirty minutes. Just keep an eye on her."

"You got it, boss."

I hang up the phone and turn to my sister. "I gotta go."

"Everything okay?"

"Yeah. Our neighbour is passed out drunk, and Blake can't find her keys." I tuck my phone in my pocket and head for the door.

"And this neighbour is…?" Hollis calls from behind me.

"Nobody, but after what happened to Aunt Zara, I'm not about to let them toss her into my room unconscious." I turn to face Hollis as I slip on my shoes.

Her face makes it clear she understands what I'm saying. "Do you want me to come with you?"

"Yes," I reply before I can change my mind. "It's just… trying to take a drunk girl home…"

Hollis gets up and sets her popcorn bowl on the table. "Give me two seconds to get a sweater. You order a car."

"Thanks, Holl."

Thirty minutes later, our ride-share pulls up in front of my house. There isn't anyone outside today, which hopefully means there aren't too many people here. My sister follows me into the house, where she's greeted by a drunken Blake.

"Hey! If it isn't Oscar's hot sister."

"Hi, Blake," Hollis replies. "Looks like you're having fun."

"A blast. You should tell your brother to try it sometime."

Hollis doesn't answer because she's set her eyes on Brad. "Oh. My. Gosh. Who is this? He's adorable!" she squeals the same way I've seen so many other girls gush over this dog.

The girls introduce him, Hollis laughs at his name, and the group of them congregate around the dog, leaving most of the single guys in the room looking miserable.

As for the unconscious girl, Frankie is curled up on the couch, covered in an unzipped hooded sweater I quickly recognize as mine. With the level of noise in here, she must really be out of it to be able to sleep. It angers and annoys me that anyone can be that irresponsible, they would just pass out in a stranger's house. I should have known she had no self-preservation instinct the moment I saw that dog.

"Holl, can you look for her keys?"

She doesn't look thrilled to leave Brad's side, but she nods and shifts my sweater off of Frankie and immediately pulls a set of keys out of her pocket.

I turn to Keith, who appears to be the least inebriated, resisting the urge to question how hard they looked. "What happened? What did you guys give her?"

He shrugs. "No clue, man. She was in the kitchen most of the night, then she came out here, sat on the couch, and knocked out."

That's not a helpful answer. I just want to know if I need to be worried about alcohol poisoning or something. I know none of the guys would allow any drugs in the house, so that's not a major concern, but there's no saying someone else wouldn't have.

The question is, would Frankie take something—either willingly or unwillingly? The thought of that makes my blood boil.

Before I get any more angry, I ask my sister to wake Frankie because I know if I try to do it, she'll bite my head off. Frankie stirs, but doesn't fully wake—she's not coherent enough to walk home, even with support. I lift her by putting one arm under her upper back and the other under her knees, then Hollis leads the way to the door, down the path, and up Frankie's porch.

"Why does she have so many locks on her door?" Hollis asks as she's fiddling with the third one.

"I guess her guard dog doesn't make her feel safe enough." I groan, realizing we've forgotten Brad. "Once we get inside, can you go get her dog?"

She finally swings the door open wide enough for me to slip in sideways. "What if he has to go out before she wakes up?"

"Holl, it's really not my problem if the dog pees in her kitchen."

"Gosh, Blake is right," she says, flicking on the front hall light.

"About?" I ask as I set Frankie on her sofa.

Hollis stares at me from the foyer. "You should really try having fun sometime."

"Just because the way I have fun looks different doesn't mean I don't. This isn't fun to me, Holl. Drinking to the point you're unconscious shouldn't be fun for anyone." Repeating the current situation just makes my anger return. "I'll go get the dog."

I walk past my sister, out the front door, and jog across the grass.

Brad is reluctant to come with me until one girl says, "He speaks Italian." She gushes, like she's impressed he's a man of culture.

This night is never ending. I went to my sister's place after work so I didn't have to deal with any of this stupidity. "Any clue how to say, 'get moving or you'll end up at the pound' in Italian?"

The brunette gasps and steps in between me and Brad. "No, he will not."

I roll my eyes. "Relax, I'm not taking him to the pound." That would require even more effort.

The girl glares at me, and I realize she's the only person in here who looks sober, so I ask, "Did you see Frankie drinking? Or… take anything?"

"Frankie?" Her dark brows furrow.

"Brad's owner? The blonde?" It takes every bit of discipline I've spent my life developing to not roll my eyes again.

"Oh. Yeah. She had a few AMFs, but if you're not used to them, they can sneak up on you."

That explains why she's so out of it. I witnessed a few girls in residence drink themselves stupid on that concoction last year. "Thanks," I answer, pulling out my phone to translate some commands into Italian.

Once I come up with the right word, Brad follows along beside me, out the door and down the path. He has to stop to do his business, but aside from that pause, he doesn't give me any trouble going home. As soon as we re-enter the house, he stops beside the sofa and nudges Frankie's hand. Again, she stirs and grumbles, but doesn't fully wake up.

"Do you think she'll be okay alone?" Hollis asks, bending down to pet Brad's head.

"She's better off here than she was. She'll sleep it off." I glance at my phone screen and notice the time. "It's almost two. We should go."

"Yeah. Okay. Bye, Brad." She gives him some vigorous scratches on the side of his neck. "Bye, Frankie. Nice to meet you."

"You know she can't hear you, right?"

"Doctors tell people to talk to anyone in a coma. Why is a drunken stupor any different?" she retorts as we walk to the door. "Oh, shoot. We'll either have to leave her door unlocked or take her keys."

I would have preferred to sneak out and Frankie never know we were in here, but Hollis is right; none of the deadbolts can be locked without a key. "For someone with three deadbolts on her door, I'm assuming she wouldn't want it left unlocked."

"Good point." Hollis takes the keys from her pocket and glances back at Frankie before stepping out the front door. As she's locking the second deadbolt, she says, "She's really pretty."

I turn to walk down the steps. "If you say so."

Hollis jogs after me, pulling even with my strides across the grass. "Oh, please. Don't pretend like you haven't noticed."

"Looks aren't everything, Holl. She's... a headache."

"Mm-hmm."

We step onto my porch, allowing me to see her smirk under the light.

"Whatever," I reply, pushing the door open.

The crowd has dwindled to only two of my roommates and two girls. Keith shrugs and tells me the other girls left after Brad did. Suits me fine.

Hollis helps me tidy up a bit in the kitchen, and by the time we're done, Austin, Keith, and their companions have disappeared. I offer Hollis my room, then set up camp on the floor beside my bed.

The house is virtually silent by the time I lie down, close to 3am, but my brain is another story. Thoughts of what could have happened to Frankie parade around my mind, followed by concern if she's okay. Maybe I should have asked Hollis to stay with her, but I didn't think about it at the time.

So, instead of sleeping, I allow my imagination to run rampant, conjuring up a variety of scenarios that could be happening on the other side of our wall.

Who left their jackhammer running in my head? I wake up from the urge to vomit, but the second I attempt to open my eyes, daggers pierce through them, straight into my skull. I force them open slowly, shielding my face from the sliver of light filtering through the curtain.

My curtains.

In my house.

How did I get home?

That question is going to have to wait. I drag myself to the powder room and empty the contents of my stomach. Brad pushes the door open behind me and peeks his head inside. He probably needs to go out, but there's no way I can do that right now.

"Sorry, buddy."

Like a good boy, he curls up on the floor beside me while I hate myself for being so stupid. With each purge of my stomach, more details return from last night. I remember feeling totally fine until, suddenly, I didn't. After that, I'm not sure what happened, but I'm glad I made it home.

I'm not sure how long I stay on the floor, huddled around the toilet. The cool tile feels soothing against my clammy skin, so I'm content to lie here for a bit. I'm supposed to be at the clinic at seven, so I pull out my phone to check the time. It's almost 9am and I have four missed calls. My battery is at six percent, but I need to call to let Rhonda know I'm going to be late… later.

"Wildflower Animal Hospital."

"Hi, Rhonda. It's Frankie."

"Oh, Frankie. Are you okay? You sound dreadful."

"I'm fine. Just…" I trail off, not wanting to lie to her, but also not wanting to admit my stupidity. Pride wins out over morals. "Stomach troubles."

"My dear, you take today off. We'll be fine here."

"I can come—"

"Get well soon. Gotta go." She doesn't give me a chance to argue further before she hangs up.

I hate missing my shift. Not only is it unprofessional, but my volunteer hours count toward my vet school applications, and I don't want to shortchange myself. I set my phone down on the floor and use my free hand to pet Brad's head. Just as I work up the energy to take him outside, a knock pounds at my front door.

Brad's ears perk up; my heart thuds in my chest, causing my stomach to churn again.

The person knocks again, louder this time. My heart pounds harder.

I use my foot to close the bathroom door, hoping they'll go away. The fact Brad isn't barking is the only thing keeping me from dialling 911. Perhaps I put too much stock in his instincts, though, because seconds later, I hear one lock disengage. Then another in quick succession. I reach up to lock the bathroom door and pick up my phone to dial 911 right as the door opens and I hear a familiar voice shout, "Frankie?"

Are you kidding me?

"Oscar?"

His footsteps track across my living room toward the bathroom door, then they stop.

Silence.

Awkwardness.

Anger.

All three hang in the air around me, more potent than the regurgitated liquor smell. I push myself to stand and turn on the faucet to splash water on my face. I look like I've been eaten by a zombie and vomited back up. That won't stop me from saying what I need to say, though.

After rinsing my mouth, so I don't have to worry about my dragon breath knocking Oscar off his feet, I open the door to confront him. "You came into my house? Uninvited?"

He crosses his arms in front of him, causing his gym bag to swing at his side. "I thought you were dead."

"If I remember right, you said you wouldn't call the coroner when my dog was in here eating my rotting corpse." I glance down at Brad, who is sitting beside me, wagging his tail.

Apparently, he doesn't know how to read a room.

"Who said I was going to call the coroner? I just came to bring back your keys." He holds up my distinct key ring I didn't realize was missing.

Granted, unless they were in the toilet, I wouldn't have looked for them. "How did you get my keys? Did you come in my house last night too? What gives you the right? Trespassing in my backyard wasn't enough for you? You had to come right through the *locked* front door?"

Oscar is the total opposite of me, standing there with a stoic glare. "No. I brought you home because you didn't have the sense to control your liquor and keep *yourself* safe, so I did."

A rush of embarrassment overtakes me, significantly stronger than the urge to vomit. No. I'm so far beyond mere embarrassment. I'm mortified. So much so, I don't have a good response.

"Listen, I'm getting really tired of being the villain in your story, so think whatever you want of me, but don't worry, I won't help again." Oscar turns and walks away with his shoulders so tense, I can clearly see as he exits through my front door.

I'm such an idiot. Not only for drinking so much, but for getting angry with him. He's right, and I should be grateful to him for his help. I can't tell him that though, because judging by how he walked away, that bridge has been incinerated. That realization causes my stomach to lurch once again, sending me scrambling back into the bathroom.

By 1:30, I'm feeling well enough to drag myself out to get some soup. I need something in my stomach, but I'm hesitant to eat any of the solid food I have.

As I lock my door from my porch, I hear the neighbour's door close too.

Great.

Instead of looking over or scanning my surroundings like I normally would, I focus on the ground in front of me and try to walk to my car as fast as I can.

"Frankie?" a female voice calls out.

The fact it's not Oscar is the only reason I look up to acknowledge her.

"How are you feeling?" the beautiful blonde stranger asks. Where my hair is an unfortunate box-dyed strawberry blonde shade, the woman in question has a stunning wheat blonde colour that complements her skin tone and blue eyes perfectly.

"Fine, thanks," I reply, not wanting to be stuck here any longer than necessary.

"I'm Hollis," she offers. A name that almost makes my stomach churn again.

I may not remember a lot from last night, but I do know Oscar was with someone named Hollis, and it's a unique enough name that her walking out their front door can't be coincidence. Plus, I recognize the T-shirt she's wearing as one I've seen Oscar in.

"Oscar is my little brother. He asked me to come with him last night to help you get home safely. We took your keys, so we didn't leave the door unlocked. Did he drop them off on his way to work?"

The level of embarrassment I felt in Oscar's presence this morning is nothing compared to how I feel now. This is worse than when I almost ran him over. Not only did I yell at him for coming into my house, I once again implied he's a criminal. I'm so ashamed of myself right now, I don't think I'll ever be able to face him again.

"I'm never drinking again," I mutter.

"Famous last words, right?" Hollis laughs as something behind me captures her attention. "Did you give Frankie her keys back?"

"I did," Oscar answers with irritation clear in his voice.

I don't turn around to look at him. At this point, I don't even think a sincere apology will do much, because I tried that when I almost hit him with my car and it accomplished nothing. My best course of action is to ignore him and hope he goes away.

Which he does, not stopping to talk to me or his sister. He breezes by me and heads up his walkway, opens the front door, and walks inside.

"Geeze. Must have had a bad day at work. He's cranky."

I look at Hollis, curious if she thinks that's unusual. I have yet to see Oscar anything *but* cranky. "Is he normally a ray of sunshine?"

She laughs again. "I wouldn't go that far, but he can be a riot when he wants to be."

That's so strange, because it's similar to what Blake said. I've seen nothing close to a riot. At least, not the fun kind of riot I assume she means. Maybe a bit of the city-burning, havoc-causing kind.

"That's news to me. He's hated me from day one. I thought it was because of my dog, but I'm pretty sure it's just me." I don't know why I blurted that out. That's something I could have gone without saying.

"Something tells me that's not the case. He went back and got Brad to bring him home for you last night. He's adorable, by the way."

It takes me a second to figure out if she's calling her brother or Brad adorable, but assume she's referring to my dog. "Thanks." I smile at her, grateful she stopped me to clear the air, since that will never happen between me and Oscar. "Do you need a ride somewhere?"

"Oh, no, that's okay. I'm going to my friend's place over on Lakeshore. That's way out of your way, I'm sure."

It is probably a twenty-five minute drive, but I wouldn't mind getting to know Hollis a bit. I'm in short supply of friends around here, so I sweeten the deal. "If you don't mind watching Brad for me while I run in somewhere to get some soup, he can come along for the drive."

"Duh. Like that's even a question." She smiles wide, brightening her face. Somehow, that makes me realize how much she and Oscar look alike, even though he's never smiled in my direction. Or even in my presence.

The two of us return to my front door, where Hollis asks about the multiple locks and I evade answering, then we grab Brad and head back to my car. The sequence of events may have been a complete and utter disaster to get here, but laughing and chatting with Hollis is the exact hangover cure I need.

18

OSCAR

That's Nasty

"**S**eriously?" I lift my shoe to confirm what I think just happened. Yep. That's a slimy pile of dog crap now squashed under the sprinkling of snow on my front path. And all over my sneaker.

I stick my foot into the small snowbank at the edge of our walkway to scrub off what I can, then march over to Frankie's house and knock on the door. There's noise inside, but after thirty seconds, she still doesn't answer. Her car is out front, so I know she's home.

"Frankie, open the door." I knock again, louder this time. I haven't seen her since she last reamed me out for coming into her house—which I stand by doing because I didn't know if she was dead or alive—but I've had enough of her active avoidance.

Another minute with no response makes me more irritated.

"I'm not going anywhere until you open the door."

Finally, the multiple locks disengage. Frankie pulls the door open, looking like she's had the life scared out of her.

"Are you okay?" I ask, no longer concerned with my poop-covered shoe.

She looks up at her ceiling and blinks her eyes several times. When she refocuses on me with a hardened glare, she replies, "Can I help you?"

Her snarky tone makes any sympathy I have quickly disappear.

"Ever heard of stoop and scoop? You know? When you pick up after your dog?"

"Oscar, I spend a lot of my time in an animal hospital. You don't even want to know the number of places I've cleaned feces out of, including my own hair. I'm familiar with the concept."

I grimace at that image, then I start imagining the kinds of scenarios that could result in washing dog poop from your hair. The most dominant thought is a dog twirling its tail like a hippo and flinging excrement around the vet office, right across the back of Frankie's head.

"Did you come to talk about dog poop for a reason?"

I give my head a subtle shake to remove that graphic scene playing out in my imagination and refocus on Frankie. "Your dog pooped on the path and now my shoe is ruined."

She doesn't budge. Her facial expression doesn't change. She just stares at me with her eyebrows pulled together. "Good joke."

"Do I look like I'm joking?" I lift my shoe to show her the evidence.

Still, she's unfazed. "Come back to me for some sympathy when you've had to clean it out of your hair. Brad hasn't even been out the front door today, and he isn't to blame for your shoe."

She attempts to close the door, but I hold my hand out to stop it. Something seems off today, and while I should relish in turning the tables and blaming her for something she didn't do, it doesn't feel as good as I thought it would.

I miss the spitfire Frankie who didn't hesitate to stand her ground. "Are you sure he didn't get out again?"

"Yes, Oscar. I'm sure. He didn't let himself out the locked front door, take a dump on your path, and lock the door behind him on his way back in. And luckily, someone broke into my backyard and patched up the fence, so he didn't get out that way either." She glares at me with a hint of the intensity she usually has, but she's not quite as feisty as I'm used to. "Do me a favour? Stick a thumbtack under your toenail and kick a wall!"

There she is. I feel better now. So much so, I can't help the victorious smile from overtaking my face. That's the final straw before Frankie closes the door and locks it behind her.

I hobble back home and remove my shoe on the front porch before heading inside. All three roommates stare at me from the living room when I enter.

"Usually, when there's snow on the ground, we wait to take our shoes off until we're inside, mate," Austin chides.

"Not when they're covered in dog crap, *mate*. I'll wash them in the sink downstairs." I smirk at him because his bedroom is the only one in the basement.

"The laundry sink. Don't use the bathroom, man. I brush my teeth there."

"No promises," I add, continuing to walk past, carrying my dirty shoes.

Before I reach the top of the steps, Austin catches up to me.

"What happened to your shoe?"

"Pretty self explanatory, no? I was looking at my phone, trying to answer a text from my mom..."

"Man, that's rough. I just shovelled thirty minutes ago, so it must have been a fresh one."

"Lucky me."

Austin continues chatting about some new app he's developing with a classmate. It's meant to be a virtual study hall, where students can make groups based on their classes and host video study sessions, as well as start conversation forums. It sounds like a great idea, so I let him ramble on while I scrub my shoe, but I struggle to stop my mind from wandering back to Frankie.

Something was off today. Maybe I should ask Blake if he knows something. Or Hollis. I know my sister has spoken to Frankie a few times, and the one time Hollis stopped in to drop off some groceries, she went next door and stayed at Frankie's for a while before she left. If something is wrong, Hollis probably knows.

But is my curiosity strong enough to risk the endless barrage of questions my sister would hurl at me because I asked? No. Nor am I desperate enough to ask Blake.

So I continue to listen to Austin explain the intricacies of app creation and answer his questions about what features I'd like to see, all while my mind is elsewhere. To be specific, it's thirty feet to the north.

Three hours later, my phone rings in the middle of me trying to finish my assigned reading for tomorrow. I glance at the phone to see "Mom" lit up on the screen and quickly remember I never got around to replying to her text.

"Hi, Mom."

"Well, I'm relieved you're alive. Don't tell me you've gotten too busy to talk to your mother."

"Never. I had an… incident and forgot to answer."

"Is everything okay? Do I need to drive down there and sort someone out?"

My siblings have forever teased me about being a momma's boy and complained endlessly about how I get special treatment. I deny it every time, but it's 100 percent true. I've never heard her offer to "sort someone out" for Hollis or Ethan.

"No need. I handled it. How are things there? How's Dad?"

"Fine. Busy. This new rec centre they're planning is taking up all of his time. That leaves me… the lonely empty-nester."

"What about Ethan?"

"He's never home. This new business is keeping him busy whenever he's not at work, so we don't see him much. You know he's more the silent type."

"Sorry, Mom. If I was cut out to be a free-loading deadbeat who lived in his parents' basement, I would, just so you could avoid the empty nest."

"That's sweet of you, honey. I am happy you're taking your own path. I'll just have to wait for grandbabies."

That sentence makes me choke on the water I'm sipping, but Mom ignores my coughing.

"Don't go making me a grandma anytime soon, though, young man. I don't care how pretty that neighbour of yours is."

Hollis better hope I never get wind of her in the proximity of anyone she could potentially date, because I'll rat her out with no remorse. Sure, I've talked about Frankie with my mom, but her appearance never came up. I have no doubt Hollis was the one who mentioned it.

"Trust me, Ma, the neighbour and I are not making any babies. We barely even talk." And when we do, neither of us has anything nice to say.

"It's the 'not talking' that a mother worries about. Trust *me*, I never got pregnant from talking."

"Ma!"

"Just proving my point."

And that marks the end of my interest in any conversation for the day. "I better get going. Hopefully Hollis and I will be able to come home for a visit soon."

Despite my intention to end the call, my mom continues talking for another twenty minutes. She tells me about my aunt's grandkids, the book club she joined, and her friend Marnie's cheating scandal.

Much like with Austin, earlier, I listen politely, all while my mind wanders elsewhere. Right to the one person I wish I could stop thinking about.

Daddy's Little Girl

"*B*ella! Oh, we've missed you," my mom gushes when I open the door. It's been almost five months since I've seen my parents, which is ten times longer than any stretch I've gone without seeing them before moving here.

"*Ciao, Mammina.*" I wait for my parents to settle inside, then call Brad over to greet them.

"Oh, he's precious. Did you talk to Devin about getting a dog?" Mom asks.

I grimace, but she's too distracted with Brad to notice. Truth be told, it didn't cross my mind to ask my landlord if he was okay with a dog before I brought Brad home. I was more focused on having companionship and protection than upsetting my aunt's boyfriend. Isn't that another perk of renting a house from soon-to-be family?

"Technically, no. But he said to make myself at home... so I did."

"Francesca," my father chides, making me feel every bit the small child he still thinks I am. "You should have called Zia Olivia before."

A knock at the door interrupts our conversation, but before I open it, I instruct Brad to go to his bed. Once he's settled, I open the door to find my aunt and her boyfriend, each holding a large paper bag. "Hey! I didn't know you guys were coming too."

Olivia is nineteen years younger than my dad, so she's closer in age to me than to him. My grandparents died when she was young, which prompted my parents to move to Canada from Italy and they raised her, so we've grown up more like sisters. She's twenty-eight, happily living with her longtime boyfriend an hour north of the city, which is what prompted his house being left empty.

Devin and Olivia walk inside, scanning my poorly decorated living room. I reach out to grab the bag from my aunt, but Devin slips off his shoes, insisting he'll handle his. My parents and Olivia settle in the living room with Brad, so Devin and I head for the kitchen.

Just past the dining room, Devin asks, "How are you liking it here?" His New Zealand accent is still very noticeable, even after living in Canada for a decade.

"It's been fine. Location is great, so my commute is short. I can't thank you enough for connecting me with Dr. Ellis' clinic." I set the brown bag on the counter, turning to face Devin.

"Anton is a good egg. I knew he'd take care of you. How are the neighbours?"

I roll my eyes, recalling Oscar's latest accusation and mine toward him. Along with all the other annoying encounters we've had. "Three out of four are nice. The other has been a thorn in my side."

Devin smiles as he unloads the prepared food they purchased. "You know that means he likes you, aye?"

"Ha! No, he doesn't. We're not in kindergarten. I wouldn't say he despises me, but whatever one step shy of that is."

"Not even. I reckon he's got a big ol' crush." Devin spins back, resting his backside against the counter and crossing his arms.

"I reckon you haven't seen our interactions. You'd change your mind pretty fast." I reach up to grab plates from the cupboard.

Devin left his dishes behind when he moved out, so I have exactly six mismatched plates courtesy of his bachelor days. He's also the reason I have a sofa, a dresser, a dining table, and almost every other piece of furniture here. A simple thank you will never be enough to express my appreciation for making this possible. My gratefulness brings me back to my mom's question.

"Do you mind that I got a dog?"

"Nah, no worries. I meant to install some security cameras and stuff around here a long time ago, but never got around to it. Having a dog is a good backup plan."

To say I'm relieved hearing that is an understatement. My dad had me worried Devin would insist I move out, but he didn't seem bothered when he walked in.

"Anton told me about the dog anyway. I knew about him months ago. If I had a problem, I would have mentioned it, but I told you to make yourself at home."

I should have known Dr. Ellis would have said something; Devin is one of his best friends.

Still, I feel bad for making an impulsive decision without running it by him. "I'm sorry I didn't ask first. It just kind of happened."

He puts a hand on my shoulder, giving me a tight-lipped smile. "It's all good. This is your home right now and you deserve to feel safe."

I thank him for understanding, then he suggests we get the food sorted, so we work together to get everything set up. Once we're finished, everyone else comes in to plate their food and we settle in the living room, since the dining table only has four chairs.

It's so foreign for me to have people inside this space. Aside from a short visit from Hollis and the brief encounters with Oscar and Blake, I haven't had any other company. I've never lived on my own before, and while this doesn't really count as hosting since it was spur-of-the-moment and my guests brought food, it still feels like a new experience. Maybe I can finally turn a new leaf. Move on and away from the life I left behind, finally focusing on my future.

This is exactly what I needed today. I'm nearing the end of my semester, and I don't think I'll be able to return home during my break, so this little visit is perfect.

Hours later, as the sun is starting to lower in the sky, all four of my guests tell me it's time for them to get going. My parents' drive is twice as long as Olivia and Devin's, so I don't want to keep them late. Especially with falling temperatures and unpredictable weather. It'll be dark before any of them even get out of the city.

Brad and I walk everyone outside. As we reach the sidewalk, a vehicle pulls into the parking spot in front of my car, and the front door of the neighbours' house opens. Hollis steps out of the back of the small SUV, onto the sidewalk.

Instead of greeting her brother, who is walking down the path, she cheers, "Brad! Frankie!"

Brad's tail starts going double-time, but he stands at my side, waiting.

I turn to face my family members, who are all watching Hollis approach. Devin is eyeing Oscar as he ambles down the front steps.

I ignore the conspiratorial smile Devin sends me and turn my attention back to Hollis. "Hey, Hollis. Babysitting duty again?" I ask, poking fun at my idiocy.

"Depends how Oscar behaves." She chuckles. "Our cousin is the head chef at *Hibiscus*, so our grandparents came down for us to surprise him and have dinner." She looks back at the car and gestures for the occupants to come out.

Oscar stops beside his sister as an elderly couple steps out of the hunter green SUV, joining us on the sidewalk. Here we are, nine people and a dog, all congregating in front of my house. This is the closest I'll ever come to having a house party. Or attending one again, for that matter.

Hollis introduces herself to my family, then her grandparents, Fred and Alanna, to my parents. They look as sweet and friendly as Hollis is, and that levity seems to lighten Oscar's usual grumpiness. We haven't spoken for over two weeks—since he accused Brad of pooping on his front path— but it's a lot of effort to avoid him. He comes and goes around the same times I do. Some days I drive by as he's walking to the bus stop and I feel bad for speeding past, but I gave him a ride once, and that largely went unappreciated. It's better for us both to keep our distance.

My thoughts are interrupted when Alanna and my mom discuss how they both live north of Toronto. My parents settled in Orillia and never left, where Alanna and Fred live in Bala. I watch their animated conversations as they talk about the annual cranberry festival in Bala and Orillia's folk music events. They become fast friends, and I can see that Hollis got her extroverted ways from her grandmother. Fred, on the other hand, is very much the strong silent type, just like his grandson. Though Fred doesn't have any complaints to hurl at me, so he's much more tolerable.

Devin introduces himself to Oscar as the homeowner and talks about his familiarity with Oscar's landlord. They chat casually for a few minutes, and none of the same animosity Oscar shows me is present. I'm not sure if it's his grandparents' presence encouraging him to play nice or if it's just me he saves his pent up frustration for. Whatever the reason, I completely tune out my parents and his grandparents chatting, as well as

Hollis and Olivia's conversation, and zero-in on Devin pointing out great date locations in the area. He doesn't pay any attention to the glare I'm giving him.

Oscar also looks like he's no longer paying attention. His focus is now on my mother, who starts discussing with Alanna about why I moved here.

Panic incapacitates me for a split second before I jump into action. "You guys should get going. You might be late for your reservation, and you"—I point at my father—"don't like to drive in the dark."

Thankfully, my over-sharing mother takes the hint. "You're right. Sorry for keeping you. It was lovely to meet you all," she says with a bright smile.

Everybody else exchanges a general farewell, then the foursome climbs into the SUV and slowly pulls away from the curb.

"He seems nice," Devin declares the second their vehicle is out of sight.

"Lucky you. I can't say I've gotten the same impression." I ignore his obnoxious smile and rush to say goodbye to everyone so they can be on their way.

As soon as both of their vehicles turn onto Queen Street in the distance, I suddenly realize how alone I am. Not to discount my loyal companion attached to the leash, but there's something to be said for genuine conversation that isn't driven by classes or work.

The problem is, I don't have the luxury of building deep, meaningful relationships right now. Thanks to Brad, I'm not alone, but returning to an empty house makes me resent the lonely reality I'm stuck in.

A pounding at the door disrupts my peaceful lunch. All three of my roommates are upstairs doing one thing or another. Based on the shouts and cheers, Blake and Austin are playing video games, but otherwise, I was enjoying my bit of quiet time. That makes whoever is at the front door my least favourite person on Earth right now.

I swing the door open to find Frankie with her hands on her hips and her hood pulled up, collecting the falling snow. "Did you come onto *my* property and move my garbage bins? I told you to—"

"Woah. Stop right there." I hold my hand up to keep her from ranting any further. "No need to repeat what you told me. I haven't been on your property since your dog ruined my shoe." Yeah, we've been over this and she vehemently declared it wasn't Brad, which I believe, but it's fun to get a rise out of her.

Only it doesn't.

She just stands frozen on the porch, letting all the cold air into my house. If not for her rapid breaths and blinking eyes, I wouldn't be able to tell she wasn't actually frozen.

"Frankie." I snap my fingers in front of her eyes, trying to get her attention. "Come inside."

"I... He... What..." She starts and stops multiple times, never completing a thought.

"We're letting the warm air out. Can you come inside?"

"This can't... There are footprints in the snow by my garbage bins."

I groan, because this is just another ridiculous situation she's going to blow out of proportion. She'll probably accuse someone else of being a criminal now.

She gives her head a shake like she's jolting her brain into action again after it stalled long enough to drop the temperature in my house by eight degrees. "You're sure you didn't go in my yard? Did any of the other guys?"

"I doubt it, but you can ask them."

"Is Blake here?"

That question feels a lot like a sucker punch to the gut. Not that I can blame her for asking for him when he's made an effort over the last few months to be friends.

"Come inside. I need to close the door." I pause, assessing her tense posture before adding, "Please?"

She glances toward her house, then steps inside, allowing me to seal in what little heat remains.

"I'll go ask the guys," I offer, putting my left foot on the bottom step.

She exhales a shaky breath, wrapping her arms around herself. "Thanks."

I glance back at her as I climb the stairs, but she's just staring into space. It seems like she's afraid of something; I'm just not sure what. Who would be so bothered by random footprints at their garbage bins? We live in an area where it's not uncommon for people to search recycling bins for glass bottles to return.

Without knocking, I walk into Blake's room, which happens to be the master bedroom. It's twice the size of mine and has enough space for a big TV and a pair of chairs. He and Austin each occupy one, playing some sniper game Blake bought as "research" for his screenplay.

"Did either of you touch Frankie's garbage bin?"

Blake pauses the game, then shifts in his chair to face me. "Is that a euphemism or something? We already talked about this, man. I'm not interested in Frankie's 'garbage bin'"—he adds air quotes and scrunches his face—"or anything else. That's the worst name I've ever heard for it."

"Don't be an idiot. I mean her actual garbage bin. She saw footprints in the snow. She came here, looking like she wanted to fight me over it, and now she seems freaked out by something."

Blake and Austin both drop their controllers, agreeing to finish their game after their classes, then walk quickly out the door and down the stairs. Frankie is still waiting at the bottom, oblivious to our appearance. She doesn't look like she's blinked since I went upstairs.

"Hey, girl. What's happening?" Blake asks, pulling her in for a hug. "Why are you shaking? What's wrong?" Suddenly, his concerned tone sets me more on edge.

"I-I don't know. Someone was in my yard."

"Okay," he replies, leading her into the living room.

She halts her steps and stiffens. "Brad!" She turns and bolts toward the door, but I stop her before she can run out.

"Frankie, chill. What's wrong with Brad?"

"He's home alone. I have to check on him." She swallows hard and tugs at her sweater.

Everything about this situation is confusing, and based on the looks Austin and Blake are giving me, they're equally lost.

"Talk to me. Why can't Brad be alone?" Blake asks, walking back to where Frankie is standing near the door.

"C-can you come w-with me?" she replies, not answering his question.

What surprises me is that I assumed she was asking Blake that question, but her eyes are on me. So are Blake's, paired with a smirk and a raised eyebrow.

Austin huffs a short laugh. "Why don't we all go? We can check things out before we have to head back to campus," he suggests, glancing at Blake.

I look over at him, wanting to laugh myself, because he's not known for his bravery. "Yeah, sure." I'm still not sure what she's afraid of or why we are being roped into this, but given the reaction she's had to a set of unknown footprints, I won't refuse.

Especially not when her face relaxes for the first time and she gives me a grateful smile.

I pull the door open, leading her out. The three of us grab our jackets and slip on shoes, then walk down our pathway and up Frankie's. She stops to show us the boot prints by her garbage and recycling bins. The tread on them is distinct and heavy—either a work boot of some sort or a winter boot. Beyond that, I don't see any other signs for concern.

"What time did you leave today?" I ask as we walk up her front steps.

"Maybe ten after nine. I had classes from 9:30 until 1:30, then I came straight home." At least she's speaking in full sentences again, not stuttering and stopping.

I left the house just before eight and got back around noon, but I didn't see anyone searching garbage bins either time. As she unlocks the multiple deadbolts on her door, I offer some reassurance. "Chances are someone was just looking for bottles to return. Times are tough. There's a guy who goes around with a bike trailer, collecting anything he can."

"That's fine when the bins are at the curb. They're fair game. But no one has the right to come onto my property to search them." She opens the door just enough to shout inside, "Brad? *Venir.*"

The dog comes to the door and sticks his nose through the narrow opening.

"*Ciao, bambino.*" Frankie bends down and scratches his ear. She appears to relax for the first time.

"Do you want us to come in?" Blake asks.

"Would you mind? Just until I check things out. I know I probably sound crazy, but—"

"You don't need to explain," Austin adds, eliciting a small smile from Frankie.

We walk inside, taking in the interior of Frankie's house that looks as though she's put less effort into decorating than we have. There's not a single thing hung on the wall, no frilly pillows or hints at her personality. There's just a couch, a TV, a bookshelf, and a dog bed with a basket of toys beside it. Short of a few textbooks on her small dining table, you can't tell anyone even lives here. When I was in here before, I didn't pay any attention to her space. I was too annoyed to bother.

"Austin and I will check the main floor. You guys check upstairs," Blake instructs, sending me a covert wink. "Don't touch the 'garbage bin'."

I shake my head and roll my eyes. "You're a moron."

"That's what Dear Ol' Dad says," he replies, walking past the stairs, into Frankie's kitchen.

Now I feel like the idiot, but before I can apologize, he's disappeared with Austin, leaving me standing with Frankie.

"Lead the way," I finally say, ignoring her one raised brow.

Her eyebrows are a lot darker than her hair, making me think this brassy blonde isn't her natural hair colour. But as she starts up the stairs in front of me, I'm no longer concerned with her hair. For the first few weeks we lived next door to each other, I saw Frankie exclusively in track pants and scrubs. The day she was picking up garbage in her yard was the first time I noticed what she was hiding underneath her baggy clothes. From this angle, these yoga pants cannot camouflage her figure.

I'm so distracted, I nearly crash into her when she comes to an abrupt stop at the top of the stairs.

I clear my throat and ask, "What's wrong?"

"Uh… nothing. I just…" Her hands clench at her sides as her eyes roam around the upstairs hallway.

"Do you want me to go first?"

She turns her head to catch my eyes, flashing a new level of vulnerability. "Please."

Whatever it is that has her afraid is a far greater evil to her than I am right now. So it may be short-lived, but I'm going to take this chance to prove to her that I'm not the villain she's made me out to be.

This is surreal. Chances are I'm being paranoid, but with my parents' recent visit, I can't ignore the possibility my garbage visitor isn't random. Perhaps the more surreal part is that Oscar is in my bedroom, about to open my closet.

"Don't look in there!" I shout, stopping him from sliding the door to the side.

He looks as surprised by my outburst as I am. I've barely strung a decent sentence together for the last twenty minutes, yet that one came out loud and clear.

"It's... I... Uh... Just..." Speaking in full sentences was short-lived. I just don't know how to tell him that I have a collection of matching bras and panties hung up on satin hangers alongside my scrubs. Having him two feet from my bed is weird enough. "I'll look." At least I know if anyone pops out of my lingerie collection, Oscar is here, and he looks like he could wrangle a grizzly.

He steps back, just far enough he can't reach the closet, but not far enough he can't look inside if I open it fully.

Instead, I open the right side, exposing my collection of colourful scrubs and hoodies, and peek behind the door. "All clear." I laugh awkwardly and smile at the guy I considered as someone who hated me thirty minutes ago. "Thank you for this… I know we're… Well, you don't like me much."

"I never said—"

"All good up here?" Blake asks, popping his head through my bedroom door.

"Yeah, everything's fine," Oscar answers. He looks at me. "Right?"

I nod to him, then to Blake. "Yep. Thanks, guys. I'm so sorry I went off the deep end."

Austin and Blake offering words of understanding wouldn't surprise me. They've been friendly and kind since day one. But it's not them who chime in with their support.

"Hollis lives alone, and she's had a few occasions where she's made me stay on the phone while she went inside. Don't sweat it. Better safe than sorry."

I blink at Oscar, questioning how we've gone from sworn mortal enemies to helpful neighbours in a matter of minutes. He's literally the last person I'd ever expect to have my back. Knowing he was willing to makes me see him a bit differently.

"Hate to run out on you, Frankie, but we both have classes in thirty minutes," Blake adds, pointing to Austin.

"Oh gosh. You should have said something. It's a thirty-minute bus ride to campus." I walk past Oscar, through my bedroom door and down the stairs, listening to the footsteps trailing me. "Take my car. I have a campus parking pass." I pull my key from my pocket, holding It out to Blake as he reaches the bottom of the stairs. "You have your license, right?"

He winks at me in his typical Blake way, swiping the key and passing it to Austin. "Don't trust me with your car. I'm not responsible enough," he adds in a mocking voice, like it's something he's heard a hundred times.

"Are you going to be okay if we leave you alone?" Austin asks, looking at my car key.

No, I don't want to be alone, but more than that, I don't want to inconvenience anyone any more than I have. "I'll—"

"I can stay," Oscar blurts.

It seems he and I are the only ones surprised by that offer, because Austin and Blake exchange a sideways glance and mirrored smirks.

Blake claps his hands together once, then reaches over to pat Oscar's back. "I guess we'll leave you two alone to deal with the garbage bin issue."

Oscar tries to interject, but Blake and Austin bound out the front door and down the stairs, leaving me confused and Oscar looking like he's ready to fight.

"Right. So… uh…" I seriously need to get a grip. I take a deep breath before continuing, "You don't have to stay. I'll be fine."

His facial expression turns hard, glowering at me. "If you want me to go, just say it."

"No!" I shout, again surprising us both. "I mean, you can if you want, but don't feel obligated to stay."

"I don't."

"Want to go or feel obligated?" I'm not sure why I felt the need to ask that.

"Neither."

I'm also not sure why that answer makes my stomach flip-flop. "Do you want something to eat? I'm not sure what I have, but I can make something."

"Nah, thanks. I'm good."

"Are you afraid I'll poison you?"

"If your cooking is as bad as your driving, then yes."

I roll my eyes, turning back toward the living room. "You're never going to let that go, are you?"

"You tried to kill me. I can't know for sure you won't use your cooking to finish the job." He drops onto my sofa, stretching one arm along the back. He instantly looks like he's at home, but one thing I've noticed about Oscar is that he never relaxes. "My diet is particular. For a few reasons," he adds, leaning his head back.

"What do you mean?" I ask, positioning myself at the other end of the couch and calling Brad up to join me.

"Nothing. It's just... I have to be careful with what I eat. No refined carbs. No food colouring. No caffeine."

"What? Why? My absolute favourite food is made up of all three of those things." Not eating them sounds like torture.

"So I'm right in declining something to eat. What's your favourite food?"

"Red velvet cupcakes. Sugar, white flour, food colouring, chocolate. They're heavenly." So much so, just mentioning them makes my mouth water. "There's a bakery in Bracebridge my parents used to take me to, and it has the *best* red velvet cupcakes. Sometimes they even do fundraisers for the animal shelter, so they decorate them with little dog faces." Mere mention of my beloved puppy cupcakes makes me feel increasingly homesick and even more frustrated by my inability to return home.

"I'll have to take your word for it," Oscar replies in a low voice, as if he's picked up on the sadness in mine.

These little hints at who Oscar the person is today have made me want to see him in a different light. No longer as the thorn in my side, who is some kind of enigma sent here to test me.

There's so much more to him than the angry killjoy with no knowledge of dog breeds. Or should I say misinformed about dog breeds? I hope now that he's been around Brad a little, he's warmed up to him.

Before I get too caught up in analyzing bits and pieces of my interactions with Oscar, I ask, "How was *Hibiscus*?"

Both of his brows raise a fraction of an inch. "It was good. Great, actually. I had lamb shanks in cream sauce," he answers with a hint of a smile on his lips.

"So clearly your diet restrictions aren't because of calories. Or was it a cheat day?"

His smile rapidly disappears, and I worry that I've said something horribly wrong.

"You don't need to explain," I rush to add, not wanting to kill this moment of neighbourliness we're having.

"I have ADHD. That's all. Certain things make it worse, so I avoid them." He shrugs one shoulder, keeping his eyes on Brad.

"Wow." I pause, waiting for him to look at me so I can gauge if he's even remotely offended by my earlier comment. It only takes a mere second before his eyes meet mine. "That's amazing you've had that level of self-awareness. It takes a lot of discipline to stick with it."

"It's easy to stick with something when the alternative is a nagging ball of nervous energy pooling in your stomach that you can't shake."

Relatable. Though, red velvet cupcakes are not to blame for my nervous energy.

"Don't discount yourself. That takes a lot of dedication. It can't always be the easy choice."

He shrugs with both shoulders this time before pushing himself to stand, then walking to the window. "So, since we're sharing, want to tell me why you got so freaked out today?"

"No," I reply immediately.

"Frankie," he says in the same low voice he used earlier, but this time, it raises the hairs on my arms.

It also prompts me to spill details I never thought I'd share with Oscar. I exhale a long breath, forcing the impending tears to stay away. "Sometime during my senior year of high school, I earned myself a stalker."

He turns himself slightly, so he's facing me, allowing me to see his widened eyes. "A stalker? Who?"

"That's the problem; I don't know. It started with him leaving notes on my car outside of my work. That was it for the first year, so I just had security walk me to my car every night. But once I started university, I'd get notes on my car in the campus parking lot."

He takes a deep swallow. "What did the notes say?"

"At first, just moderately creepy things like 'you're so beautiful,' or 'your smile makes my day.'"

"Yeah, that's beyond 'moderately' in my books." He drops back onto the sofa, now closer to Brad. "What happened after that?"

"The notes got more intimidating. The final straw was at the end of my last semester when I got a note at home saying, 'we'll be together soon.'" Just repeating those words makes me shiver. "My dad said enough is enough, and since we still have no idea who the person is, despite security cameras on campus and at work, it was safer for me to leave."

"Wow."

I guess we're both wowing each other tonight, but his situation is far more impressive. Where he's taking control of his life; I'm just a floundering victim of the unknown.

"Yeah. Kind of a nightmare. And tonight, I just freaked out because of my parents' visit. I thought maybe he followed them or something. That'd be crazy, right?"

Oscar looks me straight in the eye with a new intensity. "Safe to say he bypassed crazy the first day he left a note on your car."

That's not the reassurance I was hoping for. I was kind of hoping he'd tell me I was overreacting and I have nothing to worry about. My eyes drop to Brad, watching my terrible guard dog breathe evenly as he sleeps with his head against my hip.

"If something worries you again, you know where to find us."

Now that is exactly the reassurance I needed, but never expected to come from Oscar. Once again, he's making me think there's so much more to him than I realized.

Maybe he's not so bad after all.

OSCAR

Can't Stop me Now

"**O**zzy! You're just in time for the festivities."

I stare at the selection of liquor bottles spread across the kitchen counter, suddenly wishing my eleven-hour day could have been longer. I grumble, but decide not to argue with Blake because chances are he sent out a virtual invite days ago. It's my fault for not checking my social media notifications when he tags me in things.

The good news is, the last few times they've had people over, it hasn't been as chaotic as the first party. Still, I'm not in the mood.

"What's the big deal about tonight?" I ask, trying to pretend I'm semi-interested.

"Molly, from my screenwriting class, is coming again, but this time she said she's bringing some friends." Blake winks like he so often does when he says something ridiculous.

I have no memory of him talking about a girl from any classes. Let alone one who has been here before. "Yeah, cool. Well, I probably won't stick around because I have to work tomorrow and I had a long day."

This semester, Fridays are my longest day and consist of classes from 8:30 until 5:20, then I teach a class at 6:15. We're only two weeks into January, and I can already tell Fridays are going to take their toll. Unlike my Thursdays from last semester, obviously I won't be rewarded with an empty house and quiet, either.

"Come on, man. You haven't stuck around for a single party all year."

"Why does it matter? It's cool if you like to party, but it's not my scene."

Blake raises an eyebrow at me as Keith and Austin enter the room, talking about the hockey game they were watching last night when I got home. I tried to hang out and watch it with them, but I got bored by the first commercial break, so I went upstairs to play guitar instead.

That makes me realize how often I flake on them, yet they keep trying to include me. The least I can do is pretend I'm interested and stick around for a while.

"Fine. I need a shower and some time to... decompress. What time is everyone coming?"

Blake's face lights up. "Maybe another 'garbage bin' will grab your... attention." He winks at me again.

"Don't make me regret this," I reply as I grab my gym bag and turn to go upstairs.

"Ten," he shouts behind me, putting a short clock on the time I have to myself.

I had two hours to shower and get my head in the right space to deal with more people. It wasn't long enough. I walk down the stairs with no interest in being around another crowd, but a promise is a promise.

There are five girls in the living room, one guy on either end of one couch, none of whom I recognize, so I don't pretend I'm a welcoming host and introduce myself to any of them. I continue past into the kitchen, where I find all three of my roommates, another guy I recognize but don't know, and three more girls I can't tell apart.

"Ozzie, my man. You finally left your swamp," Keith greets.

I glare at him, trying to make sense of that. "My room is nothing like a swamp."

"No, but you're a bit like an ogre."

My attention is diverted from Keith as more bodies enter the kitchen. The girl in front, who Blake calls Molly, saunters forward to give him a hug. The third girl is tall and blonde, but the one in the middle is shorter and shielded by Molly.

Blake turns to look at me, his eyes wide. He's unbothered by virtually everything, so the number of times I can say I've seen him have a panicked look is exactly once—right now.

When the recognizable redhead steps out from behind Molly, I understand.

"Sonia," I say unenthusiastically, not interested in a conversation beyond that.

Blake sends me a pleading look, which I recognize as him begging me not to make an issue out of her being here. I couldn't care less if he wants her to stay, but that doesn't mean I will. If anyone were to be offended by her presence, I would have thought it would be him since he almost got expelled because of the situation she caused. I guess Molly is worth dealing with whatever drama Sonia might bring. Hopefully, his interest in Molly is short-lived, so after tonight, I won't have to worry about my shameless ex in my kitchen again.

I acknowledge Blake's silent request with a two-finger salute, then walk past the three girls to exit the room. Thankfully, Sonia doesn't try to stop me to chat. She's not stupid enough to think we could even salvage a friendship.

I pull out my phone to call Hollis to see if I can come hang out at her place, but before I reach the top of the stairs, I get her voicemail. There goes that plan. The gym is closed, and I'd rather not go back to campus after being there for so long already today.

Aside from hiding out in my room, I don't have a lot of options.

Except…

Before I can question my sanity, I've got my coat and shoes on, and I'm striding down the front steps. Turning right. Walking up different steps. Knocking.

"Can I come in?" I ask as soon as Frankie opens her door.

"Um… is something wrong?"

"No." I shrug. "Just not interested in partying. I got a lock for my door." I hold up the key to prove my point, even though she probably has no clue why that's important.

She pulls the door open enough for me to step inside. Brad doesn't move from his spot on his bed, wagging his tail so it knocks against the near-empty shelf beside him.

In the midst of slipping off my second shoe, I pause. "Am I interrupting anything?"

"No." She stands with her arms crossed, leaning against the wall by her front window. "We were watching TV."

I'm not sure what I was expecting when I walked over here, but watching TV is not high on my list of favourite hobbies. I'm already surprised she let me in, though, so I won't complain about her evening plans.

"Anything interesting?"

"Uh… Brad likes this show about working dogs. He's partial to the therapy dog career path," she replies as she drops into the nearest seat on the couch, hugging a pillow to her chest.

I watch Brad as I walk slowly into the room. He still doesn't move from his bed until I sit on the other end of the couch.

"*Venir*," Frankie calls, patting the couch. She looks at me as if she's posing a challenge to see if I'll object.

I don't.

Brad jumps up between us. He's a lot bigger than he was the first time I met him. I'm guessing he's around fifty pounds, so he definitely couldn't get around inside Frankie's sweater anymore.

Instead of settling next to Frankie, he sits in the middle, giving me an unnerving sideways glare. I keep an eye on him, rather than on the TV, because I don't fully trust him.

It doesn't take long before my leg starts bouncing and my hands fidget with the fabric inside my hoodie pocket. Despite the long day I've had, I still have endless energy for restlessness.

I look away from Brad to watch a brief clip about a special forces dog learning to sky dive. It's intense, seeing her in her gear—goggles and all—jump out of a plane attached to her handler's chest, then unclipped as they hit the ground so she takes off running. I look over at Brad again, picturing him in the same scenario. He looks at me and promptly curls up on the middle cushion with a groan, as if telling me he's not cut out for that line of work. Like he's trying to prove he's a lover, not a fighter.

"These dogs are amazing," Frankie says, disrupting the awkwardness hanging between us.

"They are. My brother has one."

"A Malinois? Really?"

"Yeah." I pull my eyes from the TV to look at her, and she's staring at me like she's eager to hear more. "He started his own backcountry adventure business, so he rescued this dog to go with him. Her name's Flea."

"Flea?" She laughs. It's the most at ease I've ever seen her around me.

"Long story." It's not really, but I don't want to get into it.

She takes my reply as the end of that conversation, because she hugs the pillow tighter and turns back toward the TV. I feel like an idiot, but I'm too restless to delve into a conversation I'm not interested in right now.

My hand is itching for something to do, other than pick at the pilling inside my sweater, so I reach over and touch the fur on his back. He lifts his head to look at me, but quickly drops it again, fully relaxed. I pet him for several minutes, solely focused on him. For the first time in a long time, aside from inside the muay thai gym, I feel a sense of calm.

Frankie clicks the TV off when the end credit music comes on. When I lift my eyes to look at her, she's already watching me. Specifically, her gaze trails from my hand to my face. Like we're both having a hard time believing this is happening right now.

"Do you want anything to drink? Water? Um… Water? Yeah, that's all I have that doesn't have caffeine or food colouring or refined carbs."

"Geeze. What kinds of things do you drink?" I reply, slowly removing my hand from Brad.

"Normal college student things." Then she lists them off on her fingers. "Espresso, soda, and electrolyte drinks." She pops up out of her seat. "Oh! I have some herbal tea my mom brought. No caffeine."

She doesn't wait for me to reply before she's headed into the kitchen. Brad doesn't budge, so I don't either, other than to put my hand back. I scan the room a little closer, now that Frankie isn't here, but there's not a lot that says anything about her personality. She's got a few textbooks on the shelf, but no recreational reads. No artwork. No knickknacks. Everything in here is strictly functional.

Either she's the most boring person on the face of the planet or she is intentionally minimalistic. And one thing I know for sure: Frankie isn't boring.

Oscar is in my living room. I'm not entirely sure why, out of any option he had where he could spend his time, he's chosen here. As if he wasn't enough of a mystery, now he's gone and confused me even more.

I finish making his tea and my drink, then clench and relax my fists until my hands stop shaking. This is ridiculous. I shouldn't be nervous. The clattering mugs confirm I am.

Oscar is petting Brad's back when I return, but I don't point it out. I just pretend I can't see him falling for Brad's charms. Though, I really can't wait for the day I can say, *I told you so.*

I hand him his drink and sink back into my spot on the sofa.

"What are you poisoning me with?" He smirks, looking down into the mug.

"Lavender something. I haven't tried it yet. Could be fatal."

"Are you having some?" he asks just before taking a sip, clearly not worried it will kill him.

"No, I made espresso."

"This time of night?"

I shrug. "Yeah. Why not?"

His wide eyes study me from behind his tea. "Don't you like to sleep?"

"My parents came straight from Italy. Trust me, I've been drinking espresso and wine since before I hit puberty."

He sets his tea down on the table, shifting so his one leg is bent on the cushion, resting against Brad. "What brought them here?" He pauses, looking as if he regrets his question. "My dad's parents came from Northern Italy in the sixties."

I stare at him for a moment, studying his blond hair, olive skin, and green eyes.

"My great grandparents were German. They fled to Italy in the fifties. That's why..." His words trail off, but he uses his hand to gesture at himself, once again drawing my attention to how he won the genetic lottery.

Interesting. "Have you been? I've only been to Northern Italy once, but it's beautiful. We did an eight-week trip when I was thirteen from Lyon, France, through Switzerland, as far as Milan. Lake Como is amazing."

He shakes his head slowly. "No, I haven't."

I wait for him to elaborate, but he doesn't. "My parents came from Palermo, Sicily."

Still nothing.

"My dad's parents died, so they became my aunt's legal guardians. She was only six, and it was really hard on her. Seemed the best thing to do was give her a fresh start here."

"Wow."

I know I'm not very experienced in hosting visitors and socializing, but I'm pretty sure it's not supposed to be one-sided. He doesn't even look like he's paying attention to me.

"What do neighbours do when one shows up at the other person's house without warning? Play board games? Sing karaoke? Truth or Dare?"

That last suggestion gets his attention again. "How old were you the last time you had someone over? Eleven?"

Long enough that I thought Truth or Dare was a reasonable suggestion. "Well, I don't have a karaoke machine or any board games, so... we don't have a ton of options."

He takes a sip of his tea with one hand, continuing to pet Brad with the other. "Fine. Truth or dare?"

Despite having suggested it, I find myself completely taken by surprise that he's accepted. I'm hesitant to choose either, but this could be my chance to learn more about him. "Truth."

"If you could confront your stalker, would you?"

That's a zinger of a first question, causing me to choke on my espresso. Once I clear my throat, I answer, "I don't think I'm that brave, so probably not. I'd rather take the coward's way out and hope he never finds me again."

"But what if he does?"

I live in fear of that every day, but I'm not going to sit here and give Oscar more reason to think I'm still living like a victim after all this time. "Rules are rules. Only one question. Your turn. Truth or dare?"

He sighs and takes a long sip of his tea. "Truth."

"Why did you really come here tonight?" Again, I'm not brave, so asking him that is a total departure for me. It's completely different from confronting him or arguing. This civility is foreign.

"My... uh... my ex showed up at the guys' party."

"And you couldn't ask her to leave? It's your house."

"Ah, rules are rules." He smirks again, and I find myself really enjoying it. "Only one question. Truth or dare?"

There's something about Oscar's playful personality appearing at this moment that makes me feel more brave. "Truth."

"Tell me a dating horror story. It'll make me feel better about mine." He nods toward his house, making me curious about what went so horribly wrong for him and his ex.

Unfortunately, right as I was old enough to date or had any interest, my stalker started running my life and prevented me from having that experience. To not sound like a hopeless loser, I choose the one story I have. "This guy, Callum, asked me to prom. He was in a few of my classes, but I didn't really know him. I agreed because you constantly hear 'you only get one prom,' so I felt obligated to go."

"Please, don't tell me this ends in the back seat of his parents' SUV in some shady parking lot." He throws himself back on the couch, again returning his hand to Brad's back.

"Not that kind of story. Basically, he invited me because he'd just broken up with his girlfriend and wanted to make her jealous. Why he'd ever choose me to do that, I'll never know."

Oscar lifts his head and his eyebrows, making eye contact with me. There's a question in his expression, but he doesn't voice it.

"Anyway, they got back together, sometime between the dinner and the dance. I went back home to watch reruns of *L'Amica Geniale* with my mom."

"Did your best friend end up in a fistfight with Callum's girlfriend?"

My eyebrows pinch together from yet another surprise. "No," I drawl. That would require a best friend, first of all, and I've fulfilled my obligation of answering his question. "Truth or dare?"

"Truth," he answers, not shifting his focus from Brad.

I could use this opportunity to ask him to elaborate on the fistfight, but I don't. There's something else I want to know first. "What are you studying? I know the other guys' majors, but you've never mentioned what you're taking."

"To be fair, we haven't had a lot of heart-to-heart chats. Guess."

"That's not how this is supposed to work, but fine. I'll play." I consider everything I know about Oscar and throw out the most obvious choice: "Nutrition."

He makes a buzzer sound. "Nope."

That was really my only guess, so I tease him a bit. "Um… cosmetology?"

He rolls his eyes and buzzes me again.

"Oh, interior design."

"We can't all be as talented at decorating as you are." He waves his hand around my barren room.

I don't bother telling him it's out of necessity. Out of reluctance to settle somewhere just to have my life ripped out from under me. "So glad you noticed the effort I've put into it."

We pause for a moment, him not commenting on my sarcasm and me not offering any more guesses.

"Urban planning," he finally answers.

"Really? Never would have guessed that."

He shrugs. "What can I say? I'm unpredictable."

That's an understatement. I've never met an urban planning major before, so I can't claim I know anything about the subject. I'll leave it to him to drive that conversation, though. "Okay. My turn again. Dare."

"Hmm." He lifts his chin to inspect the ceiling for a moment. "Since you were so excited about karaoke, sing the chorus of your favourite song."

I'm immediately reminded of why I hate this game. I'd rather jump in the snow naked, to be honest. There's no way I'm prepared for this level of mortification.

"Do I need to get my guitar? Help you out a bit?" he asks, now looking straight at me.

"You play guitar?"

"Ah, it's your turn, not mine. Time to pay up." His upturned lips make me consider something I never would have before.

"Fine." I clear my throat and take a sip of espresso, wishing it was coffee liqueur instead. And in what I'd describe as a complete detachment from reality, I rush through the chorus of *Peaceful Easy Feeling* by the Eagles.

Thankfully, it's a short chorus, so I put us both out of our misery faster.

Except, once I stop, Oscar is silent for way too long before stating, "Look who's unpredictable now."

I don't know if that's a good thing or not, but if we can move on without a critique of my dying cat voice, I'll feel better. "Truth or dare?"

"Dare," he replies confidently.

"I dare you to teach me a muay thai move." Ever since Blake and Hollis mentioned to me that Oscar coaches muay thai, I'd be lying if I said I wasn't curious to see what he looked like in action.

His eyes light up with an excitement I haven't seen from him before. "Okay. Stand up."

I follow his instructions, moving over to an open space in the room, fighting to control my nerves.

"Put your feet like this. One foot in front of the other. Weight on your back foot, with your leg straight. I'm going to show you a simple push kick. If someone rushes you, it's the easiest way to stop them."

"Okay." I do as he says, copying the position of his feet.

"You're going to bring your front knee up first." He uses his hands to move my knee into the right position, and his touch sends sparks from my knees, straight up my core. "Everything else kind of happens at once. You're going to bring this hand down, push your hip out, and extend your leg."

I try to follow his directions, but fail miserably. My kick wouldn't knock over a broomstick.

"Like this." He puts one hand on my hip, pushing it forward, as he drops my left arm down.

His calloused fingers create a whole new sensation, leaving a trail of goosebumps up my arm and making me gasp.

"There. You got it."

I can't stop the intense buzzing I'm feeling from his proximity. Yeah, my dating life is pathetic—non-existent—but I didn't think I was so deprived, a two-second graze of his palm would cause such a reaction. It has struck me dumb, and I can't seem to turn my brain back on.

He releases my hip and steps in front of me. "Here. Kick me in the stomach. Use the ball of your foot." He pats his flat stomach encouragingly.

"What? No. I'm not kicking you."

He snickers. "Trust me. It won't hurt."

I narrow my eyes at him. "I resent that. What if I'm playing opossum?"

"Frankie, I spend half of my time taking full-on kicks to my entire body by my students and other guys training. If I took my shirt off, you'd see the evidence."

"That sounds awful," I say, dropping my leg.

"The evidence, or me taking my shirt off?"

I gulp, not wanting to answer, though I'm sure he knows which one I meant. He's wearing a smug smile now, prompting me to put what he's taught me to the test.

I replay the steps in my mind as I go through them, positioning my feet properly, lifting my knee, delivering a half-hearted kick, which Oscar catches before it makes contact.

He stands in front of me, holding my bare foot. "That was good. Now you just need to work on your reaction time. I saw that coming from a mile away."

In this moment, I realize I didn't see this coming from two feet away. And it's hit me a lot harder than a push kick.

24

OSCAR

I Don't See 'Em

Ever since the incident with the footprints by Frankie's garbage over a month ago, I find myself on edge, watching for anyone suspicious on the street. Based on the status of our relationship before that bombshell confession, the intensity with which I feel the need to protect her is surprising. It has also not been good for my sleep schedule, because instead of dozing off, like my heavy eyes are telling me to, I'm staring out the window, the same way I have every night since leaving Frankie's last Friday.

Unlike every other night this week, this time, I spot someone lurking on the opposite side of the road, leaning against an oak tree near the entrance to the loft apartment building. If not for the headlights of a passing car lighting him up, I never would have noticed him. I watch for a minute to see if maybe he's an apartment dweller stopped for a cigarette or waiting for a ride. He doesn't move, and I'm not patient enough to keep watching him any longer.

I run down the stairs and spot Keith in the living room. "Hey, want to check something out with me? There's a guy standing across the street."

He immediately pops up. "You think it's Frankie's stalker?"

"I'm not sure. But why else would someone stand out there in the cold at this time of night?" I reply, tugging on my second shoe.

Keith grabs his coat from the hook and slides his feet into a pair of clunky winter boots, ensuring if this comes down to a foot chase, the onus is on me to catch the guy. "Let's go."

We walk out the door casually, not wanting to spook the creep before we figure out his intentions. We maintain casual conversation as we stroll down the sidewalk past Frankie's house. From here, I can't even tell if the guy is still there.

Keith attempts to justify our presence by saying, "I can't believe Blake got diarrhea in the middle of the night. Like I wouldn't rather be sleeping than listening to *that* explosion from the other side of the bathroom wall."

I arch a brow at him but play along. "He shouldn't have eaten all that con queso. He should've learned by now."

Keith lets out a natural laugh, perhaps recalling the time Blake overindulged in his favourite neon orange cheese and salsa mixture when we lived in residence last year, and none of us were able to use the bathroom for forty minutes. He wasn't nearly as bothered by the situation as we all were.

We pass the tree the guy was standing against, but from the faint light of the streetlamps, I don't see anyone.

I whisper, "All clear."

"We better go pick up some meds," Keith continues at a normal volume.

Out of nowhere, someone steps out from behind a hedge in front of us and begins speed walking down the sidewalk in the same direction we're headed. I tap Keith's arm and point. The person is about sixty feet ahead and gaining distance.

Keith takes the hint and we pick up our pace to stay in step with the stranger. From what I can tell, their jacket and body shape are the same as the person who was tucked in behind the oak tree.

"That's him," I confirm.

Keith is struggling to keep up in his clunky boots. Lucky for him, I'm fast and undeterred by creeps hiding in the shadows on our street. Especially across from Frankie's house.

"Just watch my back."

Without waiting for a reply, I speed up into a jog and start closing the gap. I'm still about forty feet away when the stranger glances over his shoulder and immediately picks up a sprint.

"Ozzie!" Keith shouts from behind me.

I'm not sure if he's trying to alert me to the perp running, or he's trying to call me back, but neither is helpful.

The only problem is, I've spent the last decade building my body to be strong, withstand blows, build endurance, and manoeuvre efficiently; I'm not a sprinter. Creepy guy seems to be a college track athlete the way he opens up more distance between us. It's demoralizing, watching him widen the gap, sprinting through the wet snow as if it were an Olympic track.

I'm not the type to give up, but when we reach Dundas Street, I slow to a stop. Only because I've lost sight of him, and there are too many footprints for me to track where he went.

Keith comes huffing behind me. "We should have stopped to get Brad."

"Brad wants to be a therapy dog," I snap. "We can't tell Frankie about this."

"Why? Wouldn't you want to know?"

"I would, yeah, because I can handle myself. It'll just freak her out. We don't even know if it was him. She hasn't gotten any notes or anything, and that was his MO before." Based on Frankie's attempts at a push kick, she's not equipped to defend herself, so the least we can do is limit her fear over the situation. "We'll have to keep a closer watch."

"Right." Keith exhales. "With our flexible schedules and free time. Shouldn't be a problem," he answers sarcastically.

He may have had my back just now—kind of—but his excuse-making frustrates me. Sure, he's studying a double major, but I'm the only one who has a proper job. All three of my roommates *do* have free time. Apparently, he doesn't have the motivation to help.

"Forget it. I'll handle it myself." I scan my surroundings one last time before I turn and head home.

Keith walks the full distance a few steps behind me, not speaking until we get to the bottom step. "You should tell her, man. She deserves to know."

I spin around when I reach the door. "She deserves some peace, and I'm not about to take that from her."

My entire class tonight, I've been thinking about how to encourage Frankie to come for some personal coaching sessions. I don't take on a lot of private clients—meaning I only have my cousin Caleb—but I'd make an exception for her. Not because I enjoyed instructing her privately way more than I should have. Definitely has nothing to do with the way she gasped when I touched her, or how she leaned into me, sending me into a sensory overload with her floral scent and the softness of her body.

It's strictly because I want her to be able to keep herself safe. Nothing else.

Totally noble intentions.

Gentlemanly, even.

Just being a good neighbour.

I grumble as I stuff the last of my equipment into my locker, deciding to call my sister. She's a single woman in the city, so even though she doesn't have a stalker, she might have some insight into how I can approach Frankie about learning some more self-defence.

"I have about seven seconds to talk," Hollis answers. "Is this an emergency?"

"Um… no. Just checking in. Everything okay?"

"Yes. No. Maybe. I'm not sure. It will be, but I need to figure out how I'll fix it."

"Anything I can do?" I ask, hoisting my gym bag onto my shoulder.

"Not yet. I'll let you know, but I think this is something I have to handle internally. Stuff at the lab is just… it's changed, and I don't feel right about it."

"If anyone can make it happen, it's you." I pause for a second, waiting for a reply, but Hollis sounds distracted by something else. "My offer stands if you need me, okay?"

"Thanks. You know Mom always taught us that if we're passionate about something, don't give up on it just because it gets hard? I'll find a way, but if I need you, it's nice to know someone has my back."

"Always. I'll let you go." Since we've gone well past her seven-second timeframe.

Hollis says a rushed goodbye and hangs up. I fiddle with my phone to put on some music and prepare myself for walking home in the freezing cold.

I'm only a few metres out the door when my mind shifts from listening to chord progressions and lyrics to thinking about Frankie. Again.

My mind races with random questions I'd ask her if we had the opportunity to play Truth or Dare ever again.

What does your ideal life look like?

If you could pursue a hobby you don't currently, what would it be and why?

Did your first kiss steal your breath and give you butterflies?

Mine didn't, but standing inches away from her did. I always thought my mom's Harlequin Romance take on that happening was a total crock sold to middle-aged women who buy into that sort of stuff. I was wrong, because one spontaneous evening with Frankie proved that it's a real thing.

As if my rampant thoughts created her out of thin air, when I round the corner to return home, I spot her and Brad walking down the sidewalk.

After the strange lurking Olympic sprinter a few nights ago, my instinct to protect her has grown even stronger. Instead of ignoring her and heading home like I did for the first many months, I continue down the sidewalk to meet her.

Tell Me Again

I thought Oscar and I had turned a corner and would be able to get along a little better after our past few encounters. That hasn't happened, though. It feels like he's been avoiding me for the past ten days, leaving me to assume he still hates me. Obviously, it was just me who was affected by our proximity when he came to my house.

Granted, aside from classes and my time at the clinic, I've basically been a shut-in.

Today, even Brad seemed to be going a little stir crazy, so I've decided to get him out for a proper walk. His outings have been limited to visits to the clinic, where I'd be willing to bet people are more excited to see him than if the real Brad Pitt walked in the door. He's a neighbourhood celebrity, and everyone who knows him adores him… except for the person who is now walking our way. A confusing thorn in my side who makes grey sweatpants and a black beanie look ridiculously appealing.

I half expect Oscar to grumble and continue walking past without acknowledging me, but he surprises me once again by stopping.

"Frankie. Brad." He looks down at my dog, but doesn't give him any more attention beyond saying his name.

"Oscar." *The Grouch*, I add silently. I want to hate him and take issue with everything he does again, but the reality is, his mere presence is making my stomach flutter.

We stand, facing each other, neither speaking for more seconds than what's comfortable. I keep glancing down at Brad, just to focus my eyes on something less awkward than Oscar's questioning gaze.

Finally, I ask, "Did you have classes early?"

"Work."

"Oh. Who said being an adult was fun, huh?" I ask, hoping my tone hints that his one-word answers are getting old.

His lips form a tight smile, but he doesn't respond otherwise.

For some unexplained reason, I turn around and start walking back toward home, making space for Oscar to fall in step beside me.

"Why muay thai? Do you compete? Like fights and whatever?"

"No." He lifts his right hand and rubs the back of his neck.

Talking to him is more work than cleaning up from a parvovirus outbreak. "But what made you choose muay thai?"

I fully expect another one-word reply, but he explains, "When I was younger, I never sat still. I couldn't focus in school and started getting into trouble because I was bored out of my mind. My parents put me in every sport you can imagine. Soccer, hockey, rugby, football, baseball, volleyball, snowboarding, golf. You name it, I tried it, but none of them helped. I was either overwhelmed or bored. No happy medium."

"Because of your ADHD?"

He flashes me a sideways glance before returning his eyes to the sidewalk ahead. "Yeah. Sometimes, on top of everything going on in my head, a lot of chaos is overwhelming, so team sports never grew on me. That's not to say other people with

ADHD can't do team sports, but I couldn't deal. My grandfather kept telling my parents to put me in karate, but my mom was worried I'd start beating up my brother because he's a sensitive guy."

"Ethan, right? Hollis says he's a bit of a hippie."

Oscar laughs; his face lit up with a small, yet brilliant smile. "Yeah, he is. He's the kind of guy who is happier in nature. He despises the city and anywhere with big crowds. Hates attention even more than I do."

It never occurred to me that Oscar hated attention. Being friends with his three roommates, who all seem to thrive in the spotlight, I assumed he was the same way, but looking back at his behaviour during each of their parties, that makes more sense. I really did make snap judgments about him, and couldn't have been more wrong.

"So your mom finally gave in and you started karate?"

"Yep. I did that for a few months, and it was the first individual sport that kept me focused. Soon enough, my coach moved me into kickboxing, so I could do most of my training with other equipment instead of having to wait around for anyone else. It went from there."

"Makes sense. What made you transition to coaching? Is this a case of 'those who can't do, teach?'"

Now he gives me an intense glare, no longer paying attention to the snowy sidewalk. "I can *do* just fine. That's not why I don't fight."

"Enlighten me, then."

He releases a deep sigh. "Around the time I started karate, I found out that my aunt had been sexually assaulted before I was born. The guy got away with a slap on the wrist, but it almost ruined her life. To be honest, I wanted to pound the guy's face in and make him pay, even as a kid, before I really understood what happened. My coach pulled me aside when I started and explained to me that wasn't the right place to focus my energy. If I wanted to make a difference, use my skills someday to teach others how to defend themselves. So that's what I do."

My steps falter, listening to his impassioned speech. That's actually... sweet. Not to mention, it makes sense why he was so willing to teach me.

"You should come to a class. Doesn't have to be my class, but a push kick alone isn't going to help much if... you know..." His words trail off as if he wants to say something else, but stops.

Now, in addition to the image of him gently instructing some gorgeous, yoga-loving natural blonde and the shocking jealousy that elicits, he's also brought my unfortunate situation to the front of my mind. I'm blaming those two things for the reason I sharply reply, "No."

"No? Why not? Frankie, if this guy shows—"

"You don't think I've thought about it? I *know* what could happen, Oscar. Trust me when I say my very active imagination has considered it a lot."

"Then why won't you let me teach you? If not me, someone. Even Blake could teach you a few things that would help."

I swallow the hundred reasons I want to blurt out, and instead, stay silent. Sure, I could tell him that the thought of anyone else touching me makes my skin crawl. That having him so close to me should have done the same, but it had the opposite effect. I could tell him that realization terrifies me, because if this guy *does* reappear, I'll likely have to up and leave my life behind again. I could also explain that my brain is so overloaded from school and my clinic hours, I can't fathom trying to learn something else, even if I recognize that it's practical.

"Frankie," he starts, saying my name the same way that made me cave to him before.

Only this time, I don't.

"Thanks for the offer, Oscar, but no. You don't have to understand, but you have to accept it." With that, we arrive at my walkway, so I follow Brad's lead up the path to my front door, ignoring the feeling of eyes on my back as I disengage the locks and walk inside.

Brad walks over to his water bowl and starts noisily lapping up the liquid. It's a reminder to hydrate myself, because I was busy all day and haven't had anything except espresso and an iced latte.

I walk toward the kitchen as I hear a slam next door. It sounded like the front door. That begs a hundred more questions. Why would he be so upset I said no? Why would he care? It's nothing personal.

Except it's entirely personal. If jealousy hadn't hijacked logic, I may have said yes.

Not to mention, after hearing what he said about his aunt, I have no interest in being his pity project. He can't hate me and try to help me at the same time just because he wants to be some kind of hero. It's one or the other, and I'm not sure which side of the fence he's on.

"You're an idiot, Francesca," I mutter.

Maybe I should ask Blake.

I shudder at the thought of him teaching me anything for several reasons. One, he is so chaotic, asking him to focus on teaching a specific thing would probably take a lot longer than necessary. Two, it's not his hands I want touching me. It's not him who has frustrated me within an inch of my sanity, only to prove that he's so much more than I gave him credit for.

But for all of those reasons, I can't take Oscar up on his offer. I'll just keep hoping that Brad, pepper spray, and a push kick will be sufficient to protect me should the need arise.

Or better yet, hope that years of no violent encounters mean that even if my stalker reemerges, that streak continues.

Another door slams, sounding like it was from the front room of the neighbour's house upstairs, and instantly jolts me back to reality. I didn't even check my house when I walked in.

If I'm going to stay safe, the first thing I need to do is stop thinking about Oscar and start taking care of myself.

25

OSCAR

Hurry Up and Wait

Reading week starts tonight, and all three of my room-mates have officially left for the break. Because of my job at the gym, I'm stuck in the city so I can keep up with those classes, but I'm looking forward to really living on my own for the first time. If I want to, I can shower with the door open, play my guitar anywhere in the house, or sleep naked in the living room and no one will say a word.

But as I walk up to my room, trying to decide which of those acts of rebellion I'll partake in first, I hear a loud bang, followed by a shrill scream and barking. I'm not 100 percent sure it came from Frankie's, but I'm not going to hide in here to wait for confirmation.

I bound out the door, down the stairs, then immediately look at Frankie's house. It's dark out, but I can see by the faint light peeking through her front door; it's open slightly. She never leaves her door open.

The fact I don't hear Brad barking now or her screaming could be a good thing, or it could be really, really bad. The smart thing to do would be to call the police, but I will not stand here and wait if this psychopath is inside with Frankie.

I push the door open a few inches and stop to listen. Nothing. The door jamb is busted, though, so it was obviously kicked in—which explains the noise I heard. I stop inside, scanning the space for any movement. Again, nothing. I walk through the entire main floor, not finding anything out of place, feeling my heart pound harder against my ribcage by the second. Then I hear a little puppy whimper that sounds like it's coming from upstairs. Frankie's house is a slightly different layout from mine, so her U-shaped stairs jut off the side of her dining room.

As I reach the landing, I hear another whimper and a faint *Shhh.*

"Frankie?" I call out. "It's Oscar."

"Os-Oscar?"

I follow the sound of her voice to the bathroom at the top of the stairs. She opens the door slowly, peeking her head around it. Her terrified red eyes relax when they land on me. She's holding a towel rod that she ripped clean out of the wall.

"Are you okay?" I ask, shifting inside without turning my back on the door because I didn't check the rest of the house.

"He-he kicked th-the door in. B-Brad sc-scared…" Her hiccoughing words trail off as she's reduced to more intense tears.

"Come here." I remove the makeshift weapon from her hand, setting it on the back of the toilet, then giving Brad a quick pat. I may not have liked him at first, but he could have just saved Frankie from an even worse outcome tonight. With no barriers between us, I hesitantly wrap my arms around her.

She collapses into me, pulling her arms in between us, so I'm fully consuming her in mine. I wasn't sure how she'd react, but her welcoming me as a safe place right now feels like a turning point.

"You're okay now. Shh."

Sirens get closer, screaming to a stop outside of Frankie's house.

Frankie looks at Brad and says, "*Stare.*"

He sits and watches her, awaiting her next command.

"Toronto Police. Is anyone here?" a woman's voice shouts from downstairs.

"Top of the stairs," I yell back.

Two officers' heads appear from the landing.

The woman asks, "Anyone else here?"

"I didn't check the bedrooms, but I don't think so."

She nods and points to her partner to go to the left as she goes to the right. A few seconds later, they both declare upstairs clear.

Frankie puts Brad in her bedroom, then we follow the officers downstairs and sit on the couch so they can ask questions. She explains that she got home about thirty minutes earlier and was just coming downstairs to make something to eat when the door flew open. Brad went running to the door, barking at the intruder. She screamed for Brad and ran upstairs into the bathroom to call 911. The dog joined her a moment later, so she assumed the person had left. Then I came in less than a minute later, and she thought I was the guy returning.

I can hear the stress in her voice as she explains everything she remembers, and I feel bad for adding to her fear. She tells the officers about her unknown stalker and the reason she left home in the first place. They're both sympathetic, but as Frankie explains she doesn't know who the person is, the male constable tells her there isn't much they can do.

An hour later, they walk out the door, not having any real solutions for Frankie going forward other than "Call us if you see anything suspicious."

I can appreciate that their hands are tied, but if this guy just kicked her door in, do they really think she'll have a chance to call again if he comes back?

"Pack a bag and grab Brad. You guys can come stay with me," I offer as soon as we're alone again.

She opens her mouth to say something, stopping before she does. After a few seconds of the same thing, she finally answers, "We can't do that."

"Why? All the guys are gone. I'm not asking you to stay in my bed, Frankie. You think you're going to stay here alone with a broken door?"

"I… We… I'm not a pet project, Oscar."

"Seriously?" I don't even know what to say to that. If that's what she thinks of me, I'm not sure how to make my intentions clear without spelling it out. Something I'm not willing to do. Her safety matters, though, so regardless of how wrong she is, that's still my priority. "Just because you think I'm a bad guy doesn't mean I am the bad guy here."

"I… No, I don't. It's just…"

Instead of trying to finish her sentence, because I know she could recall any of the many times she and I butted heads, I make an alternative offer. "You want me to call Hollis? I don't think Brad can stay in her apartment, but—"

"No!" She looks down at her beloved dog, tears welling in her eyes. "I'm not staying without him. I know you don't want him at—"

"Frankie, it's fine. At least if we're next door, we can keep an eye on things until your door is fixed."

She takes a deep swallow and uses both hands to wipe her eyes. "Okay. I need to call Devin."

It takes me a second to remember who Devin is. Not going to lie, the day I met him, I was ridiculously distracted by how happy Frankie looked. A total contrast to how she looks now.

So I make it my personal mission to return that smile to her face.

"I'll get things as secure as I can for tonight. Go pack a bag."

Sooner than I thought possible, one side of her lips lift in a forced smile. "Thanks. I owe you big time." She pats her leg to call Brad to follow her up the stairs and disappears.

A short time later, we're walking through my front door, with Frankie leading Brad and carrying his dog bed, and me hauling her small suitcase.

"You can sleep in my room because it overlooks the street. That way, if you hear anything, it's easier to look."

That sounds like a reasonable explanation. I also don't feel right giving her permission to sleep in either of the other rooms upstairs without asking the guys first. I'm sure they'll say yes, but it's still their space and not mine to offer.

But judging by Frankie's face, she's not thrilled with that plan.

"I'll sleep on the couch. Don't worry. That way I can keep an ear on things too," I reassure.

"Oh, no. That's too mu—"

"Frankie, relax. It's fine. Trust me; falling asleep on the couch isn't a hardship. I've been dying to try it out, but the guys are always here. Let me live out my couch-sleeping dreams."

Another half-smile. "Are you sure? I don't mind sleeping there."

"And take my one chance? Not happening. Even if you weren't here, I'd sleep on the couch, so think nothing of it."

She finally relaxes and drops Brad's bed beside the coffee table, which he promptly curls up on. "Okay. But if it's a problem—"

"It's not. What did Devin say when you called?" I ask, trying to change the subject.

"Oh, he mentioned before that he wanted to put in security cameras, so now seems as good a time as any. He'll let me know when he can find someone to install them."

I feel a flood of relief knowing that. Security cameras don't stop determined criminals, but they might help us pinpoint the creep targeting Frankie. "Good. I've got that part covered. If he can order them, I'll get Austin to help set them up." I have a better idea before I finish my sentence, so I pull out my phone while I'm talking. "You know what? Send Devin Austin's number and have him ask which system is best for his budget. We'll go from there."

"Really? He can do that?"

I suppress a laugh, seeing her wide eyes. "Not the physical labour, but he'll know how to do the techy stuff, yeah. The other guys and I can do the rest."

"You don't have to—"

"Frankie," I repeat, knowing I say her name too often, and it might not be accidental. "Let us help." Selfishly, I don't want her thinking my motivation has anything to do with anyone but her.

She's not a pet project. I'm not sure what she is, exactly, but I do know I'll do whatever I can to keep her safe.

All the nights I've fallen asleep alone in my house have blended together, with one anxiety-filled sleep blurring into the next. Tonight turned that anxiety up several notches. I was prepared to shove my broken towel bar through someone's forehead if the situation called for it, but I'm grateful Brad scared the person away. I can't imagine what would have happened if he wasn't there.

As scared as I was, now lying in Oscar's bed, knowing he's downstairs on the sofa keeping watch, I feel like I'm safe to fall asleep. Brad is curled up next to me, tucked in under the blanket with his head on the pillow, snoring like a furry husband. He's earned his rest tonight. And now that my residual adrenaline is working its way out of my system, it's my turn too.

My eyes peel open, and it takes me a few seconds to remember where I am. Brad is missing, which has me worried, so I climb out of Oscar's bed to look for him. All the doors upstairs are closed, so I know he didn't sneak into Keith or Blake's rooms. The only possibility is that he went downstairs. Maybe he had to go out.

In the living room, I find a scene I'm not expecting. I rub both of my eyes to make sure they're not playing tricks on me.

Oscar is lying on the floor beside the sofa, covered in a sheet, but Brad is on the couch, head on the pillow, still snoring. Whatever transpired here is worth preserving. I snap a picture so I'll have photographic evidence of their little slumber party later.

I sneak back upstairs, careful not to disturb either of them. Since I'm still exhausted and I need to figure out what to do about my door, I call Dr. Ellis and let him know I won't be able to come into the clinic today. I hate leaving them shorthanded again, but he'll understand the implications of what happened.

Our conversation is brief, and as expected, he just wants to make sure I'm okay. He offers to call Devin for me, but I let him know I've handled that.

I want to figure out how to fix and reinforce the door before I worry my parents, so I don't call them and hope Olivia won't inform them either. Knowing my parents, they'll insist I move again, but it's the middle of the semester, and aside from having the life scared out of me, I like it here. My professors are great. My lab partners pull their weight and don't talk too much. Even the neighbours are growing on me.

I sink back down into Oscar's bed, pulling the covers over me. He was willing to put himself in harm's way to check on me yesterday. Beyond that, he gave up his bed, and at some point during the night, the couch, to make sure I was safe. That's not something I take lightly.

To show my appreciation, despite how tired I am, I climb back out of bed and head downstairs, determined to make him a no-sugar, no-caffeine, no-food colouring breakfast. I have no idea what to make, since my breakfasts usually consist of a coffee and a muffin. I take to an internet search to see what I can make with the ingredients on hand.

Thank God the other guys drink coffee, though. First step is brewing myself a cup.

By the time I settle on something that sounds edible, though much less enjoyable than a muffin, Brad enters the kitchen. He walks toward the door, stopping in front of his bowl of water. I forgot to set that down for him last night, so Oscar must have. Something about that small gesture on top of everything else warms my heart and makes me determined to make this unappealing breakfast as good as it can be.

Thirty minutes later, Oscar walks into the kitchen while I'm carrying on a full conversation with my dog. Correction: *shirtless* Oscar with charcoal sweatpants and mussed hair. But I'm not looking at his hair. Heat creeps across my cheeks, which I'm blaming on the stove. Nothing to do with his entire defined upper body on display.

How does he keep all of *that* hidden under his regular clothes? He's not bulky like Keith, but he is fit. His restrictive diet is really working for him.

"Morning," he interrupts my staring with a sly smile. One that only makes him look hotter, if that's even possible.

I clear my throat. "Morning. How was your long-awaited couch sleep?" I ask, suppressing a chuckle.

"Back's a little sore, but nothing some stretching won't fix. What's all this?"

"Uh, I'm making breakfast. As a thank you."

"You didn't need to do that." He glances down, then raises an eyebrow. "How many people are you inviting?"

"Oh." I let out an awkward laugh. Maybe I went a little overboard. "Guess you'll have leftovers." I dish the poached eggs onto a bowl of sauteed kale and roasted sweet potatoes. "I'll clean all of this up, then Brad and I will head out."

"You're not eating?" His raised eyebrow inches up closer to his hairline.

"No. You've done enough. I should head ho—" My words halt when I realize I can't really go home with a broken door. "I've got to get the door sorted."

"Eat. I can fix the door. We'll need to run to the hardware store."

"It's fine. Devin said he can hire someone." Honestly, the number of favours adding up against me are getting too high to ever pay off, so a neutral third party is probably a better idea.

"That could take days." He pulls out a stool and points to it as he focuses on me. "Have breakfast. Then we'll fix the door."

After everything he's done, it feels wrong to let him do anything else. But it also feels wrong to argue with him. Mostly because I don't want to. So I dish up a serving for myself, let Brad out the back door on my way around the counter, and take a seat beside shirtless Oscar.

"Did you find coffee?" Oscar asks, stabbing a sweet potato with his fork.

"I did," I answer around a bite of egg. "I didn't consider myself a coffee snob, but it was awful."

He chuckles. "It's an endless debate here. Austin buys whatever's cheapest, so when it's his turn, Blake complains about it too."

"I knew I liked him." My words spill out without considering how they sound or the implications until they're hanging in the air between us.

Oscar sets his fork down and clears his throat. "You could do a lot worse than Blake."

"That's not—" I stare into my breakfast, begging it to send me an answer. It doesn't. "Blake isn't my type. I mean, I like him as a person. A friend. Nothing more." That over-explanation makes me resent this cardboard breakfast even more for not providing me with a less embarrassing reply. Kale is quickly becoming my least favourite food.

"Hmm," he mumbles, picking his fork back up.

We eat the rest of our meal, treading lightly with meaningless conversation. He asks about seasonings and I explain the trick to poached eggs I learned from my mom. He acts interested, but awkwardness grows with each silent second.

Once I take the last bite of my meal, I realize Brad never asked to get inside. I get up from my stool, grab my bowl and fork, set it beside the sink, then walk to the back door. "Brad?" I call, peeking my head into the small yard. "Brad?" I yell a little louder when he doesn't respond and I can't see him.

To my horror, I discover a hole under the fence leading into my backyard. The dirt-covered snow surrounding it is a clear sign of what happened.

"Brad!" I yell once more, shutting the door and running toward the front of the house.

"What happened?" Oscar calls. His footsteps sound behind me, reaching the door at nearly the same time. He places a hand on my arm. "What happened?"

A large part of me is embarrassed about the situation, since this was the exact thing that got us off on the wrong foot. Not just the wrong foot, but the wrong foot in the wrong sock in the wrong shoe.

Still, I need to get to my yard to make sure he stopped his escape there and isn't five yards over by now. "He got under the fence."

Instead of looking angry, he jumps into action, grabbing a hoodie from the hooks behind the door and sliding his feet into his shoes. The same shoes I recognize as the ones he accused Brad of ruining. I don't point that out as I grab my shoes and sweater too.

Ninety seconds later, I'm staring at my dog, who made his way into our yard and stayed there. He was waiting at the backdoor when I opened it, smiling like he's in the running for the *goodest boi* awards. He saunters inside without remorse.

I use the time to serve Brad breakfast while Oscar checks the rest of the house with strict instructions to avoid my closet. Since the front door couldn't lock, I was even more nervous to return home, but he seemed to sense that and offered before I could ask. Another favour to add to the tally.

"Guess he was hungry," Oscar states, returning to the kitchen.

"Guess so. To be fair, I'm thirty minutes late for breakfast." I stare down at my dirt-covered dog while he eats his kibble, grateful he's safe. After the stress and anxiety over the past twelve hours, my nerves can't handle anything else.

Thankfully, Oscar says the one thing that can help get things back on track. "After he's done eating, we'll get this door fixed."

The past few days have been weird. No, that's an understatement. Otherworldly, maybe? Like I'm living in an alternate universe where all of a sudden I have a girl and a dog sleeping in my roommate's bedroom, even though she has a house right next door.

She was terrified to spend the night alone after the break-in, and despite our history, I didn't have the heart to wash my hands of the issue and tell her it's not my problem. It might not be, but I've spent the last three days with her in my house, and I don't hate it.

My roommates agreed to cut their reading week short so they could come back to help get her settled back home. Austin spoke with Devin and arranged a multi-camera system he said will be more than sufficient. I didn't pay attention to any details beyond that. I trust him.

They should be home in a few hours, so I have to make sure I get all the supplies we'll need before they arrive.

I exit my bedroom just as Frankie walks out of Blake's room, wearing a pair of long satin pyjama pants and button-down shirt. He insisted she use his fancy mattress and Egyptian cotton sheets to get a good sleep before his magnificent return. His words; not mine. I think it might have worked, because for the first time in about eighty hours, she looks well rested.

"Oh. You go first." She points at the bathroom door before quickly spinning around to retreat into the master bedroom.

"It's fine. I'll use Austin's."

She pauses, then spins back to face me. "Thank—"

"You said that already. A lot."

She really has. She's thanked me about a hundred times over the past three nights.

"Right. Well… hopefully after today I'll get out of your way. I can't thank you enough—"

"Trust me. You can." The words spill out a little harsher than I mean for them to. Just the fact she hasn't clued in that I don't hate having her around yet is a little annoying. So instead of wasting any more time trying to make her realize I'm not as upset about our current living arrangement as she thinks, I turn to head down the stairs without another word.

By early afternoon, the guys have all returned home, and Frankie thanked each of them twenty-eight more times. She's also hugged each of them with an enthusiasm she's never shown me, even when I came into her house to protect her from an intruder. Each smile she gives Blake, Keith, or Austin inches my jealousy up a notch.

"Grab that wire," Austin instructs, redirecting my racing thoughts by snapping his fingers and pointing.

I grab the black wire and pass it to him.

"You not sleeping?" he asks, splicing the wire with a pocketknife.

"No less than normal. Why?"

He shrugs as he twists two pieces of wire together with a connector. "You look tired. And you seem distracted."

I roll my eyes, trying not to be annoyed with Austin for not understanding how my brain works, but it's hard sometimes. There's only so many times you can explain the same thing before it becomes pointless. It's also annoying that no one seems to point out when Blake is distracted or chaotic, because that's his permanent state. When I have an off day, people try to 'fix' me.

"Things have been a little weird around here." I shove the box toward Austin that holds one security camera he's working to install. "Back in a bit." I need some water. And a break.

Like our house, Frankie's kitchen is tucked around the back side of the stairs. When I walk past the corner, I'm surprised to find Blake, alone in the kitchen, eating a bag of corn chips and jarred con queso.

"I don't know how you eat that garbage and don't lose your mi—" I pause and watch him scoop more toxic sludge into his mouth. "Never mind."

Blake replies, "Touche," holding his chip up in a cheers gesture. "Want some?"

"Pass. Thanks." I stop at the fridge, tugging it open to grab a bottle of water. "Where's Frankie?" I ask, looking into the fridge instead of at Blake. It becomes clear that con queso and corn chips are possibly the least toxic food items Frankie has in her house.

"Thinkin' about her 'garbage bin', hmm?"

I stand straight to look over the open fridge door at this buffoon I call my best friend, resisting the urge to call him an idiot again. "Move on, guy. I'm not interested in her garb—" No, you know what? I'm not stooping to his level and using his stupid euphemisms. "Where is she?"

He wipes his mouth with the sleeve of his waffle-knit tee. "Upstairs with Keith and Brad. Installing a camera in her bedroom." He waggles his eyebrows, and that's the final straw that lands him on the list of people I'm over talking to.

Frankie's laughter reaches my ears as I approach the top of the stairs. I grit my teeth as I approach the room and find Frankie seated on her bed with Brad, watching as Keith stands precariously on a dining chair and secures a camera to the ceiling.

Her posture stiffens when she sees me, causing her to pull her shoulders back and sit upright. "Everything okay?"

Not really. This is weird. Uncomfortable. It's not that I don't want her laughing at anyone else or thanking them or hugging them. I just don't want to feel like she thinks she can't do those things around me, and I don't know how to fix that without making a fool of myself. So I grunt and nod... and immediately regret both.

Even Brad tilts his head while looking at me, as if he's asking what my problem is.

Keith drops a screwdriver, which conveniently makes my presence less awkward. I step forward to pick it up and, from my vantage point, I can see inside Frankie's closet. Returning the screwdriver to Keith is suddenly far from my mind as I glimpse the lacy fabric in a variety of colours.

"Oscar?" Keith asks, forcing me to look away.

"Yeah. Sorry." I hand him the tool, thinking back to the two other times I've been in here. I'd be lying if I said I hadn't been curious about what was in there based on her reactions. Never would I have guessed that she was hiding a lingerie collection. It would also be a lie if I said I wasn't tempted to look closer.

But with Keith in the room and Frankie's current feelings toward me, that feels fifty shades of wrong, so I reach my hand up to slide the door closed.

The soft sound of the sliding door making contact with the wall draws Frankie's attention. Pink creeps across her cheeks, and her eyes widen.

Before I can formulate a response to offer reassurance or crack a joke, Keith hops down from the chair and dusts his hands off, clapping them together. "Finished. Austin just needs to connect the wires."

I keep my eyes on Frankie instead of acknowledging him, and she's wholly focused on me. For a few seconds, it's as if we share a wordless conversation where she's begging for verification I didn't see what she knows I did, and I keep my expression neutral, not confirming either way. After a few seconds, her wide eyes transform into narrowed ones, sending an entirely different message. It's hard to keep a straight face, but years of martial arts training have prepared me for this moment. Game face on.

"You wanna go ask Austin to hook this up?" Keith interrupts. Again.

I turn enough to look at him. "Yeah, sure. He was just finishing one on the main floor." I glance at Frankie on my way out of the room and can't miss the redness that has spread down her neck.

As hard as it was to keep my face neutral, it's even harder to stop myself from picturing her in any of those lacy creations. Did she wear those when she was sleeping in the room down the hall from me? When she slept in my bed? I've acknowledged that she was gorgeous and intrigues me in a way no one else has before, but as I reach the bottom of the stairs, it's hard to deny how insanely attracted to her I am. Not just physically.

All the more reason I need to get out of here, because even after everything, she still seems to think I'm the devil incarnate. Letting myself get in any deeper with her is just going to end in disappointment, and Sonia taught me that I can't afford the distraction.

"Okay, we've got six cameras. One here"—Austin points at the camera I *helped* him with earlier—"one in that corner aimed at the front door, one outside each entrance, one in your room, and one at the top of the stairs. They're all hard-wired with battery backup, and connected to a hard drive. So even in a power outage, they'll still record footage; they just won't be able to transmit the feed to your phone. As long as your internet is on, you can check the feed from anywhere. I installed the app and connected everything, so you can change the settings from there if you want to activate the motion sensors when you're gone. Brad might set them off, though."

We all look over at Brad, who has taken up two-thirds of the couch to have his fourteenth nap since we arrived five hours ago.

"Not as much as you'd think," Frankie replies with a brief laugh. "This is amazing. Thank you guys so much." She looks straight at me and adds, "All of you. I don't know what I would have done without your help."

"Just being neighbourly. Gotta protect each other's garbage bins. Am I right, Ozzie?" Blake flashes me an irritating smile, likely knowing I want to throttle him, but I won't with this many witnesses.

Instead, I reply, "Guy, I'm going to stuff you in a garbage bin."

"Now you're talkin'!"

Keith and Austin both laugh, leaving Frankie with a twisted face.

"Thanks to the solid new door from Devin and the security bar from Oscar, no one is getting through that thing again. The cameras are just more of a deterrent, and you can see if anyone is hanging around who shouldn't be." Austin places a hand on Frankie's shoulder. "We're going to find out who this guy is."

She nods, taking a deep swallow.

"If you need anything else, you know where to find us," Keith adds. "I've got so many reading week assignments to get done before Monday, so I need to head out."

With few parting words and assurances she'll be fine on her own, the guys and I leave to head back home.

The weird thing is, even with more people, it feels more empty than it ever has.

Secret Admirer

Today was taxing. Dr. Ellis asked me to come in for a few hours after my classes tonight, so even though I don't normally work on Tuesdays, I knew he had to be desperate to ask.

We had to put down a family's dog who had been trapped in their house during a fire. It was, by far, the most heartbreaking situation I've ever dealt with in all of my years volunteering with animals. I tried to stay strong, but even I found myself sobbing alongside the family, who weren't concerned about having lost their home or all of their earthly possessions. It took me close to an hour to compose myself, because I'd picture the same scenario with Brad, then start crying all over again.

That's why I'm walking out the door, into the dark parking lot, ninety minutes past when I should have left.

The hairs on my neck immediately stand on end, and it's nothing to do with the bitterly cold February air. I turn my head from side to side, studying my surroundings. This constant state of paranoia for almost four years has left me unable to trust my own instincts.

"It's in your head, Francesca," I mutter before taking a deep breath.

With nothing out of the ordinary alerting me to present danger, I speed walk toward my car. I freeze ten feet from my bumper when I spot a bright white piece of paper tucked into my windshield wiper. The same kind of paper I've received several times before. The same handwritten notes that chased me out of my hometown, unlikely to ever return.

Instead of grabbing the paper to read it, I spin and run back inside, praying the culprit hasn't stuck around.

Rhonda pops up from behind her desk when the bell dings a little harsher than normal. "Did you forget something, dear?" she asks, tilting her head.

"Note. There's…" I run out of breath, unable to complete my sentence.

Again, I focus on taking deep breaths as Rhonda steps out from behind her desk and stops in front of me.

She places one hand on either of my arms and applies gentle pressure, like we do for a skittish animal. "Francesca, what's wrong?" The pronounced wrinkles between her eyes sink even deeper.

Finally, I rush out, "There's a note on my car."

"Oh." Rhonda's hands drop, causing anxiety to rush my system again. "Are you sure it's not just a flyer? A lot of places around here still do that."

I shrug. "It-it's possible. I didn't look."

"Okay. Well, let's not get worked up until we know. You keep watch over the phone, and I'll go look."

Now my hand shoots up to grab on to her arm, not nearly as gently as she did for me. I loosen my grip and plead with her, "Please, no. Don't go out there."

She pulls her arm from my grip and lifts her hand to pat my cheek. "Don't forget to use the proper greeting." She sends me a soft smile before turning to walk out the door.

I watch her disappear to the right, into the small parking lot, not realizing she wasn't wearing a coat until a minute later when she returns, hugging herself for warmth. It's impossible to miss her forehead creases and tense jaw.

"Please tell me it's a flyer for the denture clinic."

She turns to make sure the door closes behind her, then replies, "It's a flyer for the denture clinic."

"It is?"

"No. It's not, but you said please." She clutches the paper to her chest. "We should probably call the police."

I thought my stomach was already as tormented as possible, but I was wrong. "It's him?"

"Yes, I think so."

I drop into a chair and fold myself in half to try to settle my stomach. "This can't be happening. The police won't do anything. He broke down my front door and they couldn't help. What are they supposed to do when I don't know who he is?" My words speed up as I spew my random worries.

"Let me go get Anton and see what he suggests. There has to be something we can do." Her footsteps grow quieter until another door shuts behind her.

After a few seconds, I sit upright, only to come face to face with a bright white paper on the top of the reception desk. Against my better judgment, I pick it up, unfold it, and scan the words written in the familiar red pen.

YOU WERE HARD TO FIND. YOU STILL LOOK AS BEAUTIFUL AS YOU DID THE FIRST DAY I SAW YOU. DON'T LEAVE AGAIN, BECAUSE IF I HAVE TO FIND YOU A SECOND TIME, I WON'T BE SO NICE ABOUT IT.

XX, YOUR SECRET ADMIRER

I stand, staring into space for what feels like hours, until the bell on the front door dings, startling me back to reality. I jump at the sound and arrival of a middle-aged woman with her cat in a carrier.

Realizing Rhonda hasn't returned and that I'm still in my scrubs, I shake my personal problems from my mind long enough to ask the woman how I can help her. She's got an appointment with Dr. Chen, so I force myself to focus long enough to get her situated in an exam room and notify Dr. Chen her next patient is here.

By the time I return to the reception area, Rhonda still isn't back, so I start weighing my options. There's one person I *want* to call, but I don't think I have any right to. Just because he's come to my rescue a few times doesn't mean we're friends. Not even after he sought refuge in my house away from his ex or allowed me to sleep in his bed to keep me safe. Our status is still painfully unclear.

So I pull out my phone and type out a message to one person I'm confident is okay with me calling them my friend.

Frankie: Are you free?

I'm unsurprised by the immediate reply.

Blake: Like single? For you, always.

My head is so twisted and confused, I can't even laugh at his reply. Why in the world does he think free is a synonym for single? Because I'm single, and I don't feel *free* at all.

Frankie: Like not busy.

Blake: Sorry babe. In Kiki's class. U ok?

No, I'm not, but I'm not letting him upset his professor, no matter how chill he claims she is.

Frankie: All good. Talk later.

My next option is Hollis, but she lives quite a distance and she doesn't drive. Not to mention, she's even busier than I am, so begging her to come to my rescue would be a major inconvenience. I can't ask that of her.

My phone dings with another text message, and to my surprise, it's Blake.

Blake: I no u didnt message to say hi. Ozzie can help. Just call him.

I stare at the phone for a minute, wondering how a guy who is such a scatterbrain can be so perceptive at the same time. He is also giving me the encouragement to do exactly what I thought would be my next step. Even though we're kind of in a weird place, I think we're civil enough I can confide in him.

Right?

"Dr. Ellis just started his next surgery, so he'll be a while. Is there someone I can call for you?" Rhonda stops behind her desk but doesn't sit in the leather, orthopedic desk chair that looks more expensive than my car.

Does her calling make the scenario more or less awkward? It feels a bit like when my mom called my childhood friends to request a playdate. Only this time, I'm an adult, so having another adult handle a simple task is ridiculous.

But based on the words in that letter, I think I'm justified in being a little ridiculous right now, and I'm not sure I'll find the courage to call him myself.

"Can you call my neighbour? He might not answer, but he knows about..." I pass my phone over to Rhonda with Oscar's number displayed. "You know? This... whole situation."

Rhonda smiles while picking up her headset and positioning it over her curly hair. I hold my breath as she dials and exhale when it starts to ring.

"Oscar? Hi, my name is Rhonda. I'm calling on behalf of Francesca Moreno."

Just as I toss my hand wraps into my gym bag, my phone rings, lit up by an unknown number. It's not private, but I don't recognize it, so I'm reluctant to answer. It's 9pm, I've been out of the house and around other people since 8am. The last thing I want is any kind of conversation, but my gut tells me to answer.

"Hello?"

"Oscar? Hi, my name is Rhonda. I'm calling on behalf of Francesca Moreno."

Francesca? The name rolls around my head for a minute before I make the connection.

"Frankie?"

"Yes, yes. Sorry."

I shove the last of my stuff in my bag haphazardly and ask, "Is she okay?"

"Well, that depends. Physically she's fine, but she got a note on her car."

A combination of fury and fear adds to my confusion. "Where is she? Can I talk to her?"

"Sure, dear. One second."

I rush around to grab my coat and close my locker while mellow hold music plays over the phone.

"Hello?" Frankie's shaky voice questions as I rush out the gym door.

"Hey. You okay? What happened?"

She sniffles but keeps her voice steady to reply, "It was him."

I know she's talking about her busted door, so I don't ask her to clarify what 'it' she means. "Where are you?"

"The animal hospital. I'm sorry for—"

"Text me the address. I'll be there as fast as I can."

"You don't have—"

"Frankie. Text me the address."

She stays silent for several seconds, leaving me confused why she'd have someone else call me, but not want me to come meet her. It's only when she whispers "Okay" that I feel a little relief.

"Stay inside until I get there, okay? Then we'll figure out what to do."

She repeats "Okay" before we hang up and she sends through a text.

The amount of times she's told me I don't *have* to do something I've offered to do is reaching an astronomical number. I don't know how else to make her realize I want to keep her safe by any means necessary. If that means running over a mile in minus fifteen temperatures, then that's what I'll do.

Each heavy stride makes me regret not leaving my bag in my locker, but I need to bring my gear home to wash. Though, right now, that's hardly my priority.

My mind wanders as I speed down the plowed sidewalk, my lungs stinging from inhales of bitterly cold air. I know Frankie has questioned my motives before, but me wanting to help her has nothing to do with my aunt. Sure, even if a stranger called me for help, I'd do what I could, but I'm not sure I'd run an eight-minute mile in the snow for them. The speed I'm travelling down the sidewalk at is a direct result of my feelings for Frankie.

For some reason, the only thing scary about that is the fact she doesn't see it.

The glow of the animal hospital sign up ahead signals it's time to slow my steps to calm my breathing, take in my surroundings, and look for anything suspicious. Rather, any*one* suspicious. Nobody catches my eye or alarms me by the time I reach the front door, which is a little disappointing. It would have been nice to sort this problem once and for all tonight.

Frankie is hunched over in a chair when I enter, resting her head in her hands and her elbows on her knees. She lifts her head as the bell rings, and her expression transforms from raised brows and down-turned lips to a soft smile. The subtle shift in her demeanour brings me a little relief.

"Hey. You okay?"

"Yes. No." Her furrowed brows return. "Did you run here?"

I nod, trying my best to answer and dismiss the question simultaneously. "Show me the note?"

A woman pops up from behind the reception desk, who I didn't notice was there until now. "You must be Oscar. I'm Rhonda. I can see why Francesca asked me to call you." She giggles before turning sombre and clearing her throat. "Here's the note."

"Thanks, Rhonda." I take the paper from her hand and unfold it without looking at Frankie to gauge her reaction.

As hard as I try, I can't stop the horror from showing on my face as I scan the neatly handwritten words. My jaw falls slack and my eyes widen, reading and rereading the disturbing message. "We need to take this to the police. Find security footage from surrounding businesses. Something to figure out who this guy is." I glance at Rhonda, sending her a pleading look in hopes she'll have my back if Frankie disagrees.

She doesn't, but her suggestion starts out just as bad when she says, "Okay. I can drop you home, then I'll—"

"Not a chance. You're not going anywhere alone right now," I interrupt, then realize how controlling that sounds. The last thing I want is for her to think I'm making decisions about her life. "I wouldn't even let Blake go anywhere alone if he got a note like this. And he's a brown belt."

"Blake's a combination of wild and crazy that'd make him invite the person over for con queso and Redbull to chat about life." She lets out a little laugh, confirming she didn't take my demand the wrong way. Also confirming Blake can always make her laugh in ways I never can.

"Right." I take a long breath, refocusing on why I'm here and what she needs from me. "Where's your car?"

"Just outside." She hooks her thumb to point behind her.

"Do you have cameras out there?" I ask Rhonda.

"No, dear. Sorry. We just have them around front. Nothing on that side of the parking lot."

"Maybe you should," I snap, instantly regretting it. "Sorry, Rhonda. This guy just keeps getting away with this and I want to stop him."

She offers me a sympathetic smile. "I can see she's in good hands with you."

The phone rings, drawing her attention away from me, so I don't reply. I reach my hand down in offer to Frankie, pulling her to stand when she takes it. We're inches apart, allowing me to see her red-rimmed eyes and brows that are nowhere close to the shade of her hair, which she recently dyed again. That's not a new thing I've noticed, but it prompts a realization that never occurred to me before. "Did you dye your hair because of him?"

She nods.

"I won't let him change anything else about you." Instinctively, my arms wrap around her, and I pull her into my chest.

Frankie makes a hiccough sound before relaxing into me. Her breathing takes on an irregular rhythm, almost as if she's crying, but she's now silent.

"Let's take this to the cops, hm? Then we'll make sure everything is okay at home."

She steps back, exposing her tear-stained cheeks. Her subtle nod and drained appearance make me hate this guy even more than I did five minutes ago.

I need to put a stop to this.

Frankie entrusts me with her keys to go out and get her car, which I pull up as close to the door as I can for her to jump in. We drive in silence to the police station, with Frankie staring out the windshield in a daze.

As expected, the constable who takes Frankie's statement reiterates that there isn't much they can do about a note. The department is too strapped to assign any kind of protective detail or investigate further. He tells her she could hire a private investigator, but they're expensive, and there's no telling how long it would take for them to find the person responsible.

Basically, all I hear is *we can't help you*.

I wrap my arm around her lower back as we walk down the stairs outside of the police station. "Do you want to drive?"

She shakes her head. Her complete detachment from her surroundings over the past hour has me really concerned, so I stop her at the bottom of the steps, turning her to face me. Her breath catches when we make eye contact. Even under her thick coat, I can see the rise and fall of her chest. Her exhales disappear in a puff around us, fading into the darkness.

My mind races with a thousand thoughts. Everything from the secrets hidden in her closet to what I'd do to protect her. Mostly, how badly I want to kiss her.

But now isn't the moment for that. I don't know if there will ever be a moment for that, or if it's just something I'll torment myself with for eternity. Callum may have set the bar low on their prom date, but out front of a police station after being traumatized by her stalker might be even worse.

I need to bring this moment back to reality, not detach along with her. "You should really come to the gym. Let me teach you a few th—"

She shifts out of my hold and steps back several feet. "I already said no."

"That was before."

"Oscar, this isn't my first time through this. Trust me, it's taken up enough space in my head, I don't have room for anything else right now. *Anything* else," she emphasizes.

Keith's comment from nearly six weeks ago floats into my mind. *She deserves to know.* Maybe that will be the tipping point, so she'll start taking her own safety seriously. Because the fact this guy hasn't been violent in the past means nothing for the future.

"I saw him standing outside of your house," I blurt, not considering my delivery at all.

Her eyes widen, brightening under the streetlights, and her posture goes rigid. "What?"

"Back in January… he… uh… I saw someone standing across the street. Keith and I went after him, but he took off."

"And you didn't think to tell me? In January?" she shrieks, drawing the attention of a few police officers walking in and out of the building. "You just kept that a secret and let him bust down my front door?"

"Woah. First of all, I didn't *let* him do anything. If you can't see what's in front of you, I'm try—"

"I don't want to hear it. You shouldn't have kept that from me, Oscar. You had no right to decide I didn't deserve to know. It's *my* life." She holds out her hand. "Give me my keys."

She's upset and I get it, but I was hoping that piece of information would make her see the severity of the situation. It backfired spectacularly. So I hand over her car key and wait on the sidewalk for her to at least hint whether she wants me to join her or if I'm bussing it home.

"Get in. I'll take you home because I appreciate what you *have* done, but I don't know how to feel right now." She opens the car door, leaving me with those words and a stomach full of regret.

FRANKIE

My Life

We pull up to my parking spot, and while I should be focused on my house and checking for anything out of the ordinary, all I can think about is Oscar. Specifically, how he kept a massive secret from me, all while he pretended like he cared about my safety.

If he really cared, he would have told me about the man across the street. It turns my stomach to know he was lurking around before he busted down my front door. To know that he could have been watching me all this time.

"Do you want me to…" Oscar points at my house, but the tone of his voice tells me he wants to get away from me as quickly as possible.

"It's fine. Brad's home."

Oscar scoffs. He probably added an eye roll, but I can't see well enough in the dark car.

Truth is, I'd rather have backup to go inside, even with Brad and all the preventative security measures I've taken. The more overpowering truth is that Oscar's presence affects me too much. Distracts me and makes my heart do a weird flipping thing that feels like an arrhythmia.

So as much as I'd like him to rest his hand on my back and lead me inside, we need distance. I also need to prove to him that I can handle things myself. Having Rhonda call Oscar for me was the coward's way out. I can't be a coward now.

We have a short standoff on the sidewalk before parting ways and each heading to our own doors. He watches me from his front step as I hesitate to unlock my deadbolts. Slowly, I disengage each lock, listening inside after each one. The only sound I hear is the tippity-tap of Brad's nails on the tile entryway.

By the time I reach the final lock, Oscar has disappeared inside. I hold my breath as I inch my front door open. Thankfully, I left all of my lights on inside so I could watch the security cameras more clearly.

"*Ciao, bambino,*" I greet Brad as I walk in, though I'm scanning the room instead of looking at him. He doesn't seem anxious or upset by anything, so I hope that's a good sign.

I take a few steps toward the living room so I can look around the stairs into the kitchen. Nothing out of place. The back door looks secure.

A pounding sound behind me nearly startles me to death.

"Frankie? It's Blake."

I breathe a sigh of relief at hearing his voice. Without hesitation, I turn to open the door.

"Hey. Can I come in?" he asks, his face marked with an uncharacteristic worry.

"Sure. I just got home."

"I know. Oscar told me what happened. All of it. I… thought you might want someone to check things out with you."

That's incredibly sweet of him. I'm not sure if it's him or Oscar I need to thank, but I've spent enough time as the neighbourhood damsel in distress.

"I should be fine. Brad's here," I repeat, even though I don't have a ton of confidence in his guard dog abilities.

Blake laughs. "Right. Well, maybe I'll just stay here until you give me the all clear? Just to be sure."

"The cameras didn't pick up anything. Not even outside."

"It's not a flawless system, Frankie. And I don't trust that Brad wouldn't sell you out for a burger."

There's no point in arguing with him about this. I might as well take him up on his offer and get it over with. "Fine. This floor looks okay. Wanna come upstairs?"

"Now we're talkin'," he replies, adding a fist pump.

"Blake." I glare at him, sending a clear message.

"Right. Back to business. At your service, m'lady." He takes a dramatic bow, rolling hand and all.

Five minutes later, we've confirmed the house is empty. I feel better knowing for sure, but my nerves are still out of control.

Blake and I return to the living room, where he comes to a stop with both hands in his sweatpants' pockets. "You know, he's a good guy. He wasn't trying to keep a secret, Frankie. He was trying to keep you from worrying more than you needed to."

Clearly, Oscar really did tell him all of it.

"He should have told me. It's my life being affected by this, so I should have been aware."

"And what would you have done differently? Added *more* locks to the door? Gotten another dog? Taken more precautions? You're already doing everything you can, so the only thing you would have done is worry more."

That is a very valid point. One I don't want to admit to out loud, so I say nothing.

"Look, Keith was there. They both told me and Austin the next day. We all knew about it, so you can't be mad at him and not be mad at the rest of us. But before you hate us all, know that we did what we thought was best for you." He untucks his hands from his pockets and rocks back on his heels. "You have our numbers if anything seems off through the night. Don't be afraid to use them, okay?"

I choke back the swirling emotions coursing through me and nod. "Thank you."

"That's what neighbours are for. Never know. I might earn myself a crazy stalker chick someday, and I'll need your help in return." He shrugs as he slides his feet into his shoes.

Again, I glare at him, not appreciating him making light of the situation—even if that's his way of life and what I love about him.

"Bad joke. Sorry." He flashes me an awkward toothy grin, still managing to look handsome. It's no surprise he has his own legion of girls swooning over him. He does have a certain charm to him once you get past his obnoxious outer layer.

"It's fine. Thanks again."

With that, he unlocks the front door and walks outside, leaving me and Brad alone once again.

We settle in on the couch, too on edge to sleep upstairs. It feels safer sleeping down here with access to multiple exits.

Though sleep doesn't come, because I'm too amped up from the day's events. Instead of dozing off, I lie on the couch, running through every interaction I've ever had with Oscar, trying to figure out where we stand.

And I never come up with an answer.

Both of my shifts at the clinic this weekend have been marked with a fresh spike of anxiety. Especially when I have to leave at the end of the day. The weekend receptionist, Talia, has been walking out with me, and thankfully there haven't been any more notes.

That doesn't make me less nervous, though.

Sunday afternoon, once I'm safely in my car, I take a moment to pull up my security camera app and scroll through the footage over the last few hours. Nothing out of sorts, so I tuck my phone away, pull onto the road, and head toward home.

I have to stop for some groceries on my way, so I choose the busiest, most crowded store to shop in. More people means more opportunities to blend in and fewer to be anywhere alone. Surprisingly, the chocolate and candy aisle is relatively empty. Like no one else in this neighbourhood is trying to silence their stress with sugar. Must be nice.

Once I check out, I grab my bags and head to my car. Again, the hairs on my arms stand up, even under my thick coat, alerting me to something. I stand frozen in the middle of the parking lot, scanning the area. A few people are staring at me with scrunched up foreheads, but none of them are the source of the eerie feeling I have.

With no answers and no desire to stay here like an easy target, I walk toward my car, checking for anything on the windshield. I breathe a sigh of relief when there's nothing there. I open my door, pressing the lock button as I toss my groceries on the passenger seat and hop in before slamming the door shut. It's not much, but the safety of my car certainly feels better than being exposed in a busy parking lot.

I detour on my way home, checking my rear-view constantly to make sure nobody is following me. When I'm confident the coast is clear, I turn onto Boston Avenue and slip into my parking spot.

I don't get out of the car right away. Instead, I stare at my front door, resenting this person for taking another home I'd come to love and ruining it. I no longer feel relieved to come home at the end of the day to enjoy some peace and quiet. Even though Brad is anxiously awaiting my return, I struggle to want to go in there. It's not my sanctuary anymore, but the thought of starting over is too much to handle.

A knock on my window instantly speeds up my heart rate. I look up to see Oscar with one hand raised in surrender and the other holding a small pink box.

"Sorry," he says through the window.

I can't help but feel a little bad about how I treated him on Friday night. Even though I maintain that he should have told me about the man across the street, it's hard to stay mad at him when he looks genuinely remorseful now.

Once I grab my bags from the passenger seat, I open the door and hoist myself out, coming face to face with him.

He reaches out to grab my bags with his empty hand and passes me the box with his other. "I got this as a peace offering. To say I was sorry." Wrinkles form around his squinting eyes, and since it's gloomy and grey today, it's not from the sun.

I take the box from his hand, noticing the *Desirea's Sweets* logo on the top. "How did you get this?"

"Hollis took a trip home for the weekend. I asked her to grab it, but I wasn't sure if this was the bakery you liked."

The fact he put in the effort to have a red velvet cupcake delivered to me from a bakery two hours away is... I'm not even sure what to think. It's so beyond a simple apology, which, after talking to Blake, I would have accepted and offered my own in return. This amount of thought and effort makes me want to kiss him.

His quick dismissal makes sure that doesn't happen. "Anyway, I just wanted to say sorry. If I see anything else, I'll let you know." He turns to walk toward my door, since he's carrying my groceries, but I reach up to grab his arm.

"Apology accepted. I'm sorry too... for getting so upset. It was more the situation than you."

He sends me a tight-lipped smile and a subtle nod before walking up my front steps and setting my bags down.

I trail up the stairs behind him, stopping in front of him as he turns around.

"Enjoy your cupcake." He attempts to step past me, but again, I stop him.

"Do you want to come in?"

OSCAR

Midnight

"Yeah, sure," I answer Frankie's invitation to come inside.

Something seems off with her, but that's secondary to the real reason I said yes. I've missed her these past few days.

She flashes a brief smile as she steps past me to open her door. Methodically, she unlocks and opens it, revealing a tail-wagging Brad on the other side. "*Ciao, bambino.*"

I step in behind her, carrying the bags of groceries. "Want me to check upstairs?"

She glances over her shoulder from halfway to her kitchen. "I can do it. Just putting my cupcake somewhere safe."

Priorities. Make sure the cupcake is safe before she checks for herself. Sure, between the cameras and the dog, the chances of someone being in here are slim, but they're not zero. And I wouldn't put anything past this creep.

Still, she's just accepted my apology, so I'm not going to point any of that out.

I meet her in the kitchen with her groceries, setting them on the counter.

"Look away. I don't want you to judge me," she instructs, situating herself in front of the bags.

"Does my opinion really matter?"

She pauses with a box of mac and cheese in her right hand. "Yes."

That's a surprise. Based on the first several months of our interactions, I'd have thought she was pretty confident in her decisions and wouldn't care what I thought. Her flushed cheeks say otherwise.

"I'm not going to judge you."

She keeps herself in front of the counter as she pulls out a pack of frozen mini pizzas, packaged pierogies, and a tub of frozen whipped topping.

Okay. Maybe I will.

I watch as she unloads a bag of gummy bears, yogurt-covered raisins, and a four-pack of chocolate bars before I can't take it anymore. "How do you survive?"

"See. Judgment. I had a bad day." She gives me a stern look, lacking any intimidation factor. "I got strawberries, at least." She pulls out the container, looking quite proud of the one whole food she purchased. "Needed something for the whipped cream," she adds, turning to put the berries in the fridge.

I shake my head and step a little closer. When she stands upright again, we're closer than I realized we would be. Too close. Not close enough.

I reach my hand around her back, watching her chest expand with a sharp breath. Once my hand closes around the intended object, I step back and wave the small pink box in front of her. "Looks like you won't be needing this."

She lunges forward with a surprising speed that catches me off guard—an impressive feat. "Oscar! You can't take back a gift!"

It's not hard for me to fend her off, but I can respect her determination. She must really want this cupcake.

Even Brad gets in on the action. He jumps up at my hip and sneezes, shooting dog snot on my arm tucked behind my back.

"Ah-ha!" Frankie snatches the box from my hand the second I move it to wipe Brad's germs off. "Teamwork!" She rips open the fancy box and stuffs a bite of the cupcake in her mouth. She closes her eyes and moans as she chews, either oblivious to or ignoring the clump of icing on her lip.

I've never really been tempted by sweets... but I am right now. This seems like a perfect opportunity to taste a red velvet cupcake for the first time.

Her eyes open and land on mine as she traces her tongue across her lower lip, taking my taste-test opportunity with it. Her glossy lip looks even more appealing than the processed sugar ever could.

We stand, locked with our eyes on each other. I know what mine are saying. Hers are leaving me less confident.

Finally, Frankie breaks the trance. "I would have offered to share, but now you'll never know how amazing this is."

She has no idea how badly I wanted to try it.

"My loss." I look down at Brad, who now has all four paws back on the floor. "Not cool, man."

He tilts his head and wags his tail, making it impossible to be mad at him. He follows me upstairs to check things out, and another temptation hits. When we get to Frankie's room, I have a strong urge to peek in her closet.

Beyond the camera pointed this way that would clearly show me betraying her trust—again—I don't want to invade her privacy. There's no appeal in seeing what's in there if she doesn't *want* me to see it, anyway.

Plus, lace on a hanger does nothing compared to how it would look on her.

"Why am I doing this to myself?" I ask Brad.

He takes off back downstairs without answering.

When I return to the kitchen, Frankie has made me another cup of lavender tea. Last time I drank it, I slept better than I have in months, so I don't hesitate to down the entire contents of the cup and ask for more.

We move into the living room once I get a refill, where we slide into comfortable conversation. She thanks me for sending Blake over the other night and apologizes at least six more times. She also thanks me for the cupcake five more times, gushing over how incredible it was.

I find myself zoned in on the conversation, watching the movement of her lips, the flutter of her lashes, the pulse in her neck. Everything about her is interesting. Sitting here with her is the only place I want to be right now. More than at the muay thai gym. More than strumming my guitar. Way more than listening to my roommates bicker over whose turn it is to do the dishes.

Her presence is soothing, and I feel fully relaxed. With Brad curled up on my hip, I'm too tired to fight it.

What was that noise?

I blink myself awake, scanning my surroundings in the dim light cast from the main floor powder room. Frankie's house?

Faint footsteps near the front door stop me from questioning why I'm here and spur me into action. A shadow passes in front of the window in a blur.

I rush to the door and struggle to remove the security bar—regretting having bought it for Frankie in this moment—unlock the deadbolts and chain slide, and fling the door open. With the snow almost melted and none on the sidewalks, I don't have any way of following the footprints, so I scan across the street, to the left, then the right. No sign of anyone.

There was definitely someone here, though.

How does this guy keep disappearing into thin air? How does he keep getting so close to Frankie and not get caught?

What would have happened if I wasn't here? A hundred different rhetorical questions bounce through my head as I stand on the freezing cold porch long enough to make sure no one is around, then turn back inside.

"Oscar?" a shaky voice calls after I close the door and lock it.

Without thinking, I run up the stairs, two at a time, rushing to reassure Frankie everything is okay. When I get to the top, I'm stopped dead in my tracks.

Am I dreaming? Surely, this can't be real. I didn't really question waking up on her couch. Didn't hesitate at the intruder on the porch. But Frankie, stopped in her door frame, hugging herself, dressed in the shortest possible lace-trimmed satin shorts and matching cropped camisole, has to be a dream.

If it is, I don't want to wake up.

"Oscar?" she asks again, confirming she's not a figment of my overactive imagination.

"Uh… sorry. Yeah. A noise on the porch woke me up. I think someone was out there, but by the time I opened the door, they were gone."

Her arms drop, exposing all of her skin that is silkier than her outfit. I blow out a breath, trying to keep focused on the issue at hand.

Unsuccessfully.

She seems to just notice her outfit and crosses her arms back over her chest. "I'll check the cameras." She turns into her room, stopping to look back over her shoulder. "Can you stay? Until I check the cameras, at least?" she asks, nudging her head toward her room.

I wasn't planning on going anywhere anyway, but seeing past her to find Brad sprawled out on the bed, snoring, I'm not confident he'll be any help should there be another threat. *If there even was one in the first place.* Maybe I'm just too paranoid and thought I saw and heard something that wasn't really there.

Frankie crawls back into her bed and leans against the rattan headboard. She pulls the covers up over her chest, then reaches for her phone on the end table. "Did you lock the door?" she asks, her eyes wide.

"Yes. I didn't get the security bar back up, but it's locked."

She exhales and nods with a grateful smile. For the next several minutes, she stares at her phone screen, while I watch her expression shift through a range of reactions from my position standing beside her bed. Concern, confusion, relief, then, the most recognizable one, fear.

"What is it?"

She turns the screen to face me, paused on an image of a man on her porch. Specifically, a man dressed in a black jacket with the hood pulled up over a baseball hat and a bandana over his face.

I rewind and watch the ninety-second clip of him walking up on the porch and looking in the windows, then freezing for a split second before bolting and disappearing. "Something tells me he's not just a drunk who can't find the right house."

When I lift my eyes from the phone and pass it back to Frankie, I realize she's got tears spilling down her cheeks. I'm so tired of seeing her cry because of this guy. He better hope I never find him, but for her sake, I hope I do.

"Come here." I sit on the bed beside her and lean her into my chest.

"He's never going to stop. I—" A sob interrupts her words. Once she composes herself again, she continues, "I have to move again."

That short statement feels like a blow to my chest. "No, you don't. You can't." I take a deep breath to get my surprising emotions under control. "It's almost the end of the semester.

Don't leave now. We'll take this to the police station tomorrow, and maybe they'll finally take it seriously."

"Oscar, they couldn't do anything when he busted in my door. What will they do for a guy on my porch?"

She has a valid point. This entire situation is infuriating. I'm angry that the police department's hands are tied. I'm angry she's already had to uproot her life once and is considering it again. And I'm angry there's nothing much I can do about it.

Instead of giving her false hope or useless reassurances, I just hold her. If this is the last chance I have to make her feel safe, I'll make it worth it.

Mr. Right Now

Oscar now tops my list of people I've had the most sleepovers with. My best friend from third grade is a close second with four. My parents were never crazy about me staying at other people's houses when I was young, and they were too strict for anyone else to want to stay the night at mine.

Something tells me as much as they may have reservations about sleepovers with Oscar, if they knew the circumstances, they'd be okay with it.

I'm more than okay with it, which is the scary thing. It's not just having him as a bodyguard, either. His presence makes me feel safe, yes, but beyond that, he makes me... happy. Like I can let my guard down a little and enjoy pointless conversation. Blake was right when he told me Oscar can make you laugh harder than anyone, and he will push you beyond what you think you can do.

If my time in Toronto is coming to an end, there's one thing I never thought I could do that I suddenly have the courage to try. "Do you want to come over for dinner? Like... a date?" I blurt the words as Oscar downs a glass of water, standing in my kitchen in yesterday's clothes.

He stares at me over the glass, not giving me an answer. My stomach sinks, understanding that no reply *is* an answer. Somehow, I've totally misread the situation, and now I've made a fool of myself.

"It's fine. Never mi—"

"Yeah," he finally spits out. "Name the day." His lips turn up in a rare full smile, making my heart flutter.

"Oh. Um… What's your schedule like this week? I'm finished every day by 4:30."

"Today is the only night until Saturday I don't work at the gym. I'm usually done by nine."

I know the end of the semester is winding down. Last summer, he had big plans, working with his brother and travelling the world. There's no telling, even if I stay here until the end of exams, that he's going to stick around after the semester is over. This could be my only chance. And if we crash and burn, at least that will make leaving a little easier.

"How about tonight, then?"

His gorgeous smile never falters as he replies, "It's a date."

My stomach is flipping like an elite gymnast, and I'm suddenly lost for words.

Surprisingly, Oscar steps closer and sets his glass on the counter behind me. "My class starts at 8:30, so I have to go. I'll see you tonight." Then he leans in and brushes his lips against my cheek, leaving heat in his wake.

Or maybe that's just because my head is still reeling over him holding me until I fell asleep, rubbing my bare arm with his thumb. Whatever the reason, my face flushes and again, words evade me.

He sends me a wink, pats Brad on the head, then grabs his jacket and stops at the door. "Don't forget to lock up."

The amount of care and concern in this man has completely thrown me for a loop. Considering my first impression of him—and second, third, fourth, fifth—he's nothing like I assumed.

With a level of excitement that completely obliterates the fear the last few days have been plagued with, I reply, "See you tonight."

Unsurprisingly, I've been distracted the entire day. My lab partner, Lynne, was obviously annoyed with my incessant daydreaming. I almost confessed to her that I have a date tonight, but I don't think she'd care. She's top of the class and doesn't seem like the type to socialize. At first, I liked that about her because I was anti-social myself. Now, I just really want to talk to someone.

I walk out of my last lab at 4:20 as my phone buzzes. I pull it out of my bag to find a text from Hollis.

Hollis: *How was your cupcake?*

Just thinking about that surprise treat brings a smile to my face—which has nothing to do with the dessert itself.

Frankie: *Amazing. Thank you.*

Hollis: *That was all Oscar. He even bought me one as a bribe to go get it. It wasn't a hardship.*

I laugh as I approach my car, realizing too late that I was so distracted by my phone, I didn't look around the area.

"Hey," a deep voice says behind me.

I jump and drop my phone in the muddy, patchy grass that has felt the effects of a long winter.

"Sorry," Oscar says, stepping closer and bending down to grab my phone. "I didn't mean to scare you."

My heart rate slows as I blow out a breath and take in the handsome, casual confidence of my next-door neighbour. "You did."

"I'm sorry," he repeats gently, wiping my phone on his pant leg.

"It's fine. Just... Yeah. Years of being on edge."

He gifts me with another smile I've decided I'll never get sick of seeing. "My classes ended an hour ago. I was about to leave, but I walked past your car and thought I'd stand watch for a bit. See if he showed."

"And?" I ask, turning my head from side to side, finally scanning the area.

"If he did, there'd be an unconscious body in your trunk."

I can't tell if he's joking or not. I *think* he's kidding, but I can't be sure. Yet, after the years of torment, I can't bring myself to hate that possibility. Any sympathy I may have had for this psychopath disappeared when he chased me out of my old life.

"Want a ride?" I nod toward my car, eager to leave.

"Sure." He passes me my phone before walking around to the passenger side. "We can stop and grab dinner on the way." He climbs inside without waiting for me to reply.

I follow his lead, sinking into the driver's seat. Once I lock the doors and turn the car on, I answer, "I was going to cook. Still afraid I'll poison you?" I pull out of the parking spot, smirking instead of wearing my usual stress-induced scowl I leave with most days.

"No. You proved me wrong when you stayed at my place. I'd just rather enjoy the time we have."

There's something ominous about that sentence. On one hand, it's sweet and reassures me that I haven't misread what's happening between us. On the other, it sounds like he's resigned himself to me leaving. That our time is finite, and he knows it.

So rather than insist on making the shrimp risotto I had planned, I concede, because this could be our first and last date.

"This food is awful. I'm sorry for suggesting it," Oscar declares, dropping his fork. "My cousin Caleb warned me it was bad, but

I thought he was being judgmental because it wasn't French cuisine."

I chuckle, sprinkling more salt on my chipotle burrito bowl. It has less flavour than a cucumber. "It's not awful... but it's not good." I drop a piece of chicken on the floor for Brad, and he proceeds to turn his nose up at it. "Okay, it's awful."

"I'm not telling Caleb he was right; he'll gloat." He stands and grabs his dish, then puts his hand out to take mine. "Don't torture yourself."

It really is the worst takeout food I've ever eaten. How that place stays open is beyond me.

"Thanks," I reply, pushing my bowl forward. "I'd offer you dessert, but I only have..." My words trail off as I remember my purchases from yesterday. "Strawberries and whipped cream," I continue. "You can have the berries. I'll eat the whipped cream."

Oscar stands in front of me, holding one dish in each hand, looking like his mind is racing. "Deal."

He scrapes our uneaten meals into the food waste bin while I pull the whipped cream from the freezer and the berries from the fridge. Honestly, I don't know how typical dates usually go. Society portrays them as grand, exciting events where two people who barely know each other try to put on their best front in hopes of a second date. Well, maybe they don't hope for a second, but the entire process seems exhausting.

This, though? Having Oscar in my space, feeling comfortable with him, and knowing at least some of the less-than-ideal parts of each other, is exactly what I wanted. It may also be the exact opposite of what I need, depending on how things go over the next few weeks.

No. I'm not thinking about that right now.

"What's on your mind?" Oscar asks, sneaking up behind me as I chop the tops off of the washed berries.

It's not that I want to lie to him, but I don't want to bring up the one topic of conversation that has driven so many of our interactions thus far. "You poor thing."

"Me?" He stills behind me, pausing his hand that was reaching for a strawberry.

I spin around to face him, bringing us as close as possible without touching. "You'll never taste the amazingness of strawberries and whipped cream." I pop one in my mouth, savouring the combination of tart and sweet.

He brings his hand up, using his thumb to trace my bottom lip. "What if I want to taste it?"

Now I'm the one who freezes, minus the sharp inhale I take, which I'm sure he's noticed. He drops his hand; his gaze bounces back and forth between my eyes and my lips, seeking permission I give without hesitation.

He leans forward, drawing out each painful second. His warm breath creates a pleasure ripple from my lips to my toes. "Frankie," he utters, resting his forehead against mine.

I bite my lip, anticipating the contact I truly want, which is abruptly halted by a loud noise outside. A combination of fear and disappointment causes my heart to plummet.

Oscar doesn't hesitate before he rushes to the door, opens all the locks, and flies out onto the porch. He's not even wearing shoes, but that doesn't stop him from running down onto the path, looking in every direction. Brad races out after him, making a quick turn to the right, straight for my garbage bins.

By the time I step out onto the porch, clutching my small strawberry knife, Brad is barking at the recycling bin, jumping up against it.

"You should go inside," Oscar whispers.

I tilt an eyebrow at him. There's not much I'd put past this psycho who has dedicated years to tormenting me, but hiding in my almost-full recycling bin is pushing it. I shake my head, then hold up my knife and gesture for him to open it.

He steps forward with his phone flashlight, grabs the handle, and flips open the lid. "A raccoon?"

I peek over the railing, and sure enough, there's a pair of terrified glowing eyes staring back at me. *"Venir,"* I instruct Brad.

He walks his wagging butt up the stairs and stops behind me, looking exceptionally proud of himself.

Oscar leaves the lid flipped open and rejoins Brad and me on the porch. "Do you think he wore work boots last time?" he asks, wrapping his arms around me.

I lean my head against his chest. "Wishful thinking."

Sadly, I know this night is coming to an end, and the super-charged, intense moment we had inside is now gone. This friendly embrace feels like he's getting ready to leave. Strawberries and whipped cream have been long forgotten.

And despite the endless possibilities I'm faced with thanks to my stalker, I realize not a single one makes me okay with saying goodbye to Oscar.

34

OSCAR

My Kinda Girl

don't *want* to go home, but I should.

The guys razzed me for twenty minutes this morning when I walked in wearing yesterday's clothes. Hollis texted me last night to ask if the cupcake won Frankie over, but I was knocked out from the lavender tea, so I never replied. That prompted her to call our mother, who prepared to send out a search party, which thankfully began and ended with Blake. That gave him all the extra fuel he needed to give me a thorough grilling.

Given Frankie's visitor last night, I'm hesitant to leave for a lot of reasons, but I'm hoping if the creep is watching now, he'll see me leave, and it will embolden him to come back again. He just won't be expecting the new camera Austin installed on our house today, equipped with motion sensors, aimed at Frankie's porch.

"We're being recorded," I remind her.

She lifts her head and steps back, making my chest suddenly cold. At least physically cold. Figuratively, it's a different situation.

"Right. I forgot about that."

At this moment, I'm cursing having that camera installed, but priority needs to be keeping her safe. It's hard to convince myself that anything should take precedence over kissing her, though. Even harder to not pull her back inside and finally get my fix of strawberries and whipped cream.

"I've got a long day tomorrow," I tell myself as much as her. "Coaching. Classes. Assignments."

"I know," she replies, plastering on a smile.

The problem with our current situation is that I don't know if she's upset about me leaving because she wants *me* to stay, or if she's just afraid to be alone. I look down at Brad and remember at least she has him for backup. He's earned his keep before, so despite my initial reservations about him, I'm glad he's here.

"Text or call if you need anything. One of us will be right over," I say, stepping back inside to grab my shoes, bag, and sweater from the foyer.

Frankie walks in behind me, stopping beside the door. "Thanks. And thank you for dinner."

I chuckle, knowing full well that culinary abomination will live forever as the worst thing I've ever tasted. "Maybe next time I'll get to try dessert."

Her face flushes scarlet. "Maybe."

With one last smile and a peck on her cheek, I exit her house reluctantly to head home.

The bombardment is instantaneous as I walk through my front door. Blake peppers me with claims that he saw this coming months ago. He asks a few inappropriate questions I refuse to answer, but lucky for him, none of them include the phrase *garbage bin*.

"Thanks for the chat. I'm going to head upstairs so I can keep an eye out for this scumbag."

I hope that will be the end of the conversation, but he pops up off the couch.

"It's been almost a year since I got to take someone out—I mean, other than you," Blake adds, trailing me up the stairs. "If you want me to handle this guy too, just say the word."

I don't answer that. This guy is going to face the criminal justice system, not a semi-unhinged neighbour with zero impulse control and a knack for trouble.

"Thanks, man. Hopefully the cops can handle it this time."

Blake laugh-scoffs, and I can't say I blame him.

"So you're all in with Frankie now?"

I push my bedroom door open and toss my bag on the floor. "I don't know about 'all in', but we'll see where things go."

Blake repeats his laugh-scoff, making me turn in my dark room to look at him.

"What?" I hold my hand up, stopping him from flicking the lamp on. "No. Keep it off. Needs to be dark."

"That's what," he replies. "I don't know if you've noticed, Ozzie, but you're either all in or all out. With everything."

Of course, I've noticed. If something piques my interest, I have a tendency to go a little overboard in my enthusiasm. But I'm not irrational, and don't think that same approach can apply to a relationship.

"I'm capable of balance. Frankie isn't stopping me from anything else I'm supposed to be doing."

"She's not?" Blake flops onto my bed and watches me wheel my desk chair closer to the window. "How many assignments do you have to finish that you haven't started?"

Four. "None."

"Right." He crosses his ankles and lifts his arms up to rest behind his head. "When you dated Sonia, your priorities shifted. That's fine and all—I mean, I'm hardly one to offer relationship advice—but don't get in so deep, you can't get out."

Instead of answering, I stare out the window, lost in a flurry of thoughts.

"Listen, it's not your all-or-nothing ways I'm worried about. Sure, go all in," Blake continues, "but with Sonia, when you switched to the nothing stage, you spiralled, trying to fill that void again."

I grit my teeth, hating that he's comparing Frankie to Sonia. Though, if I'm being honest, when I was dating Sonia, I never saw things going south how they did. I don't want to imagine that with Frankie.

He makes a valid point, though.

There are any number of things I could be doing instead of watching out my window, attempting to stalk her stalker. I haven't touched my guitar for days, which is unheard of. My assignments are getting behind, and I can't allow them to be in my *nothing* column.

Maybe things are proving to be too much of a distraction. Maybe I should back off before things go sideways again. Blake was the one who suffered the most when things with Sonia went off the rails, so I owe it to him to take what he's saying seriously.

Yet, I can't convince myself to turn away from this window.

Despite staying up until 1am, I never saw anyone suspicious. The camera didn't pick up any unusual activity either, which is a good sign. It also hasn't picked up Frankie leaving for the day, and I'm afraid if I run into her, she'll make my head more of a mess while I'm trying to sort out what Blake said.

I can't delay leaving, though, because I've got to meet my cousin Caleb at the gym.

With my gym and book bags hoisted on my shoulders, I step out the front door, intending to beeline to the bus stop. Just as a breath of fresh air hits my lungs, a door closes about thirty feet to my right.

"Hey," Frankie greets. She's dressed more casually than I've seen her for a long time, holding Brad's leash.

"Morning," I reply, adjusting my bags. "I'm running a little late. Everything good?"

"Oh. Yeah, fine." She walks down her steps onto her path and pauses as I reach the same distance on ours. "Actually, I wanted to ask you something."

I make a show of checking the time on my phone, realizing how dangerously close I am to missing the bus. "Can we revisit that once I get home? I really am running late."

"It's nothing, really. I just…" She steps across the grass, giving Brad the slack to reach me first. "Can you hang on to my extra set of keys? Just in case."

Just in case what? I want to know what kind of worst-case scenarios are running through her mind, but I'm too distracted by her request. By the fact she's trusting me with something that has to be a huge deal for her. She's inviting me into her life in a way she's not asking anyone else.

And that means something.

So if my two choices with Frankie are all or nothing, it's an easy decision.

35

FRANKIE

Come See Me

I miss Brad. It's been a couple of months since he's been able to come to the clinic with me, and normally, on my typical eight-hour days, that's fine. But I'm staying a few extra hours today to make sure I exceed the volunteer hour requirements for vet school. If a decision comes down to me and someone else with the same grades, my commitment to the field has to be the difference maker.

The problem is, that means Brad has now been home for ten hours, and I worry about him. Especially while I mop up a puddle of pee off of the exam room floor, courtesy of a nervous Maltese. All it takes is imagining doing the same thing when I return home for me to pull out my phone and send a text.

Frankie: *Can you do me a huge favour? I'll owe you big time.*

I press send and immediately regret my wording. That makes it sound like I'm asking for something way more involved. The same way I did a week ago when I gave him my spare keys.

The quick reply prevents me from backpedaling.

Oscar: *Depends.*

I pull up the security camera app and check the last motion sensor notification. I feel like the world's worst fur-mom when I see Brad pacing by the back door.

Frankie: *Can you let Brad out? He's crossing his legs.*

Oscar*: Just on my way to the gym.*
Shoot. If this dog had peed fifteen minutes earlier—
Oscar*: Walking out the door now. I'll stop in.*

I'm so relieved, I type *I could kiss you* before I realize how true that statement is, preventing me from sending it. Thanks to that greedy raccoon, I lost my one opportunity and we've both been so busy, another chance hasn't presented itself.

Before I can delete my message and reply, the motion sensor notification pops up on my screen. I watch as Oscar unlocks my front door, walks into the house, bends down to pet Brad, and continues through to the backyard. It feels wrong watching, but he knows the cameras are there, so it's not like I'm some voyeur spying on him without his knowledge.

I attempt to click out of the camera app when my phone glitches. My rapid screen-tapping causes me to send the message I was trying to delete. I watch in horror as Oscar pulls his phone from the pocket of his grey sweatpants, lights up the screen, taps it, and freezes. It's like watching a car crash about to happen in slow motion. You know it's just a matter of time before impact, but there's nothing you can do to stop it and there's no knowing how bad the damage is going to be.

Mercifully, he tucks his phone back in his pocket without replying.

Two seconds later, relief is pushed away by hurt, feeling the sting of his rejection.

He stands, watching out the backdoor, waiting for Brad, and each second that ticks by makes me feel worse. Brad comes bolting back inside, ensuring Oscar takes a few seconds to pet him. Then Oscar walks up to the camera aimed at the front door. In a confident move that will keep my insides warm for the rest of the day, he blows a kiss and sends it off with a wink.

It'd be an innocent gesture in any other scenario, but after sending that message, it's a reply. To make it more clear, he sends another text.

Oscar*: There are no raccoons in the gym. I'll be there until 9.*

"All good here?" Dr. Ellis asks, scaring the breath out of me and the mop from my hands.

With my hand on my heart, I spin around to face him. "Yeah. Sorry… I was… distracted."

"Is everything okay?" he asks, walking forward with concern in his tense eyes.

"Yeah. Fine. Just tired, I guess."

"It's been a long day. Why don't you finish up here and head out?"

"Really?" I ask for confirmation with more enthusiasm than I'd usually show about leaving. It would be an outright lie if I said I wasn't intrigued by Oscar's last message.

"You're a volunteer, Frankie, not a slave. I appreciate your extra hours, but you're allowed to have a life outside of here." His voice is marked with an uncharacteristic sadness, making me a little hesitant to leave.

"Are you okay? I feel like I'm always so in my head about my own stupid drama, I don't ask that enough. How are you doing?"

He pats me on the shoulder as he walks past. "This job isn't always easy, but it is worth it. Remember that on the hard days." He reaches the door that leads to his office before turning back to add, "Go on; get out of here. We'll see you Saturday."

A small part of me feels bad for leaving. Dr. Ellis, from what I understand, is solely dedicated to his work. He doesn't have a wife or girlfriend to confide in when he gets home. I also know I'm just a volunteer here, so despite the kindness he's shown me, it doesn't mean we're friends.

Thankfully, I know someone who is. I send Devin a quick text, asking him to check in with Anton, and that makes me feel better about grabbing my stuff, saying goodbye to Rhonda, and slowly exiting into the parking lot.

Unlike the other times I've left since I found the note on my car, I don't get the immediate sensation that someone is watching me. Maybe this change to my schedule or Oscar's presence in my life has scared the guy off.

While I know that's *very* wishful thinking, if it's true, it means I have no reason to feel guilty about spending more time with him. And after all of the care and concern he's shown me, it's about time I showed some concern for something that's important to him.

I went home for three hours after my shift to spend some time with Brad. I figured it made more sense to come to the gym later so I can drive Oscar home. His classes started at 8:30 this morning, so he's had a long day too.

As I walk into the gym, I'm immediately overwhelmed by the smell of antiseptic and sweat. It's a bit like those people who think cologne is a substitute for a shower. Two powerful smells competing with each other, loud grunts and shouts, and bright lights are all an assault on my senses.

However, the sight that does the most damage is Oscar's shirtless back. He's glistening with sweat, demonstrating something to a trio of middle-aged women on a large floor mat off to the right. Each one has obvious high-end salon hair, designer workout clothes, and an enraptured stare on their faces. They watch him demonstrate some kind of footwork, except not one of them is watching his feet.

Not that I blame them, but still. I knew this was a real possibility. You'd have to be dead not to be captivated by him. Or flat out lying to yourself, like I did for many months.

He spins around, finally facing me. His wide smile helps to chase away some of the jealousy I really have no business feeling. He's doing his job, and after what he told me about his aunt, a very noble job at that.

Still, it feels good when he waves me over.

"Hey," he greets when I reach the edge of the mat. "Just finishing up here."

"I'll just watch from over here." I hook my thumb behind me and point at the ledge along the windows.

The three women eye me curiously, looking perturbed I've interrupted their class. Or their ogling. One or the other. So because the last things I want are to get Oscar in trouble or have an unwanted confrontation, I back away without hearing Oscar's reply.

I take a seat on the ledge, allowing the coolness from the window to permeate my T-shirt. I don't think my body temperature has anything to do with the heat in the building. It is entirely self-inflicted from watching Oscar fluidly move through different footwork patterns. He instructs the women to stand and they pair off. Two women move to one side of the mat, while Oscar and the happiest of the trio move to the other.

Just as he did with me, he works through instructing her how to perform whatever this move is called, and she plays dumb, so he has to repeat himself four times. They're more difficult to teach than a litter of feral kittens.

When his class finishes, the women saunter off after each sending me a scowl.

Oscar walks over, stopping several feet in front of me. "I didn't think you'd come," he states casually as he rubs a towel down his face and across his torso.

Suddenly, I'm thirstier than a Jersey cow in the Sahara. If I could form words, they'd get stuck in my dry mouth, anyway.

He steps closer. "You good?"

I never thought I'd be the type of person who was so physically attracted to someone, I'd turn stupid, but here I am.

So. Stupidly. Attracted. All I can manage is to nod and force a small smile.

"Oh-kay," he drawls. "Do you want to wait here or in my boss's office? I need to have a quick shower because… yeah. I need to shower."

Heaven help me; this is getting worse.

"I'll wait here," I reply, sounding like a shy kindergartner.

"Okay." Oscar chuckles and walks off, leaving me to stare at his back.

Hardly a punishment.

After twenty minutes, two of the ladies in Oscar's class have left and most of the other gym-goers have cleared out. The large space is virtually empty, short of a very athletic man and woman sparring in the far corner. I'm amazed by the woman's skills in both throwing and blocking punches.

"That's the boss man," Oscar tells me.

"Oh," I reply, standing to face him. "Is that his girlfriend?"

Oscar chuckles again. "No. She's getting private lessons."

I stare at them for a minute, highly doubting that's all they are. "Could have fooled me. I can feel the tension between them from here." When I tear my eyes away, I find Oscar's heated gaze on me.

His wet hair and smooth skin look just as tempting as he did thirty minutes ago. "Funny, because I can only feel the tension between us."

I blow out a long breath, trying to settle my nerves.

"Coach," a shrill voice calls from behind Oscar.

His head drops, along with his shoulders. "Another raccoon," he mutters before turning around. "Yeah?"

"Just wanted to say thank you for teaching us that… um… knee thing."

"*Khao khong.*"

"Right. That. Well, thanks again," she repeats, then saunters off.

"Sorry," he says, turning back to face me. "First class."

I'm really impressed by how much they appeared to learn in one class. Since I'll have some free time over the summer, and I'll be looking for any excuse to spend more time with Oscar, I finally cave and ask, "After exams, do you think you could give me a few private lessons?"

"We can definitely arrange something." He smiles wide, then throws his arm over my shoulders, wrapping me in a combination of spicy body wash and total comfort. "Let's get out of here."

We follow the same path as the straggler from Oscar's class, walking past the not-couple in the corner.

"Night, Tyrus. See you tomorrow."

He abandons his fighting stance and turns toward us. "See ya, Os—" His words stop short when his sparring partner throttles him across the jaw.

It doesn't knock him down, but it rattles him.

The woman shrugs, not dropping her ready position. "Never let yourself get distracted."

Oscar bursts out laughing, making no effort to hide his amusement that his boss just got clocked by his own student.

Tyrus shakes his head and lifts his fists back up. "That was cold."

Oscar and I leave the pair and walk out into the parking lot.

I don't miss the fact that I haven't felt like anyone was watching me since the porch incident. Each day, I'm starting to feel more normal. More relaxed and more at peace.

And dare I say, despite how badly I want to kiss him, with Oscar by my side, I'm more *happy*.

"**Y**ou still haven't kissed her?" Blake shouts. Like he's completely forgetting we live next door. "I know you pride yourself on being a gentleman, Ozzie, but come on! She's going to think you don't like her."

I roll my eyes, facing the other way. There's no point in explaining to him that there's some cosmic force in play, stopping me every time I get close. "A few weeks ago, you followed me up to my room to caution me about going all in. Now I'm not all in enough?"

"No, I said, 'sure, go all in.' I was just worried about when you go from all to nothing."

"Stop saying 'when,' then!" I snap. "If, sure. *If* things go south, I'll deal with it. It's really not your problem."

The hurt on Blake's face is so obvious, it's worse than landing a knee strike to his gut. "That's not really how friendship works, but okay. Don't say I didn't try to be here for you." He gets up off the couch and takes a step toward the kitchen.

"Wait. I'm sorry, man. I know you're just looking out for me. You're a way better friend than I am."

"That's obvious," he replies before turning around. When he faces me, he's wearing one of his famous Blake smiles, telling me he's already forgiven me.

That doesn't make me feel less awful, though.

"I really am sorry, man. It's not that I don't appreciate you or what you're saying. I just... really like her, and the thought of it blowing up the same way as Sonia is..." I mimic my brain exploding with my hands, because that's exactly how it would feel.

"That bad, huh? If you like her that much, you better make sure she knows." He slaps me on the shoulder and continues his trek into the kitchen, once again leaving me to consider relationship advice from the king of one-night stands.

"I have a plan, but I need you to trust me... and let me drive." I smile at Frankie, attempting to rid her face of the deepening lines between her brows.

"How far is the drive?"

"Not far. Austin will dog-sit until we get back."

My efforts have failed, because she looks more skeptical now.

"How long will we be gone?" She glances down at Brad, who is sitting dutifully at her feet.

"A few hours. Just... trust me?" I hold out my hand, hoping she'll take it.

She looks right into my eyes. "Okay." Then she steps forward and laces her fingers with mine.

That simple word says a lot more than the two syllables. Her acknowledging that she trusts me is a huge step, considering what she's been through. Even though she already put that trust into action by giving me a spare set of her keys, those four letters make a statement I'll hold on to for eternity.

"Grab his leash and whatever he needs," I tell her.

"Do I have to change? What do I need?"

I look down at her casual jeans and T-shirt, appreciating how she makes something so simple look so gorgeous. "Nothing. You're perfect."

She drops my hand and inhales a sharp breath. I can't help but notice the faint smile on her soft pink lips. Lips that are providing a major distraction right now.

I shake my head, trying to prevent myself from blowing up our entire evening by taking her right back inside. Focus. Call on that unwavering discipline. "Austin has beef jerky. Come on."

Thirty minutes later, we've left Brad relaxing on Blake's bed while he and Austin play video games, and we're in Frankie's car, headed to our location. She tells me about her shift at the clinic this morning and reminds me she has to be back at 7:30 tomorrow. Sundays are my only full day off, so I tease her about being able to sleep in, even though I won't. My body is so adjusted to early mornings and little sleep, I don't think I'm capable of sleeping in. That happened one time, the day after my certification test, when I was so mentally and physically exhausted, I crashed for twelve hours.

The vibe between us is so effortlessly relaxed by the time we pull into the parking lot of the restaurant that doubles as an arcade. After Frankie mentioned she'd never played an arcade game in her life, I knew I wanted to bring her here. I've been once before with my roommates, and we had fun—as one would expect when Blake's dad was unknowingly picking up the tab.

"*Feeding Frenzy*?" Frankie asks, looking more skeptical than she did at her front door.

"You said you'd trust me. Come on." I unclip my seatbelt, hop out of the car, and jog around to her side to open the door. "It'll be fun. Promise."

She gifts me a gorgeous smile, again drawing attention to her lips. Instead of dwelling on them, I grab her hand and lead her to the door. While I don't doubt making out in the parking lot would be a night to remember, I owe her a proper date.

Inside, there are seats in the restaurant area, at a bar, or you can eat in the arcade section. We agree to start in the restaurant and save the arcade games for later.

Frankie orders some fruity mocktail full of food colouring and sugar, swearing she's never touching another drop of alcohol as long as she lives. I order a steak salad, while Frankie indulges in a triple cheese burger.

She sips her drink and opens up a bit more as the evening progresses, and she starts talking about the only paid job she's ever held. "My last two years of high school, I worked at a swimwear and lingerie store in the mall."

I choke on a piece of arugula and have to take a sip of water to dislodge it. "Really? Tell me all about it."

"There's not much to tell." She giggles, then sips her red drink through a skinny plastic straw. "The weirdest part was when guys would come in and ask for help to pick things out for their mistresses. They had no shame in admitting that. Makes a person a little cynical, you know?"

I clench my jaw. "Yeah, I do." All too well, in fact. Though, I was the unknowing paramour in my case.

"Did I say something wrong?"

I force my jaw to relax when I notice the alarm in Frankie's eyes. "No, sorry. It's... uh... Sonia. We only dated for a few months, but it turned out she'd had another boyfriend the whole time. They were high school sweethearts, but he went to a different college." I never wanted to admit that out loud, but something about Frankie makes me think I'd confess any number of embarrassing stories to put her at ease.

Her eyes narrow, then widen again. "Is that why Blake ended up in a fistfight?"

"Did Blake tell you about that?" I ask, tensing at the thought of Blake sharing that story behind my back.

"No. You did."

I stare at her flushed cheeks and her glassy eyes, trying to gauge if she's being serious.

"When we played Truth or Dare. You asked if my best friend ended up in a fistfight with my prom date's girlfriend."

Funny how I remember everything she told me about that idiot Callum, but I don't recall that part. "Sonia's boyfriend showed up in our residence, looking for a fight. I didn't want to get expelled, and the second I knew Sonia cheated on me, I wasn't about to fight for her." I scoff at the thought. "He wouldn't give up, so finally Blake handled him."

"Wasn't Blake worried about getting expelled?"

I shrug one shoulder. "He didn't think that far ahead. He just acted. But honestly, he's grown up being told he was a perpetual disappointment. So in his words, it would have just been one more notch on his tally."

"That's really sad. He's just... eccentric."

"He's a lot of things, yeah. Eccentric is one of them. He's also a really good friend."

Frankie smiles as she pushes away the last of her meal. "He says the same thing about you."

I have my doubts about that, but I don't voice them. "That's why we rented the house instead of staying in residence again. He... uh... wasn't welcome back."

"Makes sense," she says with a laugh. "In that case, I'm glad he wasn't."

That short sentence makes me smile. "Me too."

She places her hand on the table, so I reach over and put mine on top, rubbing her thumb with mine. The simple contact makes me even more eager to kiss her. To really show her how much I like her. But I'm not about to lean over our empty plates and kiss her now, so we need to get this night moving along.

"What do you want to play first?"

She stretches her head upward to look over the dining booths toward the arcade. "Ultimate dodgeball," she replies without hesitation. She slips out of her seat and stops beside mine, holding out her hand. "We need to find another couple to play against. It's two-on-two."

Acknowledging us as a couple—in any capacity—makes me a little relieved I'm not the only one of us who's all in. Even if it is just for dodgeball.

She drags me to the entrance of the dodgeball arena, stopping in the line behind a few other people. "Oh, perfect. It looks like they'll assign us victims."

I can't hold in my laugh, seeing a combination of her excitement and confidence. This is an unexpected side of her I love seeing. With no signs of her stalker for the last few weeks, she's really started to show her true, vibrant colours, and I love every single one.

"Frankie?"

Her hand clenches mine. I give her a gentle squeeze before we both spin to see who the voice belongs to.

"Whit?" she asks of a guy who looks to be straight from a magazine photoshoot.

He smiles in return. "Funny seeing you here."

"How's... Fluffy?" She grimaces, making me more confused.

"Lovely. Mademoiselle Lovelyworth," he replies. "She's fine. No hangnails, thank God."

Frankie laughs and turns just enough I catch her eye. "Oh... Whit, this is Oscar. Whit brought his mom's cat to the vet a few months ago. Oscar is my... neighbour."

Ouch. Relegated to neighbour status as soon as a good-looking guy strikes up conversation? One thing I learned from my short relationship with Sonia is that I'm not okay with being someone's second choice. I take one step to the left, creating a bit of distance between me and their conversation. I also ignore the apologetic look from Frankie.

"Whit," a pretty blonde girl calls from behind the male model.

He turns and wraps his arm over her shoulder when she comes to a stop beside him. "Rhea, this is Frankie. Remember? From the animal hospital? Frankie, this is my little sister."

"Oh," Rhea replies, looking at Frankie, then at her brother. "I see why you were so disappointed."

Frankie blushes as she greets the newcomer to this awkward encounter. "Nice to meet you. I hope you haven't slammed your brother's hand in any more car doors."

Rhea laughs, giving her brother a side-eye glance. "No, he's learned to keep his hand off of the door frame."

"Smart." Frankie offers the sibling pair an awkward smile. Then, out of nowhere, she says, "Enjoy the rest of your night."

Without waiting for a reply, she turns in the opposite direction and walks off.

I give Rhea and Whit a confused glance, utter a lie that it was nice to meet them, then follow Frankie into the crowd.

The only thing following me is an unhealthy dose of jealousy, threatening to derail our entire evening.

Oscar stops at a distance behind me, which I deserve. I wasn't quite sure how to handle that surprise encounter, and I don't think my choice was the right one.

I reach out for his hand, but he doesn't reciprocate. My stomach sinks. "I'm sorry."

Oscar shrugs, avoiding eye contact. "It's fine."

"He asked me out," I blurt, "and I told him I was too busy to date. It felt weird being here… on a date. Like he'd know I lied."

"*Did* you lie?" Oscar asks, finally looking at me.

"Yes." I close my eyes for a second to break our eye contact. When I open them, Oscar's focus hasn't shifted. "I *was* busy, but the real reason I said no was because I wasn't interested in him. There was someone else I had stuck in my head all the time."

He continues to stare at me, not reacting to that statement.

Clearly, I need to bare my soul here. "A certain blond neighbour who drove me absolutely mad and hated my dog."

His eyes brighten under the colourful arcade lights. "How long ago was this?"

I swallow the lump in my throat and answer, "October."

Finally, he steps closer. "Why didn't you say something sooner?"

"You hated me," I answer with complete confidence.

He reaches a hand up and strokes my jaw with his thumb. "I never hated you, Frankie." He inches forward, stopping centimetres away. "If I ever hated you, I wouldn't have been so jealous when you were talking to that guy."

Hearing him admit I'm not the only one who is struggling with feeling jealous emboldens me further. "If it makes you feel any better, I had the same problem at the gym."

He raises an eyebrow. "You were jealous of the soccer moms?"

"I was jealous you were touching them," I admit, hoping it will have the right result.

It does.

His face transforms into a scheming grin as he places his opposite hand on the small of my back and pulls me against him. "I was coaching them, Frankie. Trust me; I only *want* to touch you."

Every drop of oxygen vacates my lungs. I bite my bottom lip while looking up at Oscar's. The noise and chaos around us fade into nothing, and the only thing stimulating any of my senses is Oscar.

Finally, after weeks—months—of anticipation and countless times being interrupted, Oscar presses his lips to mine. He's slow at first. Tender. Not nearly as greedy as I feel. Kissing him is every bit as amazing as I expected it to be. He responds to my desperation after a few seconds, but quickly pulls his head away.

"This is a family restaurant," he says with a breathy chuckle.

My cheeks burn when I turn my head to the left and see a horrified mother staring at us. I offer a pathetic smile before grabbing Oscar's hand and dragging him to the wide hallway between the bar and the arcade. I stop with my back against the wall.

Oscar places one hand on either side of me and leans forward. "I'm not known for being patient, but that was worth the wait."

I've already confessed too much, so I'm not about to tell him that's the only kiss I've had since a pathetic slobbery exchange with Callum that had me questioning my life's choices. He didn't set the bar high, but Oscar well and truly exceeded expectations.

For that reason, my only acknowledgement of his words is grabbing the collar of his black tee and pulling him toward me. I won't *tell* him that kissing him has unlocked a new top on my pleasure list—way above red velvet cupcakes—but I will *show* him.

His reaction time is impressive. His palm rests on my cheek, creating another point of contact that still doesn't feel like enough. It would be so easy to get lost in him, but he pulls away far too soon, sporting a cheeky grin. "Family restaurant."

"Right," I reply, looking toward the arcade to mask my disappointment. I'm relieved we haven't drawn the attention of any more mothers. "So, which game do you want me to beat you at first?"

Oscar laughs. "You've never been to an arcade before."

"Beginner's luck?" I shrug, grab his hand, and walk back into the flurry of activity surrounding the various games.

A small boy, who is maybe nine or ten, starts whooping in front of the basketball game and shouts at his dad, "In your face!"

His dejected father's expression changes quickly into a smile as he gives his son a high five.

Oscar halts beside me.

I glance at the boy and his father, then at Oscar. "I hope you'll be such a good sport when I beat you."

He responds with a one-sided smile. "Just made me realize I haven't talked to my dad for a while."

We continue our walk until he stops in front of a Skee-Ball machine, gesturing at it.

"Sure. Looks like a good one to test my beginner's luck." I smirk at Oscar, taking up my spot at the base of the game. "What does he do?"

"Hm? Who?"

"Your dad."

"Oh. He works in the town office. That's why I chose urban planning as my major."

My first ball rolls up the ramp, veers to the far left, and drops into the ten spot. I try to distract Oscar from my failure by asking, "So, you want to work with your dad?"

"No," he says with a brief laugh. He steps behind me, wrapping one arm around my waist and taking my right hand in his. "Like this."

Just like when he taught me a push kick, I'm putty in his hands. I lean into him and allow his hand to guide mine. Sure enough, the ball rolls up and drops into the hole for thirty points. It's a slight improvement, but I still have my eye on the hundred points in either corner.

"Better," he breathes into my ear.

"Are you trying to sabotage me?"

"If we were playing for something, maybe."

I'm not a betting person, but even if I was, there's nothing I want to play for. Anything with Oscar is a win.

With a final score of 180, I feel less than confident as Oscar takes aim in his lane.

Distraction is my only shot now. "So you don't want to work with your dad?"

"No." He sticks his tongue between his teeth so it pokes out the side of his mouth as he shoots a ball into the forty slot. "Not with him. Just in a small town somewhere."

"Why a small town?" I ask, leaning against the partial wall sectioning off the Skee-Ball area.

"The city isn't really my thing, I guess." He rolls another ball up, so it drops into the thirty target. "I want to help develop smaller towns that need better infrastructure without having to compromise their green space. Somewhere convenience, nature, and wildlife can all co-exist."

I wonder if this guy will ever stop surprising me. Since our first interaction, he's continued to prove my first assumptions wrong. Each thing I get to know about him makes me like him even more. And I'm already in heartbreak territory if things go south.

"It's lame, I know. But my dad has worked as the CFO for seventeen years. He used to bring me into work with him, and I just remember being fascinated by everything that goes into running a town. There are always new challenges and moving parts. It feels like somewhere I could make a difference." Now, he's abandoned throwing any balls to focus solely on me. "Once I decided that's what I wanted to do, there was no changing my mind."

"So you're saying you're stubborn." I inch toward him; more because I'm drawn to him than hoping his game will end with a measly seventy points.

"I'm saying"—he gently grabs my arm and pulls me forward, making me collapse into his chest—"when I find something interesting, not even a vicious pit bull can chase me away."

I take a hard swallow, unable to look away from Oscar's intense green eyes.

Before he can lean in any closer, the arcade game starts dinging and flashing, displaying his second-place score.

A victorious smile spreads across my lips. "In your face!"

Like a good sport, Oscar lifts his hand up to offer a high five.

I slap his hand in midair before I grab it to continue my epic defeat of the guy who's good at everything.

Hours pass while we spend time deep-sea fishing, motorcycle racing, flying fighter jets, and playing air hockey—which I'm convinced was rigged. I haven't smiled this wide or laughed this much for years. Don't get me wrong; I love Brad and he brings me a lot of joy, but it's been a long time since I was just able to let loose and have fun. It's little to do with the arcade and much to do with the company.

"Ready to go?" Oscar asks after we finish our final game, solidifying my victory.

I don't want this night to be over, but I have to be at the clinic in a little over eight hours. "I don't blame you for wanting to leave before this gets really embarrassing."

He grabs my hand as we march toward the door. I follow his eyes over to the bar, where I spot Whit and his sister seated, facing away from us.

As we step through the door, he says, "You may have shot down my jet, but I still feel like the winner tonight."

38

OSCAR

Slowly Slowly

Slow is not my speed. The only thing I want to do slowly is kiss Frankie. Otherwise, I struggle with taking anything slow. So even though Frankie and I agreed not to rush anything between us, I find her drifting into my thoughts everywhere I go.

Like now; as I try to finish an essay on catastrophic policy failures in provincial government, all I can think about is her smile, her laugh, and her lips.

"You down for one last party of the semester?" Blake asks, peeking his head into my room, stopping my daydream in its tracks.

I lean back in my desk chair and roll my eyes. "What do you think?"

"I knew we could count on you, Ozzie. We sent out invites for the fourteenth, so if you could put in a kind word with the neighbour, that'd be great. Be there or be square."

Honestly, I'd rather be square.

He pops his head out, then back in the door. "I'll get her more flowers... flower. Sweeten the deal."

There's no point trying to figure out what on Earth he's talking about, so I let him leave without asking.

I turn back to my computer and pull up the calendar, only to realize that date interferes with my study schedule. I need that entire weekend to prepare for a Monday exam. Microeconomics is my toughest class this semester, and the exam is worth three-quarters of our final grade. If it's anything like the macroeconomics exam last semester, I'm going to need every minute of that study time. Not to mention, I still have to coach during exams, and I'd rather spend free time with Frankie than partying.

Oscar: What does your exam schedule look like?

Because if she doesn't have any exams on the day of the party, I hope she'll be down for hanging out instead of letting me suffer.

Frankie: Done on the 14th. Kill me now.

Shoot. Looks like worst-case scenario.

Frankie: Worst part is, it's at 8am. Calls for at least 4 espressos.

I huff a half-laugh, half-sigh-of-relief.

Oscar: Please don't. You're too young for a heart attack.

Blake just told me they're having a party on the 14th. I was wondering if you wanted to come by... maybe have a few AMFs. For old time's sake?

Frankie: Not funny.

I laugh, picturing her narrowed eyes and look of pure indignation. I haven't brought up her drunken episode since she flipped out on me the following day—which I soon understood the real reason for her upset. But what good is having a drunken college experience if someone doesn't remind you about your stupidity every once in a while?

Another reason why I don't drink. I just like to be the one doing the reminding.

Oscar: What do you say we make our own plan? Celebrate your exams being done?

Frankie: Sounds perfect. What about tomorrow night?

Here I thought I'd have to wait to spend time with her again. If I was smart, I'd say I can't because I need to finish this paper. But smart isn't a word I'd use to describe myself when it comes to Frankie.

Oscar: *I'm all yours.*

The guys have all gone out to see some new three-hour thriller movie at the theatre. I've never sat through three hours of anything in my life, so even if I hadn't made plans with Frankie, I'd have opted to save my twelve bucks.

Since I have the house to myself, I asked her to come over here instead. Not for any reason other than I don't want her thinking she has to host me at her place all the time. I'm capable of cooking and I never got to showcase that when she stayed here over reading week.

A knock at the door interrupts me right as I'm about to put the sheet pan in the oven. I jog toward the door and swing it open. The sight that greets me makes my heart race. Frankie in a form-fitting black spaghetti-strap dress, her hair in long loose curls, and a light layer of makeup. There's never been a day I didn't think she was stunning, but she's a total knockout tonight.

"Wow. You look... way too good to stay in for dinner." I run my hand through the length of my hair, regretting my basic jeans and tee.

"Is it too much? I never get to dress up, so I figured tonight was my chance."

I reach my arm out to pull her inside, only now noticing Brad is seated on the front step beside her. He takes her movement as his cue to come in too and struts toward the kitchen. I close the door and take the opportunity to greet Frankie properly.

It's only been days since I last kissed her. Despite living next door to each other, it's been surprisingly difficult to carve out time for each other with our busy, often conflicting schedules. But the second our lips meet and she leans into it, meeting me with an equal amount of eagerness, it feels natural. Effortless. Like kissing her is the easiest thing in the world.

It also may be my favourite.

I trail my fingers down her bare arm, feeling goosebumps rise against my touch. She reacts by hooking her forearms around my back and pulling me even closer. Then she nips my bottom lip with her teeth and utters my name on a breath. Suddenly, the only thing I have an appetite for is her. I could survive on kissing her alone.

Even if she was caffeine and refined carbs and food colouring combined, I'd still choose her.

"Oscar," she repeats as she pulls back a few inches.

"Frankie."

Her cheeks flush, making her impossibly more gorgeous.

A loud clang from the kitchen interrupts our moment—thankfully after our kiss this time.

"Brad!" I shout, taking off for the kitchen. I walk in to find the sheet pan I had set beside the stove now on the floor with Brad scarfing down the uncooked food.

Frankie walks in behind me, stopping dead when she sees the metal tray and leafy greens laying on the tile. "What happened?"

"Apparently Brad doesn't like bok choi, but he likes salmon."

"Oh my gosh. Was it on the floor?"

I turn to look at her, hoping she's not serious. Judging by her horrified expression, she's really asking.

"No, Frankie. I didn't put our dinner on the floor." My words come out with more bite than they should have.

The surprise is immediately recognizable in her eyes. "Sorry. I shouldn't have brought him. He was alone all day…" Her words trail off, and I notice tears pooling in her eyes. She walks toward Brad and hooks a hand in his collar. "We should go."

"I'm sorry. Please, don't go."

"We ruined your night," she practically whispers, not releasing her dog.

I hate that my snappy reply has changed her demeanour. "The only thing that would ruin my night is if you leave. I'm not upset about the salmon. I just don't know what to feed you now."

She looks down at the floor, then at Brad. "For what it's worth, he's never stolen food before. Must have been good." She offers a weak smile, but I can tell all is not forgiven yet.

I intend to remedy that. "Look online to see what we can order to eat. I'll be right back."

Before she can argue, I rush toward the front of the house and up the stairs.

When I come back down, she's seated on the far sofa, leaning over her knees, talking to Brad at her feet. "… how you got your little hippo body—"

My arrival stops whatever she was trying to say.

She looks me over, her eyes settling on my guitar. "What's that for?"

"I've been working on something."

"When do you find the time?"

She's seen the guitar in my room, and I know I mentioned it before, but I've never wanted to play it for someone else. Let alone spent hours learning chords and lyrics for one specific purpose. I just didn't know that purpose was to make my apology loud and clear.

"When something is important, you make time. I'm not very good at it, so bear with me." I sit on the coffee table in front of her and adjust myself into a comfortable position. Without looking at her, I begin strumming the opening to *Peaceful Easy Feeling*. Once I'm through the first verse, I finally look at Frankie.

She's mouthing the words, focused on the movement of my hands.

I continue through the chorus, hoping she'll join me, but she stays quiet, listening to my sub-par singing voice. Thankfully, there's a little guitar solo to focus on, which was a lot of fun to learn.

As I strum the final cord, she lifts her dark eyes from my hands to my face.

"That was amazing." She glances away, blinking for a few seconds. "Do you know why I like that song?"

"It's a classic. Everybody likes it," I reply.

She breathes a short laugh. "After my stalker left his first note on my car, I was really on edge. Stressed and scared to go anywhere alone. One day at work, this song came on and I imagined what it would be like to have a *peaceful easy feeling* again."

That realization brings up thoughts I haven't had for a few weeks. Since her stalker hasn't appeared for a while, I'd almost started to forget about him. Even Frankie seems more at ease lately.

I lean the guitar against the coffee table and shift myself onto the couch beside her. I wrap my left arm around her shoulders, grab her hand with my right, and plant a kiss on her temple. "What about now?"

"I'm finally starting to feel peaceful again." She smiles at me with the most irresistible tilt of her lips.

And the feeling that brings me complete peace is when my mouth meets hers.

39

FRANKIE

Messin' Around

My exams are finally over. Even though I have an increased commitment for volunteer hours, my schedule is a lot more open for the next four months. I'm hoping that extra free time means more with Oscar.

There's been no sign of my stalker for six weeks, so I'm clinging to the hope he was arrested for something and is currently serving time behind bars. Or he's in a coma somewhere, and he'll wake up with amnesia. I'm not an evil person, but it's hard for me to have any sympathy for the man after everything he's put me through.

But I also recognize that the situation brought me here. Without the sequence of events happening the way they did, I never would have met Oscar. I never would have adopted Brad. So many things I'm grateful for today would have been a forever hole in my heart. Now that those things are such an important part, I can't imagine life without them.

So as much as I want to hate the man after nearly four years of torment, and wouldn't be upset if I found out he was a rotting corpse somewhere, I guess this is my way of making lemonade out of lemons.

Conveniently, my no-refined-carbs, no-food-colouring lemonade is standing on the other side of my front door.

I flick the locks and open it wide, eager to invite Oscar a place to hide from his roommate's final party of the year.

"Hi," he says, stepping inside. He closes the door behind him and flicks one lock. That's all he has time for before pulling me against him and kissing me eagerly.

Any uncertainty and anxiety just melts away with each second. Oscar's presence has changed my life in so many ways, and kissing him is an amazing bonus.

"Hi," I say on a breath once we separate.

"I've been thinking about that all day."

My heart flutters. "All day, hmm?"

"Non-stop." He hooks an arm around my waist and pulls me back against him. "I can't stay too late because I have so much studying left to do."

"I know." Not going to say I like it, but I respect his need to focus on school. "Just a few days left."

He grins and kisses me again. This time, it's quick and reassuring. "A whole summer with no parties."

"Does that mean you won't come over anymore?" I tease, but there is an unmistakable note of concern in my voice.

"You won't be able to get rid of me." His genuine smile makes my heart skip a beat.

"Luckily, I don't want to."

"Brad looks like he'd take me out if I turn my back," he says, peeking around me.

I look behind me without loosening Oscar's hold on my waist. "Don't mind him. He's a ham addict, and we ran out. He's salty about it."

Oscar drops his forehead to rest on my shoulder. "Nitrates too?"

"Hey, I don't comment on your food choices," I defend. "You keep eating your flavourless cardboard and leave us mere mortals alone."

He shakes his head, still resting it on my shoulder, and huffs a laugh. "You'll be the death of me, woman." He lifts his head and kisses me again. This time, he doesn't hold back. He brushes his tongue along my bottom lip, prompting me to relax in his arms and get lost in the sensation of his tongue mingling with mine. We get caught up for a few minutes before he pulls away. "What a way to go."

I never dreamed anyone would ever make me feel so desirable. So safe and content. Of all the negative feelings and emotions I've held onto for years, Oscar has slipped into my life and rid me of each one. Just by being him, he's completely changed my life for the better. Just by being him, he's made me fall in love with him.

"Come on. I got you strawberries and me whipped cream," I say, breaking out of his arms, then walking toward the kitchen. I need some distance to process that startling realization, because I hadn't realized how deep I was in until now.

Brad hops out of his bed and follows me, probably hoping he'll get some dessert too.

Oscar sticks to his guns, refusing to try strawberries with whipped cream. I ignore his feelings on the "chemical concoction" I love so much and enjoy my dessert.

Our time together feels comfortable. If I think back to when we first met, I never could have imagined we'd be here, talking about our goals, dreams, and fears—though, his only fear is failing his classes. My list is much more extensive. But right now, my fear isn't defining me, and I want to enjoy every minute.

"Frankie, if I don't go, I'm never going to be able to leave."

I keep my arms tight around Oscar's torso. This looming sense of dread has been hovering over me for the past hour, not wanting him to leave. "I don't see the problem."

He groans, tightening his grip around my waist. "That's cruel. You're already finished your exams. I still have two left. Trust me, I'd rather stay just like this." He traces his lips along the soft skin under my ear, making me shiver from the sensation.

"Fine." I drop my arms, reluctantly giving him permission to leave. Even though I'd rather he continue his trail of kisses, I don't want to affect his grades.

He loosens his hold, bending down until his lips meet mine. He starts out slow, allowing me to savour his touch. His body is firm everywhere my hands graze, except his lips. The juxtaposition amplifies each of my senses. I breathe in his masculine, spicy scent, absorb the feel of his fingers pressing into my back, and soak in the sounds of his moans in between breaths. Eight months ago, I never would have imagined I'd be so caught up in Oscar Luna, the grumpy neighbour who threatened my dog. He started out by invading my space, and now he's quickly invaded my heart.

"I really need to go," he says, resting his forehead against mine.

I close my eyes, trying to absorb the comfort his presence brings me. "Okay, go."

"You know I don't *want* to, right? I *have* to. These classes have been tough and I can't—"

"You don't have to explain. I understand."

"Okay." He bends down and gives me one more soft kiss, pulling away too soon. "I'll see you next Friday if I don't see you before then."

The realization that I might not see him for seven days chases away the euphoric overwhelm caused by his presence and replaces it with sadness. But I don't want to make him feel guilty for prioritizing his school work. "Okay. Good luck with your exams."

"Thanks." With that, he gives me a sad smile before walking out the door.

Even with the door open, I can't tell there's a party going on next door. I don't know if it's because most people are still dealing with exams or if a lot of their regulars have left to go back home for the summer. It's the tamest one they've had yet.

I sit back on the sofa beside Brad, pulling him onto his back between my legs so I can rub his belly. He just flops there like a big baby. With Oscar's roommates leaving to go back home for the summer, it will be weird just being the two of us around. Oscar is teaching extra classes at the gym, and I'm increasing my volunteer hours, but otherwise, we'll have a lot of spare time to spend together, including the private lessons he's going to give me.

A knock at the door interrupts my summer daydreams, but I'm not bothered because hope surges through me that Oscar has changed his mind and come back.

I swing the door open without checking, only to find an unfamiliar man on the other side. I waver between panic and logic, and after a few seconds, I say, "Party is next door."

"You don't remember me?"

Those few words strike a level of terror through me I haven't felt for weeks.

I take a step back, giving myself enough room to close the door, but attempt to pacify him first. "Oh, you're the guy from—" I stop my words short, trying to slam the door fast enough I can lock it, but he's faster.

He kicks the door open while I'm still holding it, jarring my arm and sending a shooting pain through my shoulder. Brad comes running over, snarling and barking. This time, the guy is unfazed by the angry pit bull, swinging his leg back and kicking Brad in the side with his heavy boot.

I scream out as Brad yelps and slides across the floor, lying unmoving on his side when he comes to a stop. The man doesn't give me a chance to rush to my dog's aid before he grabs my hair and pulls me toward the dining room. I let out a scream, but he quickly covers my mouth.

As he drags me backwards, I look over and see Brad is no longer where I last saw him. He has disappeared. And in this moment, I realize I've been left alone to fight for my life.

48

OSCAR

Might Be the Police

"**B**rad!" some girl cheers from the living room.

I halt my steps through the dining room, curious if some guy named Brad just showed up.

"Oscar!" Blake shouts. "Brad's limping."

I rush back into the room, spotting Brad pawing at Blake's leg. His determination makes me think it's not just because he loves Blake. Brad's eyes zero in on me, and instead of coming over, he limps back toward the door. He wasn't limping when I was over there ten minutes ago.

Terror. No amount of training or certifications could prepare me for the fear I feel at this moment.

"Oscar? What's wrong?" Blake asks, shaking me with one hand on my shoulder.

"He's here. Frankie." I say nothing else as I bolt out the door, across our shared yard and up Frankie's steps. The door is wide open when I reach it, so I don't even think about entering the house slowly.

Some lunatic wearing a phone company uniform, work boots and all, has one arm around Frankie's throat, holding her in front of him like a shield. Tears are streaming down her face, but she looks like she's staring off into space and hasn't noticed I'm here. Like she's trying to stay detached from reality, and if that's how she has to deal with this moment, I'm not going to pull her back.

So I address the guy. "Let her go and we can talk about this. Whatever you want, we can figure it out."

I'm trying to stay strong for Frankie, but when this guy pulls a knife, it takes every bit of strength in me not to collapse to my knees and beg. If I thought that would help, I would, but he doesn't seem open to talking.

Still, I keep trying. "What is it you want?"

"She was supposed to be mine. She was nice to me. Then she ran away like I meant nothing! Now you've taken what's supposed to be mine!"

This guy is even more deranged than I thought. She was nice to him? That justifies terrorizing her for years? He's unhinged, making this situation even more terrifying.

"I'm sorry about that. This is my fault, okay? If you want to punish someone, take me. Let her go and you can take me. I'm the one you want to hurt. You can get me out of the way, then you two can be together." Those words taste like bile, burning my tongue as I say them.

Frankie is still standing in front of him, looking like a zombie, but I can see his arm moving with each of her breaths. She's physically okay. If he doesn't drop that knife, I'm not sure she'll stay that way.

I step closer, trying to position myself so I can somehow get her away from him.

"Stop moving. Don't come any closer."

I put my hands up, surrendering to this man who has completely lost touch with reality.

My posture causes him to relax enough, he drops the arm holding the knife a few inches. The past decade of training my reaction time and being quick on my feet has prepared me for this moment. I promised myself the only time I'd use my skills outside of the gym was to protect someone in harm's way. Especially the woman I've come to care so much about.

I'm still ten feet away, so if I rush him, he'll have enough time to react and possibly injure Frankie. I keep talking, shuffling forward in miniscule movements, hoping they go unnoticed.

"Tell me when you guys first met." I feel sick to my stomach pandering to his delusion, but desperate times.

"She was nice to me," he repeats, this time with a crack in his voice.

"Well, that's something. She wasn't nice to me when we first met."

"I don't believe that. She's always nice!" the man shouts.

I glance at her, hoping she's still staring off into space, but her tear-filled eyes are now alert and looking at me. I can't risk setting this guy off by saying something to put Frankie at ease, so I refocus on him, continuing my slow trek forward. My only hope is to end this nightmare. "It was probably me that was the problem. Because you see... I'm not very nice."

Before he can process my words, I lunge forward and deliver a right hook to his left temple, jerking his head to the side and giving Frankie enough of an opportunity to get out of his grip. She stumbles forward, so I reach to grab her, but Keith comes out of nowhere to pull her to safety. Knowing she's safe with him, I turn back to her attacker just as he rushes me, wielding his knife. I throw out a straight-leg kick to his abdomen, doubling him over.

Then, I'm not sure what happens. The next thing I know, I'm being dragged off of the bloody attacker with an arm around my waist, and I hear Blake shouting my name.

My chest is heaving as I stare at the now unconscious man.

"You good?" Blake asks, shaking me with a tight grip on my shoulders.

I finally spin my head around, looking toward the front of the house. "Frankie? Where's Frankie?"

"She's with Keith on the porch. Austin called the cops. Go." He gestures for me to go to her. "I'll watch this guy, but you did a number on him; I doubt he's going anywhere."

If he hadn't been holding a knife to Frankie, I'd feel bad about what just happened, but I don't feel guilty at all as I rush out the door.

Keith has his arms wrapped around Frankie as she sobs against him. Her back is toward me, so Keith gently shifts her to look at her face.

"Oscar's here."

Her head swivels, finding me instantly. She jumps into my arms, wrapping hers around my neck. "I-I was s-so scared."

"I told you I wouldn't let him hurt you. Brad was a hero. He came to get me." Thinking back on the sequence of events, I'm blown away by how he knew to do that. He really is the hero tonight.

"Th-that guy kicked him!" she shouts, more outraged over that than being held captive at knifepoint herself.

A pair of police cars come tearing down the street with their lights on and sirens blaring. They screech to a stop in front of the house and four officers jump out. One starts throwing out questions as they approach the house, but as soon as we tell them the offender is subdued inside, two of them head in while the other two stop on the porch.

Frankie clings to me, not sobbing anymore, but tears still running down her face. Her breathing has regulated, thankfully, so she's able to answer the officer's questions.

When he asks how she knows the guy, she pauses for a full minute, staring off into space like she's running through a sequence of events. Suddenly, her eyes widen. "He was a customer. I used to work in retail… at a store that sold lingerie and swimsuits. He-he came in to buy something for his girlfriend. I remember helping him."

The officer continues to write things down on his notepad, stopping only to fiddle with the volume on his radio. He prompts Frankie to recall everything she can about their interaction.

She explains that she felt his behaviour was weird because he shared details about his girlfriend, then said something to contradict what he'd just said. It was as if he was making it up as he went. Based on my brief conversation with him, I'd say that's a safe assumption. She recalls him coming back a few times, stating his girlfriend was so thrilled with her choices. He'd say uncomfortable things about how his girlfriend had the same body type as Frankie, and asked her to model things, which she declined.

She reaches into her memory bank, sharing everything she can recall to the constable. As she talks, the more convinced I am that this guy needs serious medical help. He's not just evil; he's sick.

Whatever his future holds, I'm glad the situation has come to an end for Frankie.

Paramedics drive away with the culprit in an ambulance, followed by one police car. A new officer comes to question me, so Keith keeps Frankie company while I'm ushered to the far edge of the lawn to explain what happened. Basically, all I remember is seeing Frankie in danger and reacting to resolve the situation.

After everything the guy has put Frankie through, the constable still treats me like a dangerous criminal and advises me not to "leave town" until they sort through the details of what happened. They need to speak with "the victim" before deciding my fate. The entire line of questioning boils my blood. I want to point out that if they'd actually taken the threat seriously any *one* of the times Frankie went to them for help, I wouldn't have needed to settle the issue myself.

By the time I'm done answering questions, I'm so eager to get back to Frankie, I don't try to hide my frustration.

Her face drops when she sees me walk up the stairs to her porch. "What's wrong?"

"Nothing," I say, as gently as possible. I'm not about to tell her I could be facing an assault charge.

Regardless of what the outcome is, I wouldn't change how I reacted. She's safe, and that's all that matters right now. I'd spend any number of nights in jail to protect her.

The police cars pull away, leaving Oscar and me on his front lawn. The guys have all gone inside, and I don't know if it's because they're exhausted or if it was intentional to give us a minute alone.

"I'm sorry," I say into the dark, fighting back a fresh wave of tears.

"For what?" Oscar asks. He wraps his arms around my midsection a little tighter and pulls me closer. "You have nothing to be sorry for. None of this is your fault." He tucks my hair in behind my ear and kisses my forehead. "You're safe now."

"I should have taken some of your classes. Should have learned how to defend myself." That sentence is enough to make me sob once again. Not because I'm bothered I wasn't the one to resolve the situation, but because Oscar and Brad both ended up in harm's way trying to save me. There's no excuse that will ever make that okay.

"Shh. It's all over now. You did good, Babe."

Good? I froze. I was paralyzed by fear and dissociated to the point I don't even know when Oscar got there. All I know is that Oscar and Brad saved me when it should have been me protecting myself. It was *my* problem. No one else needed to be put in danger because I was too lazy to take a few classes. At the very least, I should have used the push kick Oscar taught me when the guy first came through my door. My tears slow, making way for the surge of anger I feel for putting others at risk.

"You're safe now," Oscar repeats. "I won't let him hurt you again."

Instead of comfort, those few words make me more scared. I know Oscar would do everything he could to keep that promise because he's loyal and brave, but he can't always be around. He wasn't this time, and if it hadn't been for Brad, who knows what would have happened. Nor should he have to sacrifice his own wants and dreams to act like my personal bodyguard. He deserves better than that.

Better than me.

Without another word, he ushers me into his house to face the sombre expressions and forced smiles from his roommates. Brad greets me at the door, and I nearly collapse with relief seeing that he appears okay. For several minutes, I sit on the ground and let Brad's tiny hippo body wriggle from his intense tail wags and nearly knock me over. I fend off his face licking, but he gets in a few stealthy swipes I can't stop. He finally settles in front of me, sitting on my thighs.

I rest my face against the back of his neck and breathe in his earthy dog scent. "*Grazie, bambino.*"

He may not know what the words mean, but I'm sure he understands how I feel.

I didn't even realize Oscar had walked away until he stops in front of me, holding two bottles of water.

"Let's get you two to bed. You're probably exhausted."

Truthfully, I'm so wired, there's no way I'll be able to sleep. Oscar has exams to study for, though, and he *does* look exhausted. Yet another reason he doesn't need this drama in his life. So I play along, telling him I'm eager to sleep in hopes he'll take that as an invitation to sleep himself.

As we approach the stairs, Blake calls from the living room, "Hey, Frankie?"

"Yeah?" I ask, peeking my head around the wall.

"We're all glad you're okay. That guy won't ever get near you again."

It's the most serious I've ever seen or heard Blake in the eight months I've known him. Somehow, it feels like this experience has even dulled his vibrant light.

"Thanks. Thank you all for what you did for me."

"That's what friends are for. We've got a date on the red carpet, remember?"

The little hint of a smile on Blake's face feels like a gift. An ounce of redemption I can carry with me so his grim expression won't be the last image I have of him.

"It's a date," I reply before continuing up the stairs.

Oscar gives me a pair of his track pants and a T-shirt, which are the most comfortable things I've ever worn. No wonder he wears them all the time.

Brad settles on the bed between our legs, overtop of the blankets, but Oscar reaches his arm out and pulls my back against his chest. My legs bend to accommodate Brad, who is already snoring. I allow myself a few minutes to appreciate something I'll never experience again. That thought alone starts a new wave of overwhelming emotions that leak out of my eyes.

"Shh. I won't let him hurt you again," he repeats.

But it's not me I'm worried about being hurt.

When Oscar's breathing steadies and his body goes limp, I slowly pull his arm off of my waist and manoeuvre myself from his hold. I replace my body with a pillow and press it against his chest. He must be exhausted, because he doesn't even stir.

I watch him sleep for a moment, questioning if this is the right choice. It doesn't take long for me to conclude that as much as he wants to keep me safe, I'll do anything to protect him too. Even from me.

"*Venir*," I whisper to Brad as I reach the door.

He hops out of the bed, making far more noise than I did. Oscar grumbles and flings his dropped arm back over the pillow.

I blow out a breath when he settles, content to snuggle my squishy stand-in.

He'll be okay without me. Better off, actually. My presence has only brought distraction from his studies and dangerous situations. Regardless of how he may feel about me, his freedom from my chaos will bring relief. His only fear is failing his classes, so I'm not going to stick around and allow myself to be the cause of that happening.

That's what I repeat to myself as I listen at his door for any of his roommates, then proceed to walk down the dark stairs. Again, I pause at the front door, suddenly paralyzed by fear for the umteenth time.

"He's gone, Francesca. It's fine," I whisper. I look down at Brad, who, even in the dark, I can see his eyes on me, waiting for instructions. It chokes me up that he's so loyal and loving, even after my inaction led to him being hurt.

I need to take action now to make sure that never happens again.

Marlene, the overnight receptionist, welcomes Brad and me as we walk into the clinic. We have only met in passing on a few occasions when I showed up early before my shift and she had been a few minutes late in leaving. It takes her a second to recognize me, and when she does, she walks around the desk.

"Frankie! Are you all right?"

I sniffle and take a breath, not wanting to have a complete meltdown. "Can I get Brad looked at? He..." I hesitate to say the next words because I feel so awful about it. "A man kicked him with a work boot on. He was limping, but he's not now. I just… want to be sure."

"Someone kicked him? I hope you called the cops!"

I nod, not wanting to explain the entire situation. "He was arrested. Is someone in?"

"Yeah, yeah. Dr. Chen is on call. Give me a minute." She ducks back in behind the desk and picks up the phone.

When things aren't busy, on-call vets stay in the studio apartment at the back of the clinic, where they're able to sleep or relax as needed. I hope Dr. Chen isn't being woken up for this, but I need to know Brad is okay. Really, I should have brought him here first thing, but I was so out of sorts, I wasn't thinking.

Another way I failed him.

Minutes later, Dr. Chen enters the room. "Frankie? What happened?"

She ushers me and Brad into an exam room while I explain the essential information. It doesn't sound any less awful after a few hours.

"Are you okay?" she asks, pressing a stethoscope to Brad's abdomen.

"I'm fine." Physically. The fact my life is being blown apart once again is a different story and I wouldn't say I'm okay with that.

Dr. Chen does a thorough examination of Brad, palpating his stomach and checking his legs. All signs point to him being fine, which is a slight relief. As she's finishing up, someone else rushes in a labouring cat in a complete panic that they can't handle the process on their own, so Dr. Chen runs off to help.

I stop in front of the reception desk on my way out to ask Marlene, "Do you have a piece of paper and a pen?"

She opens a drawer and pulls out both items. The paper is a cute piece of stationery with puppies and kittens surrounding the clinic name. It's one more dagger to my heart, reminding me of something else I'm leaving behind.

I write a lengthy note to Dr. Ellis, explaining what happened tonight and informing him of my plans. Because he was familiar with my situation, I don't think this will come as a huge surprise.

As I write, I realize I should give Oscar the same courtesy. Disappearing in the middle of the night without an explanation is cowardly, and I promised myself I wouldn't be that person anymore.

After I thank Marlene for her help and say goodbye, Brad and I climb in my car and head back to my house. Soon-to-be former house.

I'm surprised how emotional it makes me to pull up front to see the entire place dark. I haven't left all the lights off once in the entire time I've lived here. It's like a visual representation of the closing of another chapter. One I wasn't finished reading.

There's no movement next door, so I'm assuming no one has woken up yet. Unsurprising since it's 4am. While I have the chance, I rummage through my backseat to grab what I need, write a heartfelt note through my tears, then run inside to leave it somewhere Oscar will find it.

I only hope he'll understand.

Then, for the first time in nearly a year, I get on the highway to head north toward the hometown I never thought I'd return to.

The sun is shining through my window when I wake up. It takes me a few seconds to get my bearings, recalling everything that happened last night.

Frankie.

I scramble out of bed to check the bathroom once I realize she's not in my room. No sign of her. I run downstairs. Not here either.

"Brad?" I call out, hoping that I'll hear him somewhere in the house. After a few attempts, though, I realize he's gone too. My next effort is to call her, but it immediately goes to voicemail. "Frankie, it's me. Call me back. Please."

I grab a pair of flip-flops at the door and run outside, not caring that I don't have a shirt on. It's possible she decided to go to her shift at the clinic after all, so she brought Brad home before leaving. That's what I pray to be true while I knock and stand, waiting for some kind of sound inside.

No answer.

Idiot. I forgot her keys. In the seconds it takes me to run back home, I remember the security camera I have access to. With no signs of that loser appearing for weeks, we hadn't paid any attention to it. First, I want to check if she's home.

I run back up her front stairs and open the door slowly, calling for Frankie and Brad. Again, nothing. What's worse is that the few signs of her that *were* here are all gone. Her books. Her shoes. Brad's toy box.

The only thing that remains is a framed photo of us.

I collapse onto the sofa, holding the photo, looking at Frankie's brilliant smile. My stomach sinks. I pull up my phone to scroll through the security feed. There are several notifications of movement, so I scan past the ones I know are from the aftermath of the attack. The next one is at 2:30, when there are eight in quick succession. I watch as Frankie walks into her house, stays inside for a few minutes, comes back out with a large suitcase, then repeats the same process three more times. Brad walks at her side the entire time.

The next notification is just after 4am, when she runs inside and back out a few seconds later. Once she disappears down her pathway, she doesn't reappear.

Now, there's no denying what happened. She didn't go to the clinic. She left. And the worst part is, she left her only reminder of me behind.

"Where is he?" Hollis asks whichever one of my roommates opened the door.

"At the table," Austin answers.

Seconds later, my sister walks into the room, looking as defeated as I feel.

"Which one of them called you?" I roll my eyes to express my annoyance in case my tone doesn't make it clear.

"The real question is, why didn't you?" She pulls out a chair across the table, sits herself down, and rests her elbows in front of her.

"And say what, Holl?"

"I don't know. That you're sad, and you could use some moral support?"

"That sounds exactly like something I'd say. You're right." My words drip with sarcasm that I know she doesn't deserve.

Her chair screeches underneath her as she pushes it out to stand, reaches across the table, and slaps the side of my head. "Stop being an idiot."

"Sorry. I didn't know being upset made me an idiot. My bad."

Hollis growls like an angry pit bull, but way more terrifying. My sister inherited our mother's stubbornness and determination, so if she's set on something, you don't bet against her. Right now, it appears she's set on ridding me of my sarcasm. "It's not being upset that makes you an idiot, idiot. It's you sitting here moping, not doing anything about it that does." She drops back into her chair and leans back, crossing her arms.

"What else am I supposed to do? Hmm? She's been gone for a week. If she wants to hear from me, she knows my number, my address, my workplace. There's nothing stopping her. She left, and there's nothing I *can* do."

"This isn't the irritating, headstrong, all-or-nothing Oscar I know and love."

Her use of the same phrase Blake has used multiple times reminds me of the conversation he and I had a month ago. He predicted this would happen. The *nothing* stage when I'm left spiralling.

"This is exactly him, Holl. This is nothing Oscar." I lean back in my chair to mirror her posture. "There's nothing left for me to do."

She doesn't reply for nearly a full minute. Almost as if she's trying to concoct some genius plan that will solve the problem. Eventually, she suggests, "Maybe you should go back home for the summer and work with Ethan again. He could use some help with his new business."

"Not an option," I reply a little too quickly. It's not that I don't want to help my brother, but I can't leave. "I have a job here, and I don't want to lose it. The guys are all leaving in a few hours, so if I go home, the house will be left empty." I stop short of saying that I want to stay in case Frankie returns. Or at the very least, Devin shows up and has some answers.

"Just think about it, okay? I'd hate to see you here alone and upset. At the very least, promise me you won't isolate yourself. That means answering when I call."

"It's not that big of a deal," I lie. "We had a few weeks together, and she left."

"An eight-dollar red velvet cupcake says it's a big deal." She offers a soft smile that she also inherited from our mom. "Don't forget that you have people in your corner. You don't have to be the one fighting for everyone else all the time."

I look at Hollis with my eyebrows raised, because fighting for those without a voice is her entire MO. Not that Frankie doesn't have a voice, but it's ironic for Hollis to say that when I know she's exhausted herself to fight for others.

She gives me a cheesy grin that says she understands the irony.

"I'm fine, Holl. Thanks for your concern, but it is what it is. She left without a word. What more can I do?"

She exhales and slumps into her chair. "I wish I knew."

"Well, you don't have to be the one finding answers for everyone else all the time. Sometimes, there is no good answer."

"I guess," she concedes. "Not gonna lie. I'm a little hurt she left and changed her number without saying anything to me either."

"Me three," Blake says as he stops at the end of the table.

We allow the hurt to marinate for a few minutes until Blake chimes in with some of his overstepping, borderline inappropriate questions for Hollis. She's even more reluctant to talk about goings-on in her life than I am, and still hasn't explained what her issue was a few months ago. Whatever it was, has kept her busier than usual.

Eventually, she has to leave, then she's soon followed by Keith and Austin. We all wrapped up our exams earlier in the week, so my roommates stuck around just long enough to confirm they passed everything before heading home.

While I'm happy they all passed their classes, I'm not as excited as I thought I'd be that they're leaving. With just me and Blake left in the house, he drags his suitcase down the stairs and stops at the bottom.

The realization I'm going to be alone for the first time in my life is unsettling. It's not *being* alone I'm worried about; it's feeling lonely that's the hard part.

"Are you sure you don't want me to stay?" he asks, standing frozen in the foyer.

"Your mom needs you right now, man. Don't worry about me."

"You think news that Fletcher knocked up a twenty-three-year-old chick is going to bother her? You're overestimating how much she cares." It's obvious from Blake's dry delivery that *he* cares, but he won't admit it. He also wouldn't admit that even if his mom is fine, he needs her right now.

Oddly enough, we're all dealing with the realities of being abandoned by someone we love, even if neither of us will admit that truth out loud.

"Get out of here. I'll be fine." I grab his duffle bag from behind him and hoist it onto my shoulder. "Four months will fly by."

"I can always come back sooner."

"Thanks, man." I clap him on the back to urge him out the door. "Honest. I'm fine."

We load Blake's things in the trunk of the waiting ride-share, and soon enough, he's gone too.

I walk back inside to our silent, empty house and quickly realize the severity of my lie. I'm not fine. Not even a little. And the one person who can fix it disappeared from my life without a word.

My bags are officially packed. Dr. Ellis signed off on Brad's travel documents. My passport and boarding pass are in my purse. Everything is ready to pursue this new, unexpected path.

It doesn't feel good, though. Most people would be excited about a semester in Rome. Since I have family in Italy and speak a healthy amount of Italian, it shouldn't feel as scary as it does. But it's nothing to do with flying across an ocean or leaving my parents again that makes the prospect terrifying. It's the reality that getting on that flight will mean I'm officially leaving Oscar behind.

I should have stayed and explained things to him instead of sneaking out and leaving him a lame note. He'd have convinced me it would all be fine, though. No doubt, he'd lean in to kiss me, making me forget about the entire situation—temporarily.

That's the thing, though. Oscar and I were just temporary. We're too young and have too much life left to figure out. Feelings that strong in our early-twenties are terrifying. We were intense. Combustible, like a firecracker with a short fuse. Now the show is over.

"Are you sure about this, *Bella*?" Mom asks, stopping just inside my bedroom door.

"Not really, but I need to do it. I need to figure out who I am now."

Mom steps farther into my butter yellow bedroom, coming to sit on the bed beside me. "You've always known who you are. This does not change, Francesca. That man cannot change you. Your hair, your address, your school, he made you change those things, but who you are has always been the same."

"I feel different. Completely."

"My *Bella*, you have grown. That is all. You're no longer a little girl with little dreams. You're a young woman with unlimited potential."

That's entirely unhelpful. Because unlimited potential means unlimited choices. An endless list of things I could pursue, and I'm not sure I'm capable of making the right decision. Before, having a stalker limited everything I could do, which, in a way, has made me afraid of everything outside of my fear-limited box. Living in fear, ironically, has made me afraid of freedom.

This man is still winning. Still controlling my life, even from inside a jail cell.

"It's time for me to start living my life, then. No more holding back because I'm afraid."

"If that is what you wish, know we'll always support you. It has been the greatest joy of my life to watch you grow, my *Bella*." Tears trickle down her olive cheeks, but she swipes them away quickly. "And I am happy to see you back with your natural hair colour. You're beautiful no matter what, but this is my Francesca. Who you were born to be." With that, my mom kisses the top of my head as she stands, then approaches my door. "Brad has requested a ham sandwich for the flight. Do you want anything?"

That one sentence wipes away any lingering emotions I have over our conversation. "*Mammina*, no. He'll be so gassy for the entire trip."

"Ah, there are too few pleasures in life. Let him have this." She exits into the hallway before shouting back that she's lacing the sandwich with the medication Dr. Ellis suggested to help Brad sleep for the flight.

I laugh at her determination, realizing there's nothing I could say to stop her from spoiling her fur-grandbaby.

It feels good to laugh again. I don't think I've even cracked a smile for the past ten days. Instead of reliving the traumatic situation of having a knife held to my throat, I've been lost in thoughts about whether Oscar completed all of his exams. Wondering how he did on them and if he was able to study. I know how worried he was about microeconomics, so I hope I didn't derail his preparation. That is the opposite of what my intentions were.

Now, with a tear trailing down my face, I confirm that I'm making the right decision. He'll be better off now that he can focus on his schoolwork and achieve the dreams he laid out for himself.

I stand at the edge of my bed, check the time, then begin the long journey toward my future. One without Oscar in it.

Palermo is even more beautiful than I remember. I'm fortunate to have family to stay with to get acclimated to Italian life before heading to Rome for my next semester. I never imagined I'd have the chance to partake in the Research Abroad Programme when I first transferred schools, but I'm excited about it.

Zia Paola, my mom's younger sister, has two sons of her own, who are both close to my age. Today, Nico and Luca are taking me and Brad to the beach with a group of their friends. Something I would have been unlikely to do in Canada. I'm having to relearn everything about living with freedom. It's not second nature for me to go do things like this—fun things. At least not without prompting. But the fact my cousins and their friends are willing to drive an hour to go to a dog-friendly beach just to get me out of the house says a lot about the impression I've made.

"Are you ready for some 'fun in the sun'?" Nico asks, appearing next to me out of thin air.

Brad wags his whole bum at the sight of my younger cousin. It is clear who has been the cause of Brad's weight gain since we arrived a week ago. Nico was immediately pegged as the weakest link, so Brad chooses him as his target to beg from at every meal. Safe to say it's working.

"Ready. Are you driving?"

"Nah, Luca gets scared when I drive along the coast."

Based on the one time I went anywhere with Nico, I can see why. That's why I asked.

"Okay. Ready whenever you are." I walk over to grab Brad's leash from the basket by the door, making his tail pick up speed.

"He looks like he's ready to find some bi—"

"Nico, I know you are not about to say something crass in front of your cousin," Zia Paola calls from somewhere else in the house.

Nico's eyes widen as he looks straight at me. "I didn't even know she was home." He grabs Brad's leash and ducks out the door before his mother appears.

Right on time, she pokes her head out of the kitchen doorway. "I taught him better than that, Francesca. That boy will age me."

I pinch my lips together to stop a laugh from spilling out. Nico reminds me a lot of Blake with his chaotic personality and affinity for finding the fun in any situation. There's something endearing about someone who just knows how to enjoy life.

"Not to worry. He's reminding me how to laugh."

Her kind smile communicates more than anything she could say. While I haven't explained the whole story about what happened at home, I know my mom has relayed the main points.

"I'm glad, *Bella*. He is good at that. Go have some fun." She waves a linen dish towel at the door, encouraging me to follow her son. "We'll have dinner when you return."

"*Grazie,* Zia. You're sure you don't want to come?"

She laughs, creasing the deep lines around her eyes. "Go have fun. Make sure that Felicia stays away from my Luca, yes? She's no good for him."

I have no idea who Felicia is, but I want to ask why Zia is adamant she's no good for her son. What makes a mother so sure of that? How well does she know this Felicia girl to make that decision? What would Oscar's mom have thought of me? Or worse… what does she think of me now after everything that has happened? I'm sure she'd feel the same way.

So instead of asking any of the questions that spring to mind, I nod, smile, and finally turn out the door.

My cousins try their best to make our afternoon an entertaining one. Nico is the life of the party and every time he cracks a joke, his laugh reminds me more of Blake. Luca, on the other hand, is much more like Oscar. He's reserved. Observant. Protective. I notice him scanning the water occasionally, as if he's checking to make sure everyone is safe. He picks up the trash his group of friends leave on the beach before it blows away. He constantly asks if I'm okay or if I need anything. I appreciate him, but each reminder is a stab to the heart because he serves as a reminder of what I ran away from.

I try my best to refocus my attention on Brad, who is having the time of his life. He seems to have left our former life behind in exchange for extra table scraps and Sicilian sunshine. I wish I was as good at focusing on the bright spots and living in the now as he is.

Because as much as I tell myself that being here is the right thing—that Oscar deserves better than the stress I bring to his life, or that this opportunity could be the best thing to happen to me—the truth is, I know the best thing already came and went. Rather, I left it behind in exchange for an ocean of regret.

44

OSCAR

Took My Love

Frankie has been gone for thirty-three days. That's almost as long as the time between our first official date and the day she left. It only took me a month to realize how special she was to me, and that hasn't changed after a month apart. No amount of time in the gym will allow me to forget.

Every insufferable soccer mom who conveniently can't remember the basic steps of a push kick only reminds me of Frankie. Of the first time I was close enough to touch her.

So does every Pitbull song that blasts through the gym speakers.

Each time I see a strawberry.

Whenever I walk past her empty house.

She embedded herself in my head, and nothing is working to get her out. Possibly because deep down, I don't want to.

"You seem distracted," Tyrus interrupts my staring out the front window.

I turn to face him. "Me? Nah, I'm good. Just thinking about tomorrow's class."

"Mm-hmm. That's the same excuse I use."

"It's not an excuse," I respond suspiciously fast.

Tyrus smirks, enhancing the scar above his eyebrow. "If you need an ear, I'm here. But for now, shower and go home. Take tomorrow off."

I try to argue, but he isn't having it. He puts up his hand to stop me. The last thing I want is a day at home alone with unlimited time for my mind to wander, but he's the boss.

My thoughts race in the shower, unable to settle on a single idea. I've run through countless haphazard plans to find Frankie, but none of them feel right. Not going to the animal clinic. Nor turning the security camera back on to watch for Devin to appear. Least of all, going to her hometown and asking complete strangers if they know where her parents live. I'm not about to turn myself into her new stalker.

No, if she wanted to get in touch with me, she would. She knows where and how to find me. The reality is, she chose to leave, and she chose to ghost me.

It's time to take a hint.

I dawdle home instead of jogging—which I could use because a physically exhausted body is more likely to sleep. Even that doesn't allow me to escape this crappy reality I find myself in, though. Frankie works her way into my dreams. Even Brad is usually there. There's no escaping either of them, so not being able to sleep makes no difference in my overall mood.

My racing thoughts halt as I approach my front door. There is a cacophony of voices inside. Multiple loud voices trying to talk over each other. Familiar voices.

I open the door to find all three of my roommates arguing over the remote with music playing in the background. They freeze when I enter.

"You're home early," Blake states, pausing mid-remote-grab.

"So are you." Considering I wasn't expecting them for another three months.

"Yeah, about that…" He gets up from his spot on the far sofa and walks toward me. Without waiting for an invitation, he pulls me in for an unreciprocated hug tight enough I could almost mistake it for a collar choke.

I tap his arm to signal that I'm ready for him to release his hold.

He lets go, but the concern on his face doesn't relax. "Your mom called."

"She didn't."

"She did." He laughs. "Actually, she talked to my mom for a while and came up with some creative solutions for Fletcher. I figured it was better to do what she wanted and not risk her wrath."

Knowing my mom, she probably took her outrage to the next level and came up with some scheme to dismember Fletcher with her electric turkey knife. A plan she'd never follow through with, but she's pretty descriptive when she's mad and comes up with stuff that would make the mafia blush. Blake should run to her for his next screenwriting idea.

"You didn't have to come here. She was just being dramatic," I offer.

"Best not to take chances with Lexi Luna. We all kind of missed being here anyway, so as soon as I called, they were down to tag along." He hooks his thumb to point at Austin and Keith. "Austin has something to tell you."

I immediately assume he has news about the app he was working on, but if that's what he wants to tell me, he wouldn't look so nervous.

"I have an idea how to find Frankie," Austin blurts.

My eyes snap to him like a trained laser. "What idea? How?"

"Hear me out," he starts, clasping his hands together in front of his chin. "She signed up for the app I was developing... and gave me her email address. If I put my hacking skills to use, I can use that to pinpoint where she's—"

"No." My stomach drops at the thought of what he's suggesting.

He lowers his hands. Once he takes a beat to process my harsh interruption, he continues, "I'll just reverse—"

"No."

His eyes narrow. "Don't you want to find her?"

I lower myself onto the couch, throwing my head back to look at the ceiling. "I don't want to find her if she doesn't want to be found, Austin. She ran from a stalker. What kind of guy does that make me if I hunt her down too? Against her will. Why do you think I haven't gone to the clinic or tried to speak to her parents? She doesn't *want* me to find her."

The cushion beside me sinks as someone sits down. We all stay silent for a full minute, allowing the truth of what I just said to sink in. I know none of them have a good argument because it's all true.

"More than anything, I want to know she's safe, but if she wanted me to know that, she'd tell me herself. I want to matter enough to her, I don't have to guess."

Blake blows out a long breath, then squeezes my shoulders with his left arm draped around me. "I get what you're saying, Ozzie, but don't compare yourself to that lunatic. You searching for her and him stalking her are not the same."

"They're not, but it's still an invasion of her privacy."

"Give her some time. She'll come around. I refuse to accept that she would just disappear without a trace like that."

It's already been over a month, and not even Hollis has heard from her. It wasn't just me she ran away from. The guys and my sister were good friends to her, and she abandoned us all. If she cared, she would have checked in with someone by now.

But that's the thing I need to come to terms with. I *want* to matter enough, but I don't.

The guys kept me busy all weekend. With no coaching sessions to focus on, I would have been sitting at home, dwelling on everything I could have done or said differently to change the outcome with Frankie. None of which would be helpful with anything, so it was a good thing they distracted me.

Despite the hours at a driving range, a baseball game, bowling, and watching an MMA fight at a pub, with them all leaving now, I'm back where I started.

Alone and even more lonely.

Maybe I should get myself a dog. That seems to work for everyone else.

"Ozzie?"

I blink away the thought and focus on Austin. "Yeah?"

"Let me know if you change your mind. I know what you said, but she doesn't even have to know. It can just be for your own peace of mind."

I smile at my curly-haired roommate, grateful for the offer. My mind won't change on the matter, but I don't tell him that. I just thank him and let everyone leave on a pleasant note.

Once I'm officially alone, I pull out my phone to scroll through social media. At least if Frankie had some kind of internet presence, I could get a glimpse at where she is or if she's okay. Unfortunately, her stalker ensured she'd never feel safe online, so she's a digital ghost.

That knowledge makes me doubt my eyes even more when I see her name pop up in my email inbox.

45

OSCAR

Across the World

Oscar,

I know this email is probably too little, too late, but selfishly, I just wanted to know you're okay. I never wanted you or anyone else to get hurt. If I could take it all back, I would.

Even more than the surprise I'm feeling right now, that sentence *she'd take it all back* stings with a much stronger intensity. I take a few seconds to push the hurt down, then continue reading.

Brad and I are spending the next semester in Rome for an international research credit. My aunt and cousins are letting me stay with them until my programme starts again. Palermo is beautiful, but I miss home.

The whole semester? That means it will be at least seven months before she returns, and who knows which home she's referring to. Maybe she misses her parents' home.

Reluctantly, I continue reading.

I'm sorry for leaving with nothing more than a stupid note. You deserved better than that. Since I haven't heard from you, I'll take it as my hint that you haven't forgiven me, which I deserve, but I want you to know how sorry I am for everything.

Take care,

Frankie

Woah, woah, woah. A stupid note? What note? She hasn't heard from me? How did she expect me to get in touch with her when she had her phone disconnected and I didn't know her email address until just now?

Curiosity gets the best of me and I return to my room to start digging around to see if she left a note I've somehow missed for a month.

Nothing. I would have seen it by now.

My eyes land on the back side of the picture frame holding the photo of me and Frankie. I couldn't look at it anymore but wasn't ready to throw it out, so I laid it down on my desk weeks ago.

I pull the back of the frame off and a small picture of Brad sleeping on my couch and me on the floor falls out, followed by a piece of folded light pink paper. Frankie's messy handwriting fills more than half of the page. She hid it in plain sight all this time, and I had no idea.

Oscar,

If you're wondering where I am, I don't have an answer for you. I was watching you sleep, sick to my stomach that I put you in harm's way, and I realized the best thing I can do to protect you is to leave.

As scared as I was last night, imagining you getting hurt was the scariest part. I couldn't live with myself if something happened to you, and I don't want to distract you from what's important.

I'm not strong enough to drive away if I try to have this conversation in person, Oscar. You might think I'm crazy, but I really care about you and want nothing more than for you to be happy. Please understand that.

You'll be happier without me.

The time we spent together was the happiest I've ever been in my life. Not just the big things—like beating you at Skee-

Ball—but the quiet nights in too. Even when the food was awful. This photo represents our happy memories, so I wanted you to have a copy, selfishly hoping that you'll choose to remember the happy moments too.

If or when you want to get in touch, you can always send me an email. If not, I'll understand.

Yours,

Frankie

There's so much to unpack in this letter. The tear stains that smudged the ink around her name. The fact she says she cares and *wants* me to get in touch. Knowing this picture is a copy means she didn't leave her only reminder of me behind. Perhaps, most alarming, is the change in how she signed off each message; she's giving up.

This changes everything.

"Are you crazy?" Hollis shrieks. Her outrage is obviously a front, because her smile doesn't match her tone at all.

"Probably. I'm also broke now because a summer flight to Sicily isn't cheap."

"This is a way bigger deal than a cupcake."

"Well, it might just be a waste of time, because she hasn't replied to my email. I'm not even sure where she is. How big is Palermo?"

Hollis drops onto my bed beside my suitcase. "No clue. This might be the most impulsive thing you've ever done."

"Don't—"

"I love it. Whatever you need from me, name it. I'm all the way in."

I breathe out a sigh and close my eyes for a moment, trying to let my sister's words settle the nerves in my stomach. "Thanks, Holl. Right now, I just need a ride to the airport."

"Didn't you say your flight is at 6:40?"

"Yeah."

"It's barely after noon. You want to go now?"

"Oh." I glance out the window to see the sun high in the sky. "Might as well. No sense waiting here." Truth be told, I know Hollis has better things to do today, and the fact she raced over here when I didn't answer my phone all morning is enough of an inconvenience for her.

"Okay. Never met anyone who *wanted* to wait around an airport, but who am I to argue?" She taps her phone with both thumbs, typing out a message. A few seconds later, she continues, "There. Special order ride-share. My friend moonlights as a driver, so she'll come pick you up."

"Thanks, Holl," I repeat. "Can you grab my passport from that drawer? And do me one more favour?"

"I told you; just name it," she replies, standing to approach my desk.

"Don't tell Mom."

She laughs as she hands me my passport. "Wouldn't dream of it."

Right now, I don't need to deal with the thousand questions my mother would have, nor the jacked up phone bill from her refusal to respect international roaming fees. I just need to keep myself focused and come up with a plan to find Frankie once I get there if she doesn't reply.

As we're walking down the stairs, Hollis in front of me, tapping on her phone, she randomly says, "Six hundred, seventy-three thousand."

"What?"

"The population of Palermo. I'd say that makes your search a needle in a haystack, little brother."

I pause on the third-last step as Hollis reaches the foyer. "Is this stupid? I can just wait for her to reply to my email. There's no reason to fly half-way around the world to see her."

"Except..."

I wait a few seconds for Hollis to continue, but she stares at me expectantly instead. "Except... I want to see her. Even if that means flying half-way around the world and asking six hundred thousand strangers if they've seen her." I pat my pocket to make sure I have my phone, which has a picture of our picture, plus the actual photo tucked inside the case.

"There's a significant shortage of grand romantic gestures happening in this world, so if you want to fly across an ocean to find her, I'm not the person to stop you."

"Good. I wouldn't want to have to fight you." I smile at my sister, soaking in her seal of approval.

Yes, I know this whole plan—or lack thereof—is crazy, but as someone who has always tried to tamp down my ADHD and force myself to be "normal," today, I'm letting my impulsivity lead. Hopefully, it leads me to Frankie.

Hollis was right. My plan to wait around at the airport has only left me free time to doubt this scheme I cooked up at some point between midnight and 3am. Something tells me the four-hour layover in Zurich is going to feel much the same. I've turned fourteen hours of travel into almost twenty, hoping I wouldn't be able to talk myself out of this once I got here. Instead, waiting around has only made me doubt myself more.

Her email was clear though, right? She cares... *a lot*. That has to mean something, even if she hasn't responded to me yet. She won't be upset by me showing up, will she? Or think I'm anything like her stalker?

All of these doubts race through my mind until I'm on the flight, seated beside a mom and her young teenage daughter, who both look like this is their first time on an airplane. Not that I've travelled a lot, but I've been on enough flights, I'm not nervous about it. I'm more concerned about my potential to crash and burn once I arrive in Italy.

I take a minute to talk to them and try to ease their minds until the flight attendant goes through his safety demonstration. The mom pulls out the instruction manual and follows along, looking more nervous by the second.

Instead of focusing on my own doubts and worries, I tuck my phone in my pocket and carry on conversation with the mom-daughter duo. Before I know it, we're being instructed to put our phones in flight mode because we're ready for takeoff. Now, I have no choice but to stop refreshing my inbox every thirty seconds.

All I can do is hope there will be a response waiting when I arrive.

International Love

My email to Oscar has gone unanswered for five days now. I know he doesn't check it obsessively like some people, but it's safe to assume he doesn't want to hear from me anymore. Not even staring out at the majestic waters of the Tyrrhenian Sea can bring me any sense of comfort.

I royally stuffed up, and it's too late for me to go back.

I've tried to spend the last few weeks focusing on the bright side of being here, but aside from Brad's newfound love for digging in beach sand and pebbles, I haven't found a lot of positives. It's getting exhausting putting on a front around Zia Paola, pretending like I'm okay when I'm not. My cousins are easier to talk to. At least they don't worry like their mother, and they don't relay their concerns back to my mom, either. But I still feel like an outsider. Like I don't belong here, and it's nothing to do with the location or my living situation.

It's because I miss *him*. More than just the way he made me laugh or how he made mundane things exciting. I miss how he made me feel. His effortless way of making me comfortable being myself. I feel like a shell of myself without him.

Just being in his orbit made life better. Nothing can replace that.

"Brad? Come on, buddy. Time to go home," I finally call my filthy dog, knowing the sun is going to set soon. I may be on the other side of the Atlantic from my stalker, but I'm not at ease walking the streets of Palermo after dark. He's not the only evil human lurking about.

Brad and I begin our fifteen-minute walk toward my aunt's house. We only make it about four minutes before Brad starts barking, tugging me in the opposite direction. He's pretty much fully grown now and is solid muscle, so as hard as I try, I can't stop him. After a minute of trying to drag him home and him refusing, he pulls the leash clean out of my hands. To my horror, Brad goes running down the sidewalk, back toward the beach. He moves deceptively fast for a tiny hippo.

I take off running, calling his name, but he's intent on going back to dig up more fish guts or whatever it is he's so obsessed with. He rounds a corner about fifty feet ahead of me, increasing my anxiety when I lose sight of him. I try to pick up speed, but my tired legs feel heavy and ill-prepared for a sprint.

When I round the corner, instead of seeing Brad crossing the busy street—or worse—I spot him on the sidewalk twenty feet ahead, jumping at someone's legs. His back end is bouncing and his front paws reach up past the person's waist. My eyes trail up the familiar form and land on the same face I've been dreaming about for over a month.

"Oscar?" I whisper as I walk closer, so I don't make a fool of myself if I'm imagining him.

"Your dog is a menace," he says, wearing a hesitant smile. A smile that grows wider and more confident the closer I get.

I stop a few feet in front of him, baffled by the entire situation. How did Brad know he was here? How did Oscar know I was here? *How* is he here?

"What are you doing here?"

He reaches one hand up and rubs the back of his neck, continuing to pat Brad's head with the other. "I wanted to see you. So… I took a flight."

My heart flutters, making me inhale a sharp breath. But I'm still so confused. "You never emailed me… but you took a ten-hour flight?"

He grimaces. "I've been looking for you for three days, but I didn't know where to start. I got on the plane thinking I had replied to your email, but it turns out, it was waiting in my draft folder. I couldn't get connected to wi-fi once I got here, so I've just been… searching. Funny thing is, I've been showing this picture, asking if anyone has seen this blonde girl… not a gorgeous brunette." He smirks, holding up the photo I left him.

Brad finally drops his front paws back onto the sidewalk, wagging his tail like he's proud of himself. Yeah, I should give him trouble for running off on me, but I can't bring myself to be mad.

I bend down to pick up his leash as I step closer to Oscar. "This is my real hair colour. I hardly recognize myself anymore."

"You look stunning with any colour, but this is my favourite. The real Francesca."

I pull in a deep breath, trying not to melt. I can't cave to his sweet words and compliments. There's a reason I left, and I stand by my choice. Even if staring at him right now is making me question everything. "I can't believe you came all this way… for me."

"Well, I wanted to ask you to be *mi ragazza*, and that wasn't something I could do in an email."

My stomach flip-flops. Paired with my sweaty palms and fluttering heart, I think I've now achieved the swoony trifecta. "You flew across an ocean to ask me to be your girlfriend?"

"I flew across an ocean while listening to a beginner's Italian course and working up the courage to ask." He flashes me a meek smile.

"I thought Oscar Luna was only afraid of one thing."

"Not true." He moves a few inches closer, and his proximity alone makes me reach sensory overload. "When Brad limped into my house that day, I was scared. When I ran to your house, I was terrified. But when I woke up the next day and you were gone, I'd never been so scared in my life."

I take a deep gulp, completely gutted by the look in his eyes. One of fear and vulnerability that he hasn't shown before. Words fail me, and the only thing I can think to do is to kiss him. But I don't, because my own fears hold me back.

"I watched my cousin walk away from the woman he loved when he was nineteen and he was never the same without her. I don't want that to be our story, Frankie."

Now my mouth goes totally dry. Maybe I'm reaching, but I think he's saying he loves me. I clear my throat before replying, "Where is he now?"

"Righting the wrongs of his past. I just don't want to wait that long." Oscar steps forward and places a gentle hand on my tricep. "You may think I'm crazy," he starts, mimicking the words of my email, "but I love you, Francesca Moreno. A trans-Atlantic flight is the least of what I'll do to prove that to you."

Internally, I'm screaming for joy. Dying to shout the words back at him that I fell hard and fast for him too. I want to validate the big crazy feelings I've had for him and re-write the ending to our story. Doubts and my desire to protect him from me stop me from doing that. "Oscar..."

His shoulders drop, along with his hand.

"We're still young. We both have so much to experience, and I'm going to be here until December. You don't want a long-distance relationship at this point in your life. Nobody does."

At this moment, Brad, who has been silent for several minutes, lets out a long whimper.

Oscar's expression morphs into one of conviction and determination. He sets his jaw and softens his eyes. "All due respect, Frankie, I'm telling you what I want. And I wouldn't have paid three grand or flown to a different continent if I wasn't one hundred percent sure. The distance isn't something that scares me."

Looking into his green eyes now, I don't doubt a single word he's saying. My only doubts come from myself.

"If you're not sure about us, just tell me and I'll go. I'm not here to guilt you into choosing me or make you do something you don't want. That's not my intention. I came here because I thought maybe we both wanted the same thing, and we didn't get a chance to say that before you left."

"It's not *you* I'm not sure about, Oscar." I take a deep breath, preparing myself to say the words I wasn't going to utter out loud. "I love you too. So much, it scares me."

His expression softens with a small smile as he places his hand on my forearm. "Then what's holding you back? I'm here; ready and willing. Your stalker is being held without bail, by the way. Tyrus's brother checked up on the situation for me. He's not getting out, Frankie. Not without a whole heap of mental health evaluations and treatment. You don't have to be afraid to come home."

Home. That elusive concept that I haven't felt since I arrived here. One that has evaded me many times in my life; all thanks to said stalker. The thought of returning to my home on Boston Avenue warms my heart almost as much as hearing Oscar say he loves me.

And I do love him too. Enough, I am considering something I tried to convince myself was a virtual impossibility.

"Listen," Oscar adds, trailing his hand up my bare arm, "I can't promise that things will be smooth sailing or that there won't be days when you want to throw a push kick my way, but that doesn't mean it's not worth trying." He looks down at Brad, whose tail is now wagging.

I smile at my perceptive pup, then lock my eyes onto Oscar's. "That's hardly a selling point."

"Just being honest." He steps forward, placing his other hand on my left arm, holding me firmly in place. "You still love Brad when he knocks a tray of salmon on the floor and has a feast. Or when he busts through the fence to terrorize a neighbour. You love him even when things go wrong or he makes mistakes."

I shake my head and laugh. It's true, but my definition of "terrorize" and Oscar's are vastly different.

"There will be bumps in the road, but we'll have bumps if we aren't together too. The only difference is, we won't be able to help each other over them."

I inch closer until Oscar's arms wrap around me and my head is resting on his chest. He's right. All that comes from being apart is heartache. Compared to all that came from our time together, my answer is really a no-brainer.

"Will you be *il mio ragazzo*, Oscar Luna?"

"If that means what I think it means, you already know the answer. I'm yours, Frankie. Whether you're next door or an ocean away."

Finally, like we're magnetic forces that have resisted the pull for too long, I lift my head and meet Oscar's lips with mine. The spark is incendiary. The fire grows between us with each movement of our mouths until we're both short of breath.

"I really missed that. Missed you," he says, resting his forehead against mine but keeping his eyes closed.

"We missed you too," I reply, feeling Brad's front paws against my hip. I rub the top of his head, realizing how excited he is to see Oscar again too. "Where are you staying?"

His eyes pop open. "That's not the kind of reunion I—"

"No, you goof." I slap his chest. "It's getting dark, so I need to get back, but I want to be able to find you tomorrow."

His face falls as he lifts his head away from mine. "I'm staying in a short-term apartment beside the car rental place. But... uh... tomorrow is my last full day here."

Those words create a rock in my gut. Just when he found me and we've reunited, the long distance part of our relationship already starts. This won't be easy going forward, but one thing I know is that I want to try.

So there's a simple solution. We make the most of our time together before it runs out. "Want to come meet my aunt and cousins? If I'm not in by sunset, Aunt Paola will send them out searching for me."

He nods with a heart-melting smile, reaching down to scratch Brad's ears. "Yeah. Let me walk you home."

"You'll love Nico. He reminds me so much of Blake."

Oscar laughs, reaching to grab my hand. "You know, I kind of miss having the guy around. He misses you too, by the way. So does Hollis."

Thirty minutes ago, those words would have made me feel terribly guilty, but now? Now I feel like the distance is a short-term problem with an eventual solution. "We'll be reunited soon," I reply, tugging Oscar and Brad to head toward Zia Paola's house.

With Oscar's free hand, he gestures for Brad's leash. "Can I?"

Without hesitating, I hand over the leash and squeeze Oscar's hand tighter.

Then the three of us begin walking through the darkening streets of Palermo, the sun setting behind us, and finally, it feels like home.

The best part is, after years of stress, heartache, and fear, I can confidently say, I have that *peaceful easy feeling*.

THE END

If you enjoyed this book, please consider leaving a review on Amazon or the retailer's website where you purchased the book from. I love hearing from my readers.

If you'd like to hear from me, find all of my links here: linktr.ee/TiffanyAndrea.

Thank you for making it this far. If you've gotten to this point, I sincerely hope you enjoyed Oscar and Frankie's story.

Thank you to Rebecca and Elena for speed-reading through my early draft to help me craft this story into what it is now. Oscar and Frankie were hard for me because I'm far removed from my college years, so your feedback made a world of difference.

To my husband and daughters, you guys will forever and always be my reason for doing anything. Thank you for allowing me the time and giving me the support to tell these stories.

As with all of my books, I always decide on a chapter theme before starting out. Then I come up with chapter titles, and begin to craft a story from there. I often use the body of work of a musical artist to guide the story's structure. Naturally, for Pitty Party, I had to use Pitbull. That being said, I have zero affiliation with Pitbull or his record label, and have taken great care to respect copyright laws and his work. Still, I want to give credit where it is due.

Here is my list of Pitbull songs that helped make Pitty Party what it is today. You can find the playlist on my Spotify playlist at linktr.ee/TiffanyAndrea.

Call of the Wild
Time of Our Lives – Ne-Yo
On No He Didn't – Cubo
Shut It Down – Akon
Fireball – John Ryan
Guilty By Association
Rain Over Me – Marc Anthony
Get It Started – Shakira
Go Girl – Trina, Young Bo
Come N Go – Enrique Iglesias
I Wonder – Oobie
Game On – TZKEE, Dario G
Hey You Girl
Everybody Get Up – Pretty Ricky
Back Up
That's Nasty – Lil Jon, Fat Joe
Daddy's Little Girl – Slim
Pause
Rock Bottom – Bun B, Cubo
Can't Stop Me Now – Jamie Foxx
I Don't See 'Em – Cubo, Aim
Tell Me Again – Prince Royce, Ludacris
Hurry Up and Wait
Don't Mind – Kent Jones, Lil Wayne
Be Quiet
Secret Admirer – Lloyd
Better On Me – Ty Dolla $ign
My Life – Jason Derulo
Midnight – Casely
Mr. Right Now – Akon, DJ Frank E
My Kinda Girl – Nelly
Come See Me
We Run the Night – Havana Brown
Fun – Chris Brown

Slowly Slowly – Guru Randhawa, DJ Blackout, DJ Money Willz
Messin' Around – Enrique Iglesias
Might Be the Police – Brisco
Options – Stephen Marley
Get Up/Levantate
The Truth (Interlude)
Took My Love – Redfoo, Vein, David Rush
Across the World – B.o.B
International Love – Chris Brown

Honourable Mentions
Timber – Kesha
I Know You Want Me

You Are Enough Series:
We're All a Little Broken: Book 1 (Zara's story)
We're All a Little Overwhelmed: Book 1.5 (Zara's extended epilogue)
We're All a Little Guarded: Book 2 (Chelsea's story)
We're All a Little Tired: Book 2.5 (Chelsea's extended epilogue)
We're All a Little Scared: Book 3 (Isla's story)
We're All a Little Determined: Short Story Collection (Available free on my website)

This women's fiction series focuses on various aspects of mental health and overcoming trauma. It addresses anxiety, depression, panic disorders, miscarriage, adoption, grief and loss, racism, discrimination, and more, but in a light hearted way that will also make you laugh. The entire series is set in Muskoka/Bracebridge, Ontario.

A New Leash on Life Series:
This series will consist of twenty interconnected standalone romances of various genres, each featuring a cuddly canine companion.

Total Bull (Angel and Damian)
Ay Chihuahua (Dina and Holden)
Tell-Tail Sign (Sophie and Boyd)
The Pugly Truth (Hannah and Caleb)
Pitty Party (Frankie and Oscar)
Chemistry Lab (Hollis and Myer) *Coming Soon*
Good Fur Nothing (Gwen and Ethan) *Coming Soon*

Dear Sister, Never Again: This women's fiction novella was shortlisted in Wattpad's annual novella contest. It explores the journey to realizing DNA isn't the only thing that makes family.

Suburban Watchdogs: This nonsensical comedy features four longtime friends and their slobbery dog on a mission to save their town from being overrun by a trio of bumbling criminals.

Con Artist: This standalone romantic comedy follows the story of an FBI agent tasked with investigating an art theft ring. The only thing his number one suspect makes away with, is his heart.

Trip and Fall: This standalone road trip romance follows two twenty-somethings who each have a different reason for wanting to leave town and explore the countryside. One out of a sense of wonder; the other, a sense of desperation. Will they find more than the adventure they were looking for? *Coming Soon*

Sign up for my newsletter, access my website, or follow me on social media to keep up to date with new releases and sneak peeks.
Linktr.ee/TiffanyAndrea